The Second Strain

John Burke

ROBERT HALE · LONDON

First published in Great Britain 2002

ISBN 0 7090 7150 7

Robert Hale Limited
Clerkenwell House
Clerkenwell Green
London EC1R 0HT

The right of John Burke to be identified as
author of this work has been asserted by him
in accordance with the Copyright, Design and
Patents Act 1988.

2 4 6 8 10 9 7 5 3 1

Typeset by
Derek Doyle & Associates, Liverpool.
Printed in Great Britain by
St Edmundsbury Press Ltd, Bury St Edmunds, Suffolk.
Bound by Woolnough Bookbinding Ltd.

What passion cannot Music raise and quell?

(Dryden: *St Cecilia's Day*)

Part 1
COUNTERPOINT

1

Any town the size of Kilstane must over the years acquire any number of skeletons in its cupboards. But even the dourest and most pessimistic inhabitants would hardly have expected to find one walled up in the tower of their most cherished seat of learning.

And when the tower gave up its secret, there was a more recent casualty. It would be quite some time before Adam Lowther would dare make jokes about the shattering effect of his wife's top notes.

The late April rain had been beating a fierce tattoo on the front windows, and wind howled along the narrow pend below. He was trying to drown it out by listening to a CD of Takemitsu's sea music, but those gentle oceans were no match for a braw Scottish gale rampaging in from the Borders valley. When the doorbell rang he thought at first it was just an odd discord made by a sudden gust against the glass of the side door. But it persisted. Who the hell would want to be out on a night like this? Possible that Nora might have forgotten her front door key – it wouldn't have been the first time – but it was far too early for her to be back.

He went downstairs and braced himself to hold the door against the wind funnelled under the low roof of the pend.

The light above it shone down on Deirdre Maxwell.

Whenever they came across each other in the *Buccleuch Arms,* her bright golden hair was most often newly washed and shining, sometimes pulled back into a pony-tail held tight with a scarlet ribbon, sometimes loose and dull but at the same time agreeable in its untidiness. This evening, if she hadn't been wearing that familiar green raincoat of hers, you'd have thought she was standing in a shower with the jet full on: her blonde hair had darkened into sodden streaks before she reached the shelter of the pend, while water still trickled down her forehead and into her eyes.

'I thought you`d be round at the pub.' She made it sound like an accusation.

'In *this*?'

'I was wanting to talk to you.'

Nothing for it but to open the door wide and let her in. She squeezed against him in the confined space, dripping against his sleeve and on to his slippers before climbing the flight to the first-floor sitting-room. Inside, he took her coat, making himself even damper in the process, and took it out to drape over the back of a kitchen chair.

When he came back she was blinking at herself in the mirror over the fireplace, shoving her hair back and then wiping her hand down her jeans. He handed her a box of tissues and turned off the music. She sat down, dabbing at her face.

'Adam, we've got to talk,' she said.

'Have we?'

'It's time we did. About us. And about Duncan and your Nora.'

'What about them?'

Even from several feet away he could smell the whisky on her breath, and could visualize her sitting there in the *Buccleuch Arms* on her usual stool, in her usual position slumped against the edge of the bar, chain-smoking and glancing petulantly from side to side. Sometimes she would be eager to talk, sometimes hostile towards anyone who tried to chat her up. Right now her mood was as sticky as her hair, and resentful. Obviously she had been waiting for him to show up in the pub, which he often did

10

when Nora was out rehearsing; and when he didn't she must have fretted herself into quite a state to want to walk this far in this weather.

Perhaps he ought not to have offered any more drink, the way she was, but it came automatically: 'You'd fancy a dram?'

She shrugged in pretended indifference, but then held out her hand for the glass of Glenmorangie, gulped it down in two breaths, and went on again.

'What are they up to, those two?'

He kept it light and level. 'So far as I know, they're up to the usual Wednesday practice.'

'Practice?' Her voice grated. 'Should be perfect at *something* by now, after all that practice.'

'Come off it, Deirdre. You know it's all to do with the festival and—'

'Bloody festival. Bloody rubbish. Just an excuse. People are starting to talk, ye ken.'

No, he didn't ken. He said: 'In this town they're always dreaming up some nonsense to keep their silly little minds occupied.'

'You should never have let it start. Why couldn't *you* accompany Nora? You're a better pianist than my dismal Duncan any day.'

'Thanks. But it's like teaching your wife to drive a car. Best to let someone else cope with the aggro. And in this case her music isn't the sort I'm best at. Duncan gets along with her much more smoothly than I would.'

'That's just the point. Don't you *see*?' She had taken a cigarette packet out and was looking for an ashtray. 'It's all right if I smoke, isn't it?'

'Nora doesn't like the smell.'

'Och, dear me. And it would never do for her to come home and wonder who'd been here, would it?' She stared up at him, and her swing of mood confirmed that he ought not to have given her that generous tot of whisky. 'Isn't it about time we gave her something to wonder about?'

11

'Deirdre—'

'I'd like to hear you say that with a bit more meaning.' She stretched out her arms to him and tried to stand up, but couldn't manage it without using her arms to push against the sofa.

He said: 'It's never been like that, and you know it.'

'You had one hell of a way of looking at me in the street when we were still at the Academy.'

'Every lad looked at you.'

'Yes, but *you* . . .' She aimed for the ashtray and sprayed ash on the fireside rug. Abruptly she coughed: 'Nora's never really settled in here, has she?'

'It's all still a bit strange to her,' he admitted.

'After four years? Christ, how long does she need?'.

'Look, I'll get the car out and drive you home.'

'Bloody gallant, aren't you?'

He had always enjoyed her company in small doses, but never fancied her. He was trying to find some way of saying this that wouldn't be offensive, when the doorbell rang again.

This time it was Duncan Maxwell.

He said: 'Where the hell is she?'

Adam Lowther had no reason to feel guilty, but that accusing tone of voice was as bad as Deirdre's had been a little while ago. And then Deirdre coughed again, and Adam found himself saying ridiculously: 'She came in out of the rain.'

'I don't believe this.' Duncan stormed past him and pounded up the stairs into the sitting-room. 'What's going on?'

'Nothing,' said his wife, 'unfortunately. And what's been going on with *you*? And Nora?'

'That's what I'm here for.' He was a big, broad-shouldered man, and took up a lot of space as he swung towards Adam. 'About Nora. Where is she?'

'She's with you.'

'I wouldnae be asking if she was, would I?'

'I don't get it.' Adam tried to find a secure space for himself on his own sitting-room carpet. 'She went out to the practice—'

'She never showed up.'

'That's crazy. Where else would she have gone?'

Equally baffled, only still more so by the presence of his own wife, Duncan stared from one to the other. 'Look' – he swung back on to the offensive – 'just what *is* going on?'

'I was just going to drive Deirdre home when you—'

'Oh, you were, were you?'

Deirdre snuggled down deeper into the sofa, looking pleased rather than scared by the blundering antagonism for which she was apparently responsible.

A sudden gust of wind thumped against the front of the house. It was followed by another ring – this time the telephone.

'Mr Lowther?'

'Speaking.'

'Mr Lowther, Kilstane Hospital here. Please don't be too alarmed, but I'm afraid your wife has been involved in an accident.'

'She's . . . an accident. . . ?'

'Nothing to be too upset about, sir. Fortunately it's not too serious. But if you'd like to come up and see her—'

'I'm on my way. But what happened? How. . . ?'

'She must have been passing the Academy,' said the woman's level, soothing voice, 'when the tower collapsed. A few stones hit her. Caught her only a few glancing blows, but she must have been lying in the rain for some minutes before the noise brought someone to investigate. But she'll be fine, Mr Lowther, just fine.'

By the next morning they were talking of letting Nora out. Only a few scratches and bruises, and a slightly sprained left ankle. Her husband could collect her late that afternoon.

Propped up in bed, Nora looked pink and demurely healthy, but wistful – just the way she had done after her miscarriage three years ago. The dressings at her neck and the blue bruise above her left cheek only emphasized the whiteness of her throat and the lightness of her pale brown hair. She accepted his kiss as a well-deserved trophy. He felt a rush of affection for her. She was so transparent, and for a moment as vulnerable as the

13

pensive young widow he had married. It was rather sweet to see how she was already intending to enjoy herself. Everyone would be commiserating with her; out of hospital, she would be a centre of attention.

'I'll pick you up at three.' He leaned over and kissed her, and she responded with more than the usual routine peck.

'That'll be lovely.'

He drove back round the curve of the hill and down towards the Academy. The side road past the school gates, a familiar short cut which Nora must have taken a score of times recently, had been closed off by a red and white barrier. Beyond it a JCB was manoeuvring into the yard and poising itself above the hard hats of three workmen picking their way cautiously around the fringes of the rubble.

The tower and its school bell had been the gift of a nineteenth-century pupil who had gone on from Kilstane to make a fortune from Indian railways and wanted a memorial to himself in his home town. Tacked on to the original foursquare Academy building, it sported a cupola on top which some said made it look like a distillery. Others, more widely travelled, preferred to call it Italianate and even used the word 'campanile' to impress their acquaintances. Most of the townsfolk referred to it as MacLean's Stump.

Now it really was little more than a stump, with most of its stones strewn widely over what had been the schoolyard until the authorities decreed that pupils should be bussed some miles away to a larger school, leaving the premises to be converted into a furniture store.

Adam parked near the junction and ducked under the barrier.

Two fellow members of his committee were already there, inside the yard, close to railings which had been slotted into place around the rubble. An impartial observer might have considered it wiser to set the railing between the two of them rather than allow them both on the same side.

Councillor Enoch Buchanan's vans advertised his trade as Builder, Funeral Director and, in sinister juxtaposition, Heating

Engineer. He had short red hair and a short temper, and the doom-laden voice of a Wee Free preacher, accustomed to predicting heavenly retribution at breast-beating sessions of his church. He set himself up as a sternly incorruptible man who was nevertheless charitably prepared to bring dignity to the funerals of folk of any denomination other than Roman Catholic, but would not himself set foot in a Church of Scotland or Episcopalian place of worship. Rather than lay himself open to contamination he would wait impassively outside – in the hope, it was rumoured, that the Lord's holy lightning might strike the unrighteous within and thereby give His righteous servant Buchanan a bit more trade.

'If my tender for the restoration had been accepted,' he was raging now at full volume, 'this shambles wouldnae have happened.'

'If your work all those years ago hadn't been skimped, just like those rickety houses you built on the marsh, my men wouldn't have had to cope with such shoddy fabric.'

William Kerr was in his late twenties, and away at school had acquired an English accent which infuriated Buchanan even when the younger man merely said 'Good morning' – which he frequently did in a slightly condescending tone.

'If we'd been allowed to use my methods instead of yon fancy—'

'Methods? It took me way over time and over budget to undo all the damage your cowboys did way back, and get the whole place safe for the concerts.'

'Safe, would that be? Except that yon tower's come down. And where does that leave our festival?'

Adam reluctantly joined them at the railing. 'There'll have to be an emergency committee meeting.'

'Aye, there will indeed. And I'll ha' plenty to say. And right now I'll be awa' to ring Sir Nicholas. Though likely he'll be down here the moment he hears.'

'I doubt it,' said young Kerr smugly.

'And why would ye be doubting it?'

'Something else you've overlooked. He's on his way up to Sutherland, remember? To see about bringing Erskine back.'

'Erskine!' Buchanan glared at the crumpled masonry as if someone had just tossed a further load of rubbish on top of it.

Adam Lowther felt a twitch of anger. He had had to work hard to persuade the locals that Daniel Erskine had become a great man and ought to be honoured in his birthplace. But still there were groups of diehard Philistines who remembered only the malicious rumours about the man, and still resented the idea of him being welcomed to the festival.

One of the workmen picking a cautious way round the ragged edge of stonework still standing came to a halt. He steadied himself with a wary hand against the uneven stretch of low wall, and peered over it. Then he waved frantically.

'Mr Kerr. I think you'd better . . . can you come round here, sir?'

Ignoring Buchanan's contemptuous grunts, Kerr eased his way between two sections of railing and trod carefully through the jumbled fragments. It took him a full thirty seconds to take in what he was seeing. Then he straightened up and stared back at Buchanan.

'There's something here,' he said, 'that really does date back to your restoration work.'

Emerging from the debris was the bone of a human elbow, jutting up as if to brace itself and heave its owner out into the open air. Half covered beside it was what might have been a fragment of shoulder-blade impacted into a twist of metal and a lump of concrete.

There would indeed have to be an emergency committee meeting.

2

Within a couple of weeks of agreeing to become Chairman of The Kilstane Gathering committee, Nick Torrance had known that he had made a mistake. Now, all these weeks later, irritation at his own gullibility nagged at him all the way through what should otherwise have been a heartwarming choral concert in the Usher Hall. That night he slept badly, driving through a half dream so that he was already tired when he set out on the actual journey. Just how many more complications had he let himself in for?

It ought really to have been Adam Lowther on this road, crossing the Forth Bridge and accelerating along the motorway through Fife. Lowther was the one who worshipped Erskine's music and could have answered any challenge on it. Amazing how much tightly controlled enthusiasm there could be in that lean, lanky frame. He always looked so puzzled, slightly diffident; but once he got his teeth into something, they really got a grip.

But would Erskine have let him in over the doorstep?

Or, rather, would Mairi McLeod have let him in?

Nick could only hope that Mairi, after so many years, wasn't going to be one of the complications.

Before leaving Black Knowe he had slotted three CDs into the player in the Laguna's boot. One was a recital of Erskine's orchestral rhapsodies, to help prepare him for the encounter. When he was clear of Perth and traffic had slackened off, he reached for the selector and began with *The Storm Child*, the legend of a child with green strands of skin washed up after a shipwreck, writhing in agony when christened, and continually summoned back by the voices of her sisters until at last she returns to the sea during another gale.

Above an insistent, threatening rhythm the main theme depicting the girl was a pentatonic melody, supplemented by the sisters' voices in a perverse-sounding organum of thirds instead of fourths and fifths. The isorhythmic lurches made it difficult to concentrate. It wasn't easygoing in-car listening: too intricate to be followed through the pulse of the engine and the buzz of tyres on the road. After ten minutes Nick gave up and switched off.

Sunlight touched the tops of the hills and sparkled in the river as the road took a long, leisurely sweep above the valley of the winding Tay. He tried to enjoy the music within the landscape itself, so that he would arrive relaxed and ready to explain the festival and what Erskine's presence would mean to them. He could only hope that Mairi would not, with a fine toss of that streaming hair of hers, laugh that tinpot little festivals and gatherings of this kind were a bit behind the times, weren't they?

It had to be admitted that the Borders town of Kilstane had been behind the times during most periods of its history. Its provost had been late in signifying loyalty to William III and had been forced to flee into the Highlands, where as a despised Lowlander he had been put to death by the ever rapacious killers of Argyll. Townsfolk had been so slow to decide for or against the Jacobite Rising of the '45 that Bonnie Prince Charlie was on his dismal way back from England before they could make up their minds. They had escaped serious penalties because the Hanoverians, exhausted by their slaughters in the Highlands, were too drugged by bloodshed to make up their minds either.

In the twentieth century the borough council allowed itself to be swallowed up by a regional octopus whose tentacles grasped riches in the form of grants from the Lottery, the EU, and Scottish

18

Enterprise. A small clique of councillors soon learned to manipulate these to the benefit of their own pockets rather than those of the local ratepayers. In the aftermath of a misguided Common Riding ceremony which had blighted Nick's first year in his tower of Black Knowe, the Community Council looked around for a cause which could command respect – and cash.

In the far reaches of Galloway, Wigtown had received grants to set itself up as a Book Town. Kirkcudbright, always a haunt of painters, potters and poseurs, began issuing postcards and maps proclaiming itself an Artists' Town.

So what was left?

Later, thought Nick wryly, it was going to be difficult to remember who first mooted the idea of Kilstane as a Music Town. And there had been one hell of an argument over launching the project with a concert devoted to the works of that now distinguished composer who had been born and brought up here. If the first stages proved a success, every little fusspot on the council would claim the credit. If it was a flop, they would all be passing the buck, just the way they did after the Common Riding fiasco.

And the shit, he thought with growing glumness, would most likely land in his own lap, with just a bit of it splashing over on to Adam Lowther for so fervently pushing the case of Daniel Erskine.

He pulled off the main road for coffee at Killiekrankie, and before setting off again selected a less demanding CD which he had engineered himself before inheriting his baronetcy and moving to Kilstane. Then he found the first few bars of the first track just as unsettling as the Erskine piece, in a quite different way. It brought Mairi vividly – too vividly – back into his life. Against the hulking shoulders of the Easter Ross hills the memory of Mairi's honey-smelling shoulders drifted across a brief vision of the window of the Holland Park flat where they had loved, and wrestled, and quarrelled. The view of the austere yet glittering crags and slopes ahead was becoming dangerously distorted by this other face, this other figure.

Again he switched off the music abruptly. Whatever lay ahead, there must be no elements lingering from the past.

It was disconcerting to find that, just as the only way to rid one's mind of a persistent melody was by overlaying it with another, he could dismiss the always greedy, grasping shape of Mairi only by remembering the trim, dismissive shape of the young woman who had refused to grasp the offer he had made to her.

For all the good it was, thinking of either of them.

He looked for the turn-off to an eaterie somewhere south of Inverness.

'The Superintendent will see you now.'

The secretary's face gave nothing away, though she must know whether it was going to be good news or bad news for Detective Inspector Gunn.

Lesley Gunn went into the Super's office.

'Ah, yes. Inspector. Do sit down.'

Her skills in analysing works of art, looking for flaws and forgeries or subtle identification marks, all too often leaked over into her study of living beings. Although it was important – vital at this stage in her career – that she should listen intently to what Superintendent Maitland had to say, she could not help seeing a sort of seedy Rembrandt in him: the blotchy features, the cluster of dried-up spots beside his left ear, red jowls as if he had clumsily scraped the skin with his razor this morning, and a pallid patch below his left eye as if the painter had run out of colour before putting the finishing touches to the portrait.

Then she was jolted into listening to what he was saying.

'Well, Gunn, this matter of your promotion. Afraid you've been kept waiting for a decision, eh?'

'Quite a time, sir, yes.'

'Yes, well, that's the way o' these things.' He drew a deep breath and pretended to consult some papers on his desk; and she knew that the encouraging half promises were not going to add up. 'I'm afraid,' he said, 'we're in no position to make you up to DCI at this moment in time.'

'I see.' Actually, Lesley didn't see.

'It's all very unfortunate. With all these recent cutbacks, there is no room on our strength for a Fine Arts specialist at Chief Inspector level.'

As quietly as possible she ventured: 'I thought, sir, there'd been a lot of talk recently about a big increase in funding for the police.'

'Aye, talk. A lot of talk, I grant you. But we've had instructions from up above' – Maitland raised his eyes to the ceiling as if some stern God was sitting in the room above listening to every word – 'that our resources have to be deployed more widely. The functions of CID Special Operations Unit are rather too specialized for a rural force such as ours.'

'All the most vulnerable country mansions do tend to be in rural areas.'

She half expected a reprimand for insolence. Instead he grinned and said: 'Well, I'm afraid we're more interested in drugs nowadays than in old works of art. Well, then. Your function now has to be incorporated into normal procedures. Which means no lowering of your status or your usefulness, of course.' It was a smooth, smug way of saying she should be grateful she wasn't going to be demoted or sent to look after the filing system. 'It's just that unfortunately there's no immediate prospect of your achieving your well-merited promotion to DCI.' He waited for her to speak. When he saw that she still had nothing to offer, he went on with a kind of off handed matiness: 'Wasn't there some talk of your being offered a civilian appointment by . . . um . . . Sir Nicholas Torrance, wasn't it?'

He knew damn well there had been.

'There was, sir. I preferred to stay in the Force.'

'Ah, yes. Good for you.'

But had it been good for her?

'It's a bit of a disappointment,' she said, 'to find that all my work hasn't been properly assessed and appreciated.'

'Not at all. By no means. It's simply a matter of coping with difficult times. I can quite understand you feeling a bit down.

21

Happens to all of us on the way up. But while you sort things out in your own mind, we have an interesting little assignment for you.' Superintendent Maitland became loudly benevolent. 'Just up your street.'

She waited, resigned to some routine job designed to keep her quiet and out of everybody's way. Some *objets d'art* stolen from a country house? Fakes being smuggled in via Leith docks?

Maitland said: 'There's been a death. Not recent, so there's no panic. Just a corpse that needs identifying, date of death, foul play or just a weird accident. Loose ends to be tidied up.'

She was puzzled. 'Just up my street, sir?'

'You know the neighbourhood pretty well. Kilstane.'

She tried not to look as sick and incredulous as she felt inside.

'Did some damn shrewd work over that Common Riding farce,' he was booming on. 'You know your way around. DCI Rutherford will brief you, but we're happy for you to handle it as you see fit. As I've said, it's not a recent death, so we won't have the tabloids breathing all over us. Take your time.'

Take your time.

In other words, don't hurry back. Just give us an excuse for easing you gently out. Or renew your acquaintanceship with Sir Nicholas Torrance, and this time grab that job he once offered you.

She thought of having to face up to Nick and his silent accusation – he would be too discreet to say it out loud – that she had been stupid to turn down his offer, and look where it had got her.

Too late now.

'If you need a gofer,' Maitland was saying, 'you can call on Sergeant Elliot from Rowanbie. He's on light duties after being hit by a car thief. Don`t overtax him.'

The scrape of his chair on the floor told her that this was the end of the interview. She was destined to return to Kilstane and was expected to be thankful for it – to return to those people who had first sneered at her and then blamed her for ruining one of their most treasured fantasies.

She made herself say it: 'Thank you, sir.'

*

The sky across the Sutherland wilderness had turned sullen, with a dull copper glow suggesting a heat wave that was unlikely at this time of year. As Nick slowed on a twist of the narrow road, his mobile phone on the passenger seat began a faint tinkling. He pulled on to the grass and reached for it, but there was only a confused spluttering. The message, wherever it came from, was breaking up. Out here, with not a house or cottage in sight, there was obviously a dead spot. It probably spread out for miles.

He drove on. Whoever had been trying to contact him, it couldn't be urgent. His housekeeper had his mobile number, and he had given it to Adam Lowther, who had perhaps thought of yet more enthusiastic remarks to pass on to Daniel Erskine.

It could wait. He might ring from the hotel when he got there.

The final lap of the journey took longer than he had expected. The road became single track, with passing places marked by poles, most of which had long since shed their lettered lozenges from the top. In the dusk the turns and twists of the road, even narrower at unexpected intervals where a stream had undermined the verges or a rocky outcrop threatened to scrape the panels of the car, demanded an eye-aching concentration.

At last there was a glimmer of light ahead. On the map was the name of Altnalarach and the symbol for a hotel. The white-harled building looked absurdly out of place in this vast expanse of bog and scrub, saved from encroachment by a palisade of spruce. Fanatical fishermen and deer stalkers must be its main trade.

And somewhere over towards that hazy mountain like a lion crouched along the western horizon, Daniel Erskine had chosen to flee from the world and concentrate on his music. Distractions must certainly be few.

Nick drove into the car park and rubbed his eyes. He thought of ringing Kilstane, but decided against it. He was dead tired, he didn't want to hear of any second thoughts or unresolved arguments across so many miles. A drink, a snack – if they were prepared to serve anything this late – and bed.

The snack presented no problem. Out here they were used to fishermen, stalkers, backpackers and other eccentrics rolling up at ungodly hours. He gratefully knocked back a nightcap of a large Clynelish from the nearest regional distillery, and went to bed.

And dreamed uneasily of Mairi McLeod being arrested by Lesley Gunn and being ruthlessly questioned about their past relationship.

3

They assembled on the first floor of the Tolbooth, grumbling. Ian MacKenzie complained that this was his late evening opening and he was having to pay his niece overtime to look after the shop at such short notice. When it was suggested that he might rely on the rest of the committee to make sensible decisions in his absence, he at once made it clear that he wasn't going to allow decisions of any kind to be pushed through behind his back.

Mrs Cynthia Scott-Fraser arrived late as usual, screeching that she had had to dash away from an important regional council meeting on traffic calming, and would have to dash off again as soon as possible to meet the chairman of another committee. She was a rangy fifty-year-old, in the habit of stooping from her six-foot height and dabbing her head forward to emphasize every word she spoke. Each assertive remark disclosed protruding teeth which went well with her presidency of the Rowanbie Pony Club.

When they had all finished complaining and had scraped their chairs into a semicircle facing the mahogany table below the platform, Adam Lowther as Convener Depute called the meeting to order and apologized for the unavoidable absence of Sir Nicholas Torrance.

'Aye, he'd be a sight better attending to things here instead o' gallivanting off to meet that scunner Erskine.' Buchanan's objections to the return of the composer to his hometown had been overruled weeks ago, but he wasn't going to let them forget those objections. When things went wrong, he would certainly not allow them to forget.

Adam rapped on the table with his knuckles. He ought really to have acquired one of those little lecterns and the sort of gavel which so many of those present used in various capacities at Rotary, Probus and the Incorporated Crafts functions, with a clipboard under one arm and chains of office bouncing on their chests.

He said as authoritatively as possible: 'Obviously we've had no time to prepare an agenda for this meeting. But I'm sure we're all agreed that we have to deal as swiftly as possible with the situation which has arisen. The basic fact is that a corner of the Academy in which we planned our main concerts has been rendered unsafe—'

'Because of slapdash alterations by unqualified workmen,' said Buchanan.

'Because of structural failings camouflaged by earlier contractors,' said Kerr.

It was unfortunate that both men should be sitting on this committee. It had come about because Kerr's offer of free advice on refurbishment of the Academy and the provision of tents and portaloos for the open-air features was immediately matched by Buchanan insisting on his right to be included 'to give the proceedings a proper balance', by which he meant that he represented the concerns of the more sober townspeople. In effect he was the self-appointed censor alert for potential rowdiness and vandalism which must not be allowed to ruin the tranquillity of God-fearing folk. Somewhere he had picked up the word 'rave' and knew there was something about it which demanded constant vigilance.

Before there could be any more bickering, Adam said: 'Whatever may have happened in the past, right here and now we've got to decide what to do about the loss of those essential premises. Any suggestions?'

There was a long silence.

At last MacKenzie said: 'There was a time we had some gey fine music in Black Knowe. Maybe Sir Nicholas would let us use his hall again.'

'Fine for chamber music or solo recitals,' said Adam, 'but not for a full orchestra.'

'We could maybe do without the full orchestra?'

'Cancel the booking?'

'Aye.'

'The Westermarch Sinfonia doesn't come cheap. I don't think we could stand the cost of paying them off and returning ticket money. Or, for that matter, the groups booked for the Folk Revel on the haughs. Some of these rockers and rappers can turn very nasty when it comes to missing out on the money.'

Cynthia Scott-Fraser was anxious to put it on record that, like Buchanan, she had expressed certain doubts of her own. 'I was never happy about the introduction of elements like that. One has only to read of the goings-on at Glastonbury and annual debauches of that kind – drugs everywhere, men and women running about naked . . .'

'Running around all bare?' grinned Kerr: 'Here, with that wind off the braes?'

'Nevertheless' – Mrs Scott-Fraser remembered her responsibilities as representative appointed by the regional council, whose grant was allied with that of the Scottish Arts Council and some Lottery money – 'since the commitment has, however rashly, been made, we'll find it difficult to withdraw without suffering severe penalties.'

'And why should we at all be needing to withdraw from that part of it, anyway?' MacKenzie had been opposed to Mrs Scott-Fraser and everything she stood for since she had stood against his planning application for an extension to his grocer's shop and an awning with the word DELICATESSEN in large red lettering on a tartan background. 'At least *they'll* bring some trade into the town.'

Adam reasserted himself. 'We would also have to consider refunding money to booking agents for tickets already sold.'

27

'It may be forced on us. If the Procurator Fiscal insists on us calling the function off while the police investigate this unfortunate incident—'

'Because of an ancient corpse? Hardly an urgent murder hunt.'

'Maybe news of the corpse will be an additional attraction.'

Heads turned towards Duncan Maxwell. Working in the Tourist Office during the season and as a supply teacher during the winter, he was regarded with mild contempt by most of those present, and this sort of remark didn't endear him to them.

MacKenzie was the only one to offer positive approval. 'Aye, could be this will bring more folk into the town.' He might already be calculating how many extra tins to order of his Bonnie Prince Charlie shortbread, made according to a secret Jacobite recipe.

'So,' Adam persevered, 'on the assumption that we're still committed to going ahead with our plans, what do we do about the loss of the Academy hall for the main concerts?'

They all fidgeted on their seats. Adam tilted his chair back, and above their heads contemplated other heads – the dark oil paintings of past provosts, town clerks and similar civic worthies, most of them with vast black beards and eyebrows to match. The absence of beards nowadays, apart from Buchanan's fading ginger tuft, robbed their successors of that awesome dignity.

Duncan Maxwell cleared his throat. Peeved by the derisive looks he had been given, and in a mood to keep stirring, he waved at the platform along the west end of the chamber, dominated by the sheriff's bench and the great chair bearing the burgh coat of arms. 'We could shift the bench and take down the curtains at the back. Should just about accommodate the sinfonia.'

The fidgety silence gave way to a babble of outrage. 'There's no way the provost would stand for that.'

Nor, thought Adam, would the ghosts of all those grave legislators staring down in judgment on these present unworthy successors.

'And anyway, there'd still be no' enough room.'

'In any case,' said Adam decisively, 'the acoustics here are dreadful.'

Cynthia Scott-Fraser's teeth jutted in a domineering smile. 'I'm sure I could use my influence with the governors of Rowanbie school. The new gymnasium there would be ideal. It's only a few miles away, and could easily be incorporated into the concept of The Gathering.'

'And we all ken fine why it's got a new gymnasium,' growled Buchanan. 'Fine for Rowanbie weans, while our own haven't had anything since—'

'Kilstane pupils can use the gymnasium and other facilities on the same level as Rowanbie children.'

'Except that the school bus leaves before they can take part in any activities like that.'

'Mr Buchanan, we went through all this years ago when it was decided for sound economic reasons that the junior school here had to be closed and the children bussed to—'

'Sound economic reasons, aye. So that there was more money for councillors to increase their own salaries and expenses, and flit off to London and foreign places for consultations – isn't that what ye call your sinful jaunts?'

The current jargon, thought Adam, is *freebies*. But in any case it was widely known that Buchanan's main objection was that the headmistress at Rowanbie was an Episcopalian and encouraged singing at morning assembly. He hurried on: 'The whole concept, actually, of Kilstane as a Music Town means that all functions should be integrated within the town jurisdiction. This festival is only the beginning. We have to establish the name as a regular annual event. Performers and the public must come to think of The Kilstane Gathering as something not to be missed – an essential date in the musical calendar from now on. I don't think our brief is to consider extra-mural activities at this stage.'

A few voices had the courage to mutter vague agreement. Kilstane considered that Rowanbie already received too many handouts from the regional council, including a grossly inflated grant for that very gym, because the Scott-Frasers lived there and made their presence felt on every committee.

'Very well.' The teeth receded. 'At least you'll bear in mind that I made the offer. Perhaps you'll incorporate that in the minutes, Mr Lowther.'

Adam knew he would pay for his ruling. The next time he went to tune Captain Scott-Fraser's piano, the condescension would be even chillier than usual, and the niggling criticisms more pungent. Scott-Fraser insisted on being addressed as 'Captain' even though his military service long after World War Two had lasted only a couple of years before he shot himself in the leg and was invalided out. He also insisted on having his grand piano tuned every month, claiming to have painfully critical hearing. Whenever Adam arrived to carry out the task there would be a volume of Beethoven sonatas open on the piano, though in fact the Captain could play only by ear, and then only some sentimental songs all in the key of C major.

Kerr was on his feet. 'Does the Convener have any idea what reaction Sir Nicholas is getting from Daniel Erskine? It would be a bit embarrassing to bring him all the way down here if there's no scope for proper performance of his work.'

'I tried twice to contact him before this meeting. Either his mobile is switched off or he's in a dead spot. And we know there's no way of phoning the house. The composer has made a point of shutting himself away from normal life.'

Buchanan wasn't going to miss such a chance. 'And we ken fine why, don't we? Scuttling away from Kilstane nursing his wounds. Well-deserved wounds.'

'He had finished his employment at the Academy,' said Adam, 'and he had work of his own to do. Great creative work.'

'Creative? And hadn't he done plenty o' that hereabouts? Just be looking at the faces o' some o' those weans down the vennels, and ye'll soon see what he was good at creating. Look at that slut who pretends her second lad's an Irvine like the rest of them. Ye've only to look at his face to see who planted *that* one.'

'Mr Buchanan, we're here to discuss—'

'Huh! Him and that Communist friend of his, at the dirrydans with every girl they could get their hands on.'

'Communist?'

'That Polish brat.'

'He wasnae Polish,' said MacKenzie. 'He was a Czech. His dad got killed in the RAF, fighting the Nazis.'

'All the same, all of them.'

Vainly Adam said: 'Mr Buchanan, I don't think you fully appreciate—'

'The wages of sin is death.'

'Stupid puddock,' muttered a voice from the back.

Cynthia Scott-Fraser's face had gone dead, as it always did whenever a conversation did not involve her and was not dominated by her. She began pushing herself up out of her chair. 'Frightfully sorry, but I do have to dash. The Open Spaces committee. Do let me know' – from the door she directed a polite snarl at Adam – 'if you feel you *do* need premises in Rowanbie after all.'

There were a few shared sighs after the door had closed behind her.

Adam had a sudden incongruous vision of Captain Scott-Fraser making love to his Cynthia. That must have taken some courage, especially if she was continually leaping up and saying they must cut the session short because she had to dash off to an urgent meeting of the Police Committee on Sexual Abuse.

'Well. Let's sum up exactly where we are.'

Apart from the problem of the Academy hall, everything else seemed to be in order. Kerr confirmed that the tents, portaloos and band platforms were already assembled and ready for erection in a matter of hours. Adam himself would be installing the amplification for those not bringing their own equipment. A specific ruling had at last been obtained from the police and the Civic Amenities watchdog that no more than four strolling players at a time would be allowed to serenade passers-by in the streets between 10 a.m. and 4 p.m. A brass quartet would also be allowed to perform for an hour each evening on the balcony of the Tolbooth, above the main square.

The haugh along the Leister Water was still waterlogged after the recent rains, but ought to have dried out in time for the pop concerts there.

'Which still leaves us with the question of our concert hall.'

Duncan Maxwell said: 'Is the main body of the Academy actually affected by the collapse of the tower?'

'There might be an intrinsic weakness that we couldn't risk—'

'It wouldnae take me long to find out where that weakness came from,' grunted Buchanan.

'You of all people have good reason to know where it is,' said Kerr.

Wearily Adam supposed this was all in the good Scots tradition of family blood feud, carried on through the generations. He said: 'It's not the business of this meeting to apportion blame. We simply need to discuss an alternative venue. If any.'

Kerr said: 'I still maintain that the main fabric is in perfectly good condition. It's simply a matter of closing off the short passage into the tower, which anyway hasn't been used since the place was converted into a furniture store.'

'Except that the lavatories are along there, and half the audience will be wanting a piss in the interval,' said Duncan Maxwell chirpily.

'The toilets are in the hall end of the passage. They're still intact, and the tower end is blocked off. No problem.'

Buchanan said: 'If you ask me . . .'

Which nobody had. Adam was beginning to feel himself drifting away, looking at them all from a distance, looking at them mouthing things and clenching and unclenching their fists, seeing them not here but in their everyday lives. In their present incarnation they were swollen with a self-importance they could never quite achieve outside the council chamber. Shaking himself back into the present, he looked at the clock above the double doors of the chamber. 'Very well. In the absence of alternative suggestions, may I have your approval for an approach to the Borough Surveyor for a safety assessment? And in the meantime, if anybody *does* have a bright idea for other possibilities, you know where to find me.'

'And Sir Nicholas should be back soon?' said MacKenzie slyly.

'I'll make another attempt to contact him first thing in the morning. His housekeeper must have a hotel address, or some notion of when he'll be contacting *her*.'

They began making their way down the carpeted but creaking staircase to the ground floor. Halfway down, Duncan Maxwell caught up with Adam.

'Fancy a pint in the *Buccleuch*?'

Adam didn't really fancy any such thing. Duncan was never very good company in a pub. Coming back to Scotland after years away, Adam had sadly learned that most Scots did not go into a pub for a chat with friends, but simply to get owlishly drunk and boast next day of how much they had put back. But the contemptuous glare which Buchanan shot at Duncan provoked Adam into agreeing. He wasn't going to give silent assent to the pettiness of that particular clique.

'Mustn't stay long,' he said as they crossed the street. 'I want to tell Nora how things are going.'

He found there was no need to go home to do that. Nora and Deirdre were sitting close together on stools at the bar. Deirdre looked at home, with her usual glass of gin in her hand. Nora looked awkward, sipping some concoction with a greenish tinge.

'Hello, hello,' said Duncan with a jocularity several degrees over the top. In his wife's company he always seemed at a disadvantage.

Adam looked at Nora. 'Ought you to be out? I mean, so soon . . .'

'I lured her out,' said Deirdre breezily. 'Do her good. I'm looking after her.'

She reached out to drag another stool closer, and waved to Adam to sit beside her. Her shirt was deliberately unbuttoned almost to her navel, and her skirt was hitched up as if by accident when she writhed into position on her bar stool, to show

33

legs that she knew were well worth showing. It would take a man's hand only a few inches to slide under the hem of that skirt. She knew it, of course, but wanted the pretence of being taken unawares.

Certainly she had made it clear with suggestive shrugs and pouts that Adam Lowther was one she particularly wanted to explore her and find how exciting she could be. It was blatant, yet her husband never reacted with anything more than dispirited grouchiness.

How on earth had she and heavy-going Duncan got together in the first place?

But then, how had he and Nora got together in the first place?

He tried to lean forward and smile at Nora. She managed a wan smile in return before being obscured by Duncan's podgy shoulders. 'Well enough to get round to that rehearsal?' Duncan was saying. 'We really ought to get that Hebridean song off pat as an encore.'

'Encore?' squealed Deirdre, pinching Adam's wrist. 'If any.'

Adam didn't care to tell them that the version they intended to use was a reduction of an old ballad in an eccentric rhythm which had been tidied up into a parlour-posh version with run-of-the-mill harmonies in the accompaniment.

Duncan was saying: 'Wasn't there some talk of the BBC cameras coming along for a *Songs of Praise* programme? That could make a nice feature in it.'

Perhaps trying to draw Deirdre's attention away from her husband, Nora leaned towards her. 'Music's all they really think of all the time, isn't it?'

'Time we changed all that.' Deirdre was still looking directly at Adam.

The landlord plonked his elbows on the counter. Sid Carleton was a Carlisle man who had settled long enough in the Borders for his two daughters to have a good local accent, while he himself had never lost the characteristic half-Cumbrian, half-Lancashire whine of the city. 'Been meaning to make you an offer, Mr Lowther. All got to play our part in the festivities, right?

And we hear things are a bit sticky about accommodating some of the players after that business round at the Academy.'

'We've been discussing that, yes.'

'If you want a room for a jazz group or anything of that kind' – Carleton jerked a meaty thumb over his shoulder – 'we've got that function room out back there. You'd be welcome to use it.'

And the beer and the drams would flow very profitably, thought Adam. But it was still a useful idea. And live music, no matter how strident, would be better for the whole concept than the insistent thud of pop music pounding out of the speakers at the moment.

'I think we'll be taking you up on that.'

'Drop in any time and we'll talk it over. And you could back my application for an extension.' Carleton reached for a cloth and mopped up drips of beer. 'Any idea why that tower did come to collapse like that?'

'Rain, of course,' contributed a voice from further along the bar. 'What else would ye expect, after all that rain swilling down off the brae in March? Undermined the whole playground, I'd say.'

'Aye, well . . .'

'And that corpse, now.'

It must have been the main topic of conversation in this bar since the news broke.

'A nauchtie pupil, maybe? The tawse not good enough – they had to wall him up to keep him oot o' the Rector's hair.'

Nora wriggled on her stool, a sign that she wanted to go home. Adam slid from his own stool, brushing against Deirdre as she leaned at a perilous angle towards him.

'See you, then.'

He took Nora's arm, and they went out of the buzz and jangle of the bar into the sudden silence of the street. It was a clear, still evening. Street lamps trickled smears of light across the faint dew on the pavement. The only sound was a faint rustle from the newsagent's on the corner, where a two-day-old poster promising revelations about a council rates scandal had worked loose. Then there was a brief clatter as a crumpled Coke can rolled lazily into the gutter. A shadow which might have been a cat scurried across the road.

He had been so happy to come back, after the years away. He had never understood how his father could bear to leave Kilstane on such an abrupt impulse and look for work down in the depths of England.

He would still be happy if it weren't for Nora's frequent wistfulness. Just as, when a boy, he had never wanted to leave, she as a young married woman had never really wanted to come here. He looked down at the pale prettiness of her cheek, level with his shoulder – her narrow but puckish face affectionate yet always tinged with melancholy – and realized that although they were arm in arm, his mind had been far away. It was filled with daydreams, of Mr Erskine teaching him the rudiments of music, and his father so weirdly antagonistic to the whole idea. It had been *Mr* Erskine then, not the reverent 'Erskine' one used later when referring to a great man. Had any pupil ever spoken of Mr Elgar or Mr Bach? And now the daydreams were becoming evening dreams – of concerts soon to be held in the favourite settings of his childhood; a string quartet here, a free-and-easy improvisation there, and an evening of light music when he could encourage Nora to enjoy singing in spite of her deficiencies – deficiencies which a local audience would be unlikely to regard too critically.

They wouldn't laugh at her. Nobody would laugh. He knew her failings. But he would never let her be humiliated by anybody else.

He squeezed her arm. 'Feel well enough to set up your practising with Duncan? Have to make up for lost time?'

She managed the faintest of smiles. 'Music is all that really matters to you, isn't it, Adam?'

In bed, he put his arm round her, wanting her to feel close to him and the ideas that kept him going.

She was warm and cosy, but he felt her stiffen.

'Need bringing back to life?' he murmured into her ear.

'Oh, I don't know.' Then, grudging but submissive: 'Oh, all right, then.'

And, having started it, he found her willingness not enough. To finish it, he had to visualize Deirdre, even though he didn't really want Deirdre herself, but could summon up the rhythm of what he guessed the movements of that body of hers would be – movements all the boys at the Academy had been obsessed by, mentally stripping her and sweating over her. And in the end it had been lumpish Duncan she had married.

When he had finished, and kissed Nora's neck, and was lying back with his arm round her shoulders, she said quite amiably: 'What were you thinking of, Adam? Some concerto with a lot of drumbeats, or something?'

4

It was ten o'clock in the morning when Nick approached the isolated stone house below a hummock which must shelter it from the winds across the wilderness. The morning sky had changed from cool grey to pallid mauve, with a drift of cloud like an emaciated dragon sprawled across it. There was a moment when he felt an absurd premonition, an impulse to turn and drive away, and be done with this whole business Why the hell had he allowed himself to be talked into this visit?

Before he could lift the pitted iron knocker on the door, Mairi McLeod opened it.

'Nick.'

As she held the door open for him to go in past her, an almost animal heat came off her. Just as he remembered.

'But of course it's Sir Nicholas now, isn't it?'

'Not to you,' he heard himself saying. 'Just call me what you always did.'

'After all this time? Not sure that'd be wise.'

Her hair was shorter and less wild than he remembered, but the colours were still ravishingly the same – sunshine on ripe barley, with a few strands of chestnut like an inlay of darker marquetry. At the back she had pulled a loosely woven plait through a rough leather toggle, thrusting out clear of her long, pale neck.

The room into which she showed him was surprisingly long

for a Highland house, and was obviously the result of two smaller rooms being knocked together. A deep inglenook set into the side wall held a large open grate with a gently crackling fire, and two columns of peat blocks stacked to either side. No attempt had been made to mask the stonework with a wooden cladding to carry paint or wallpaper.

Facing the fireplace were two battered leather armchairs. And beyond them, a grand piano with a standard lamp, its neck tilted to throw light on the music desk. No television set anywhere you might expect to find one. No telephone in view – but then, he already knew that Erskine wasn't on the phone. Writing to his amanuensis and playing on old acquaintanceship had been the only way of making contact.

Mairi waved him towards one of the chairs and pushed a small coffee table between them. 'Coffee? Or something stronger?'

'Coffee, yes. It's a bit early for the other.'

'Daniel won't agree with that, when he manages to totter in.'

'He drinks a lot?'

'After what he's been through, do you blame him?'

'I suppose not.'

She went out with that lithe, unselfconscious swing of the hips he remembered. She was an incongruous, alien creature to be caged out here, so far from her old haunts: too exotic for an audience to be denied any glimpses of her.

Nick got up and went to glance at the music propped open on the piano.

There was about three-quarters of a sheet of manuscript covered with an untidy but legible piano part, blotched by a few corrections and some conflicting expression marks. Instinctively he slid on to the piano stool and began playing. The rhythm was baffling. After a few bars he went back to the beginning, and counted a few steady, disciplined beats before starting again. Again the music fought against the beat. Discords unravelled and then struggled through another cadence, like a swiftly flowing burn plashing into a barrier and seeking another outlet.

Behind him, Mairi put a tray down on the coffee table and said: 'You're counting sevens instead of four-plus-three.'

'Ah, I get you.' He played the unfinished bars on the last stave. 'And what comes next?'

'We haven't worked it out yet.'

'Sounds way beyond the sort of music you used to play in the old days. But there *is* a sort of folk rhythm – something going way back.'

'Daniel has sunk himself in old music to produce . . . well, new music. A new language.'

'But you have to transcribe it all for him.'

'Being laird of Kilstane, you'll know why.'

'Before my time, but yes, I know.'

That had been the reason for Daniel Erskine finally quitting his home town. Although it had happened years ago, Nick still came across resonances of it in the town. Like all the Border families, with their rivalries and ancient grudges, Kilstane folk did not forget easily. For every Adam Lowther who revered the image of Daniel Erskine as a great composer with local roots, there were far more who gloated over him getting the comeuppance he so richly deserved. Those hands he used for playing the piano and for writing music had strayed into too many other places, and hardly anyone disapproved of the jealous husband who had smashed both those hands with a sledgehammer. Most of them deplored the sentencing of the attacker to five years in prison. No wonder Erskine had fled in despair and shut himself away.

Mairi said: 'Did that bastard go back to Kilstane after he was released?'

'Not that I know of. It's not something I've thought of asking.'

'Before your time,' she echoed. 'And they wouldn't be likely to tell an incomer.'

'So that's what I am?'

'You may be the laird by inheritance, but from what Daniel tells me about his fellow townsfolk, you'll always be an incomer.'

40

'Do you suppose, if you bring Erskine back—'

'I told you when I wrote, that's a very big *if*. Ten to one you've had a wasted journey.'

'But you didn't actually forbid me to come.'

'No. We don't welcome a lot of visitors. I thought you'd be an exceptional one. And I did put your ideas to Daniel, so at least he's prepared.'

She sipped her coffee and stared into the fire as it stirred and settled, releasing a lazy drift of sparks. The smell of the peat was soporific. Nick, studying her almost aquiline profile above that incredibly graceful neck, wondered whether the whole atmosphere of this place acted as a sedative, damping down memories of another world, a dangerous past, out there.

'Where did you meet Erskine?'

She hesitated for a moment, then said briskly: 'At a folk concert. When he was trying to put as big a distance between himself and Kilstane as possible.'

'You were playing there?'

'Yes.'

He thought of her impassioned fiddle playing and the heat she generated by her sheer presence and the way her head shook fiercely, rhythmically as if urging herself on to yet another chorus, another wild improvisation.

'And you gave up your own career just to become Erskine's handmaiden?'

'Nick, you make it sound like some terrible sacrifice. Don't you realize, the folk circuit was just that: a circuit. Couldn't even say it was coming to a dead end, because there wasn't any end – just going on and on, round and round, playing what they expected you to play. If I'd written a violin concerto, who'd have listened? With Daniel . . . it's a real quest, a challenge every day. Never knowing where we're going to end up. At last I've been able to contribute to bringing something real to life.'

He looked over his shoulder towards the music on the piano,

'And that's waiting there for him to tell you how to proceed – how to work out at the keyboard—'

41

'The second strain,' she said.

'Second strain?'

'All part of the old fiddling tradition. Most of the old folk songs ran to only eight bars. After you've played the melody once and then repeated it, you need some contrast. Insert a new melody of your own – a second strain.'

'Like the middle eight in an old pop song?'

'Only more so. Leap off into a different key, change the mood. Often a conflict between the old theme and the intruder.'

She slid out of the armchair and moved past the piano to a violin case propped against the wall. Taking the violin out, she did a quick, impatient tuning, tucked it under her chin and began improvising, more along the lines of an old reel, with a dancing rhythm and some showy double-stopping. Nick pushed himself up out of his chair and went back to the piano stool, intuitively picking out a chord here, a chord there, to supplement the pentatonic theme. As she approached the end of the second repeated phrase he waited, sensing that this was where the second strain would come in. And she was off into an unrelated key without any modulation, leaping as if from a springboard into the air – a totally different air.

'And what's that supposed to be?'

The voice was gravelly, discordant even within itself, grating harshly enough into their music to bring it to an abrupt halt.

Daniel Erskine stood in the inner doorway.

He was a hunched figure of a man, stooped but with his large head jutting forward as if to ward off any possible attack. His hair was a great grey mop, but his lowering eyebrows remained startlingly black. His shirt and slacks were expensive but crumpled and greasy. Having issued his rasping challenge, he stood waiting for someone else to make a move.

Nick took a step towards him and automatically put out a hand to shake hands. Then his gaze fell towards fingerless gloves, and he froze, wondering how to retreat, how to get himself out of the *faux pas*. But Erskine extended his right hand,

42

and let the kid-glove softness linger for a few seconds between Nick's fingers.

'Shall I make some more coffee?' Mairi asked.

'A large malt would be a damn sight more acceptable. Or two large malts, hm?'

Erskine settled himself in the armchair which Mairi had been occupying a few minutes earlier. The sun, moving slowly across the world outside, cast a fuzzy halo across the back of his head and made a dark silhouette of it, staring facelessly at his visitor.

'You've come a long way, Sir Nicholas, on what is almost certainly a fruitless mission.'

'I hope that won't be so. We want to see you in Kilstane and celebrate your music, where so much of it must have begun.'

'We?'

Nick explained the concept of the Kilstane Gathering, interrupted by little intakes and expulsions of breath which might have been half repressed sniggers. He leaned forward in the hope of seeing more of Erskine's face.

'You know there were two programmes of your work on Radio 3 two months ago?'

'We don't have a radio.' Suddenly his voice rose and he jerked his head so that Nick got a glimpse of his huge profile and the thrust of his chin. 'Damn it, where's my bloody dram?'

Mairi put a large crystal tumbler on the coffee table. The glow of the fire made tiny flames dance in the amber liquid. 'About bloody time.' Erskine slowly clenched both gloves round the tumbler and lifted it as if testing its weight before risking moving it too far. He managed a long gulp and let the tang of the spirit run along the back of his lips before lowering the tumbler as carefully as he had lifted it.

Nick continued warily. 'It would certainly be better to hear the music live. Which is what we all want.'

'We?' said Erskine again, 'All my dear old friends and admirers in that shithouse of a town?'

'Times have changed. People have begun to appreciate—'

'That lot? Appreciate? The world really *has* changed.'

43

'You obviously don't get many opportunities up here to hear what your music really sounds like.'

Erskine's right hand strayed on to his knee, and twitched briefly as if there was still some life in the shattered fingers to reach out for a keyboard and play what had just come into his head. But he scowled and said: 'And don't want to. If I can't perform it myself, I don't want to hear it. And I don't much want to hear even myself performing it. Once I've conceived a piece, I hear it in my head better than anyone can possibly play it.'

Mairi put her hand on his shoulder – in reproof, or affection, it was hard to guess. 'Daniel, don't say more than—'

'Maybe it's time to say a hell of a lot.' Erskine went through the slow ritual with his glass again.

'Ernest Newman would have agreed with you,' said Nick. 'Towards the end of his life he said he would rather read a score and hear a perfect performance in his mind than attend a concert or opera.'

'Newman? Fond of Wagner, wasn't he?'

'Very much so.'

'Bloody fool.'

A shrill but faint stuttering began in Nick's pocket. With an apologetic nod he pulled out his mobile phone. All he could hear was a blurred to-and-fro of crackling. 'Seem to be in a real dead area here.'

'Those damn things,' Erskine exploded, dribbling whisky between his mouth and the tumbler. 'Either turn it off or get out of here.'

'I'm sorry, I was just hoping for a brief—'

'I don't give a damn what you were hoping for. I won't have one of those abominations nosing its way into my house. Damn glad to hear this is a dead area. I intend to keep it that way. One good reason for my staying put. Not going out if I can help it. Damn stupid things like that bleating away.'

Nick switched the mobile off before slipping it back into his pocket. Hastily he said: 'Sorry about that. But I promise we'll shield you from any annoyances of that kind when you come to Kilstane.'

'Who said I was going to Kilstane? And what for?'

'As a conductor, possibly? Or simply as an honoured guest.'

'Honoured? By those barbarians?'

Mairi said: 'I did warn you, Sir Nicholas, that your ideas wouldn't appeal.'

Erskine emitted an evil chuckle. 'Hoped to play the old pals' act, eh? Wheedle your way in through the good offices of an old . . . er . . . acquaintance. Wasting your time. Accept it, and run off home.' Then he glanced from one to the other, and chuckled again. 'Tell you what, Torrance. Take the girl out for lunch. She doesn't stand many opportunities like that with me around. Give her lunch, and then clear off.'

'Could I persuade you to join us?'

'Like hell. That hotel will be just as bad as everywhere else nowadays. Wherever you go, there's canned rubbish blasting out from speakers. Mind-numbing. Numbing the faculties so persistently that in the end the ear is unable to take in and appreciate real music of any kind.'

'Even up here?'

'Yes. Even up here. Another reason for staying where I am.'

Erskine saw Mairi and Nick to the door. There was an impatience about him that suggested he could hardly wait to get them off the premises before stumbling back towards the bottle and the tumbler.

With his hand on the passenger door of the Laguna to let Mairi in, Nick made one last attempt. 'Please think about it. About all the people who really do want you to be a part of the Gathering.'

'I'm in no mood to become a circus act at my time of life.'

Mairi waited before ducking into the car. 'We won't be long.'

'No need to rush. I'm perfectly capable of looking after myself.'

As Nick swung the car away from the house on to the cinder path and then the single-track road, Mairi said: 'I truly mustn't be too long. He'll grope about until he can get the bottle open. Maybe he'll drop it, or spill half of it. And one day I'm afraid he'll manage to set fire to the place.'

'Our friend is certainly set against the world outside. Telephones, radios—'

'Mozart managed without a radio. Even as late as Sibelius, I think one could sit in the forests and not give a damn for a lot of chatter on the airwaves.'

In the hotel they sat in the bar, waiting for the menu.

'He's pretty far advanced as an alcoholic, isn't he?'

'He likes his malt. People in these parts are used to it.'

'If he drinks heavily—'

'I didn't say that.'

'If he does,' Nick persisted, 'how do you get the music out of him?'

'Eric Fenby got it out of Delius when he was blind and paralysed by syphilis. Alcohol's nothing compared with that.'

He looked at the swell of cashmere over her breasts. And looking down the menu, she was half secretively mouthing the names of the dishes. Her lips were as full and sensuously slack as ever. He remembered her impassioned performances of old Romanian melodies she had discovered, old songs from the Hebrides, and the bend of her head over the violin bow, just the way it was now bent over that menu. And he wondered if she remembered rooms they had shared, beds they had shared. Wondered· if she was wondering about his hotel room upstairs, and whether he was intending to do anything about it this afternoon.

He wasn't going to do anything about it.

'I still don't really understand,' he said, 'why you've given up your career to wait on that old crock. He's a boor. How you can coax music of such significance out of him, the way you have done, rather than pursue your own career—'

'Come off it, Nick. I've told you already, I'd got tired of going round and round with what I could do. Nowhere to go. No way to break out.'

46

'Why should you have to? Lots of folk artists go on repeating themselves and making a fortune. The public like them to churn out the old favourites, with just a few new pieces not too—'

'Not too adventurous. Not *too* new. Stuck in the same old rut. Like I said, nowhere to go.'

'But you had other lines you could have developed.'

'Never quite good enough. And nobody was ever going to take an ex-folksinger seriously as a composer. Or even as a violinist. Or anything much else. If I'd really tried to set myself up in a different field, can you imagine the reviews? Imagine the sneers, the clever-clever critics.'

'So you're content just to transcribe somebody else's work?'

'When it's someone like Daniel Erskine, yes.'

'Look . . . what *is* there about his music? One of my committee members is utterly hooked on it. As if it was some new world – or at least a very different and exciting country.'

'Yes. Another country. Not open to everybody. No tourist visas available.'

The waiter approached. Mairi hurriedly focused on the menu. But he had not come to take their order. 'Sir Nicholas?'

Mairi smiled to herself, and seemed to be mouthing the title in a silent, mocking echo.

'There's a phone call for you, sir. Along the passage, first on the right.'

Nick went to take the call. Adam Lowther had found his number from Mrs Robson. It took him time to take in the news. At first it seemed grotesque, way outside his ken. But then he knew there were things which really had to be dealt with. He hurried back to the bar. 'Sorry. Something rather disturbing. I've got to leave. Right now.'

'Oh, so I'm being stood up?'

'Mairi, I'm awfully sorry. Bloody catastrophe. Our main concert venue has collapsed. I really must start back right away.'

'So you won't be needing Daniel anyway.'

'I won't know just what the situation is until I get back and can sum up just where we stand. Cancel some bookings and God

47

knows what else. Look, give me a minute to pick up my things and settle the bill, and I'll drop you off at the house on the way.'

At the house he got out, held her door open, and kissed her briefly as she got out. Her familiar crooked smile tugged again at his memory.

She said: 'Sorry you've had a wasted journey.'

'It was great seeing you again,' he said banally.

'Was it?' She walked towards the house, looking back once over her shoulder. 'I think it's just as well you couldn't tempt Daniel to go back to Kilstane, anyway. From what I've heard of the place, I wouldn't have fancied being around there for too long.'

The veiled withdrawal, almost antagonism, in her hazel eyes struck a chord in him that could only have resonated between people who had known one another intimately and were now ill at ease but still intimate.

He said: 'You don't want him to come, do you? *You're* the one who doesn't want him to come.'

'It's been lovely seeing you again, Nick.' It might have been a sardonic echo of his own remark. 'Sorry it's all come to nothing.'

5

Detective Inspector Lesley Gunn drove into the cramped car park beside Kilstane police station and sat in it for a few moments, taking deep breaths and trying to persuade herself that she was perfectly capable of facing the snide grins and mutterings her return was bound to provoke.

The desk sergeant confirmed her worst suspicions. He greeted her courteously but with a conspiratorial grin showing that he remembered her all right.

'Glad to see you back, inspector. We'd heard you'd be visiting us again.'

Yes, you could bet they had.

A young man in a leather jacket, pink striped shirt and chalky chinos had been sitting on the bench facing the desk. He might have been someone waiting to be charged, or a relative come to bail out a suspect. Instead, when he saw her, he got up and said: 'Good morning, guv. Sergeant Elliot.'

He had a pleasant face with sandy freckles, marred only by a deep purple scar down one cheek.

'I was told I could call on you if necessary,' said Lesley. 'Didn't expect you to be on the spot when I got here.'

'Thought I'd like to welcome you to our patch. And I get bored just sitting at home.'

'Oh, one of those. Always fidgeting to get down to the nitty-gritty?'

'I'm afraid so, guv.'

'Well, I've been told not to give you a relapse. Let's take it slowly. And first of all, let's find someone to fill us in on the situation.'

'I've already done a bit of a recce.'

There was nothing pushy or complacent about it. She could tell at once that he was conscientious by nature, and would have done as much of the groundwork as possible because that was his job, and he was committed to his job.

'Right,' she said. 'Let's sit down somewhere and go over what we've got.'

The police surgeon's report was the obvious starting point. 'Only a stopgap, until they've chipped the body out,' said Elliot.

'Chipped it out?'

'You'd better come and see, guv.'

Elliot's car was outside, waiting. In his quiet way he did seem to have organized everything without waiting to be asked.

Kilstane Community Hospital mortuary did not usually accommodate corpses in quite such a weighty shroud. Lesley had expected a body damaged by falling masonry, but this one was not the least like that. It was encased in concrete, which was itself enclosed in a wide, twisted metal tube. Not enough of the head was visible to attempt any identification.

Elliot anticipated her thoughts. 'There's every likelihood that a lot of the head and body will be crushed out of recognition.'

'Dental records?'

'When we can get down to what's left of his mouth.'

'Is someone assigned to that?'

'He's due to be carted off to the pathology lab in Gilliskirk this afternoon.'

Lesley studied the twisted conglomeration of human remains, concrete, and metal. It would take time and a great deal of care to remove first the tubular casing and then the concrete shroud without damaging the contents further. She had heard of gangland killings when the victim was weighted down with concrete and dumped into a river, but killings by feuding gangs in the Borders belonged to an earlier century.

'Shifting that must have taken some doing,' she mused.

'Shovelling him down that pipe and then pouring concrete in on him.' The sergeant nodded agreement. 'I wouldn't have thought one man could do it on his own.'

'No. And where was this mish-mash found?'

Elliot drove her back into town and parked alongside the Academy railings. A pump was thudding away, draining water from under the playground. A young man in a tweed suit, supervising the work, watched the car draw up, and nodded recognition at the sergeant.

'Back on the beat, Rab? Not ready for early retirement?'

'Not yet, Mr Kerr.' He stood aside to let Lesley move forward. 'This is Detective Inspector Gunn. Mr William Kerr.'

'Ah, yes.' Kerr shook hands with what threatened to become a knowing squeeze. 'You were the one who dug out a few little fallacies in our Common Riding, right?'

Lesley had known even before she got here that she wouldn't be popular. After the part she had played in exposing the folly of their annual charade she would be regarded either as a bad joke or as a wretched destroyer of tradition. There was no way she was going to be popular. Her only course was to be tough with them before they could decide how to make things difficult for her. Tough from the word go. Let them get the measure of it right from the start.

'I've seen the tubing and what's in it.' She waved towards the pump. 'As you seem to be in charge of operations here, Mr Kerr, perhaps you can suggest how that came to be in the building.'

'I had no responsibility for the tower end of the building. That work was done a few years ago. Current renovations have been mainly connected with inserting larger windows in the hall and providing a direct entrance from the old playground. The passage to the back door, past what had once been the outside lavatories, was removed at the time of Buchanan's work. Before I was involved,' Kerr added heavily.

'And when was that?

'That would have been in 1981.' There was no hesitation in Kerr's answer. It implied an accusation.

51

'The metal surround to the concrete and the . . . the remains. Where would that have come from?'

'It was obviously the extractor from the old kitchens on that side.'

'But how could anyone have shoved a body into it and then been able to pour concrete into it? I mean, if it was above the kitchens, it must have been at a certain height. You can't heave a concrete mixer up on your shoulders and start pouring.'

'At the time of those earlier renovations, there would have been scaffolding up the whole side of the building. Bound to have been a mixer up there at some stage. You'll have to ask Buchanan.' It was said with a touch of anticipatory malice.

Lesley glanced at Sergeant Elliot. He smiled a silent assurance that this, too, could be arranged without difficulty.

Enoch Buchanan's premises had been a familiar eyesore when Lesley Gunn did her probationary period in Kilstane, and when she came back for the Black Knowe theft investigation. If it had changed at all since those early encounters, it was only by an accumulation of recent dust and sawdust on the rigid tidiness which the owner imposed on everything in the world under his command. His office was an oblong shed constructed long before the days of portakabins, propped on stilts against one wall of the yard with six steps and a polished handrail up to it.

Buchanan opened the door as Lesley set foot on the top step. He nodded curt recognition at Elliot, but didn't wait for the sergeant to make any introductions.

'Och, aye.' He was a broader, more bristling Scot than young Kerr. 'And wouldn't I be remembering you as—'

'I'm sure you would.' She bristled right back at him. 'But what I'd like you to remember right now, Mr Buchanan, is exactly what could have enabled somebody – or somebodies – to insert a corpse into the renovations I understand you were carrying out in 1981.'

'And who'd ha' been giving ye to understand that?'

She wasn't going to get involved in local squabbles. 'The important point, Mr Buchanan, is that it couldn't have been an

accident. So do you remember who was working on the site at
the time and would have had the facilities to kill someone and
conceal the body in an aluminium flue without your being
aware of it.'

'I can't be everywhere at every minute of the day.'

'Of course not. But I was hoping you might remember something unusual – odd behaviour on the part of one or two of your
employees around that time, signs of a shortage of material, any
rumours that might have been floating around.'

'I've had plenty of different men working for me since then.
Cannae keep track of each and every one. Nae staying power,
these youngsters nowadays.'

Patiently Lesley said: 'I presume you have records of your
employees at certain periods.'

'If they haven't all been thrown out.'

'Mr Buchanan, I'd be most grateful if you could take the time
to go through your records and let me know anything that
strikes you. Something or someone you may have forgotten, and
then all at once you get to remembering.'

'And where would I be finding the time to do that? I've got a
business to run, ye ken.'

DS Elliot said: 'I'd be happy to sit in with you, Mr Buchanan.
Save a lot of time that way.'

'Well, I'm nae sure that—'

'Sergeant Elliot's trained eye would be a great asset,' said
Lesley.

'Hmph. Well.' It was neither an acceptance nor a refusal.
Buchanan was not a man to give way gracefully. 'And what'll be
the point of it all? Someone dead all those years back – what
would that have to do with us now?'

'That's what we intend to find out. It's not simply a matter of
someone having a heart attack on a hillside and lying there
undiscovered for ages. Nor was it an industrial accident that
someone's tried to cover up. At least, I assume that's not the
case?'

'And what would ye be implying by that, miss? There's

precious few accidents on any of my jobs, let me tell you that. And nane of them would be covered up.'

'In which case,' Lesley persevered, 'we have to start looking around for a different sort of murder suspect. Because murder it has to be. That body wasn't trapped by accident. It was squeezed into the metal cylinder—'

'The old school kitchen flue,' Buchanan reluctantly corroborated.

'Why did nobody notice it was no longer functioning properly?'

'It wasnae meant to. Not any longer. Our brief at the time was to modernize the rest of the building, do away with the outside lavatories and install new ones, and extend the school hall. For all the good *that* turned out to be. All that money spent, and then only these few years later they were turning it into a warehouse and bussing the weans to Rowanbie. Of all the half-witted—'

'Yes.' Lesley steered him back to the matter in hand. 'The kitchen flue, Mr Buchanan.'

'Aye, well. The kitchens were gutted and new ones added in that single-storey extension. There was no way of using the tower, which was always a bit of a nuisance anyway, the way old MacLean just jammed it on. The flue went through it. Not worth the trouble of stripping the flue out and having to make good. Just seal up the outer end.'

Lesley had a brief vision of how young Kerr would have reacted to that admission.

'And before that was done,' she said, 'it would have been possible for someone to get up the scaffolding and pour concrete in? Which must have been a tricky operation. You must have wondered about it recently, once the body was discovered.'

'Aye, everyone's done a fine lot o' wondering.'

'And you haven't had time to think of anybody you know who might have disappeared around that time?'

Buchanan made a show of heaving a large file off a rickety shelf and flicking through it without enthusiasm. A faint wisp of dust drifted across the office like a cluster of midges.

Suddenly he pushed the file away and began tugging at the

spiny hairs below his left ear. 'Now, I'd not be wanting to say there was anything to it . . .'

'To what, Mr Buchanan?'

'It could have been about that time that Jamie Lowther went south. Though I dinna see what—'

'Lowther? Do you know where he's living now?'

'From what I heard, he died some years back. And then his son came back.'

'His son?'

'Young Lowther. Adam. Married down there, then brought her back here.'

'Where might I find him?'

'The music shop along the way,' said Elliot. 'Used to be a bookshop, but there was a fire about the time of . . .' He stopped, embarrassed.

Buchanan was far from embarrassed. 'Aye, ye'll remember the bookshop, lass? All tied in with that trouble ye stirred up.'

Lesley remembered. It was irrelevant. Struggling to keep things on track, she said: 'Did this Jamie Lowther work for you?'

'Kept our accounts, aye. Good at drawing up contracts, and keeping an eye on things. Left me in a spot, going off as quickly as he did. But,' he finished piously, 'I'd not be wishing to make ill surmises about the dead.'

The phone rang. Buchanan grunted a response, then put his hand over the mouthpiece. 'This will take some time.' It was a clear request for them to get off the premises.

Crossing the yard, Elliot said: 'Incidentally it was young Lowther's wife who was first on the scene when the tower came down. Got laid out by a few chunks of it.'

'One of those weird coincidences? Anyway, I think it might be worth checking whether there were any Mispers circulating locally around the time this Lowther quit town, which might tie in with the date of that flue being blocked off.'

The window of the music shop had a display of classical CDs up both sides, and a more widely spaced selection along the front.

The most prominent were recordings of Daniel Erskine's music, and behind them was propped up an open score of a composition by Erskine called *The Drummer of Cortachy*.

There had been some alterations to the building since she last saw it. The outer flight of steps to the first floor had been removed, and a new access sheltered under the covered pend on the other side. The shop door had been widened, and its glass pane was filled with a poster announcing a concert of Daniel Erskine's music. As Elliot opened it to let her in, they were greeted by a spiky string serenade from two speakers hanging on the far wall. Racks of piano music filled the space between the speakers, and to her right was a glass cabinet with violin and guitar strings, clarinet reeds, and a couple of recorders. CDs and cassettes rose halfway up the wall to her left. Stacked in one corner as if to keep them well away from more serious musical items were three stratocasters with glistening multi-coloured metal inlays. An upright piano sheltered behind a screen which she suspected the owner might have made at school, covered with a collage of cut-out pictures of composers, conductors, and instruments. In every space on the walls were posters announcing the forthcoming Gathering or advertising recordings of Daniel Erskine's compositions.

'Can I help you?'

From the shadows at the back of the shop a youngish middle-aged man stepped out into the light. Lesley summed him up swiftly into one of her artistic categories. This one in the manner of John Hazlitt's portrait of his brother William, intense and earnest, with faint permanent shadows under the eyes and a tendency to hold his head sideways, as if listening critically with his left ear.

She held out her warrant card. 'Detective Inspector Gunn. And this is Sergeant Elliot.'

'Oh.' It conveyed neither surprise nor alarm as he shook hands. 'Adam Lowther. You're here about our corpse, I suppose.' He could be simply disappointed that she wasn't about to buy some sheet music or a recent CD.

'Yes. We're trying to identify it, or to collect information which may lead to identification and a possible reason for its – er – incarceration.'

'I don't know that I can help. We've all discussed it, of course – the whole town, I mean – but it's all a mystery. I've no more idea than anybody else.'

'Mr Buchanan said your wife was injured when the tower collapsed.'

'Only slightly, yes.'

'He thought you might be able to shed some light on it.'

'Did he?' Lowther looked irritated. 'Why should he suppose that?'

'Your father was Jamie Lowther?'

'He *was*. He died four years ago.'

'Oh, I'm sorry.'

Lowther looked around vaguely, and dragged forward the only chair in the shop. Lesley shook her head with a polite smile. There was an awkward pause. She broke it:

'You and your father were here at the time of the . . . mysterious death?'

'Were we? I mean, you know when it happened, then?'

'It seems reasonable to suppose that it was during the conversions carried on by Mr Buchanan and his builders. I gather your father worked for him.'

'He did. In the office.'

'And you?'

'I was still at the Academy. Having a few music lessons,' he said with a surge of pride, 'with Mr Erskine. Before he became famous.'

Lesley caught a flash of interest in Sergeant Elliot's eye. But, like herself, he knew better than to give any suppositions away.

Adam Lowther was obviously glad of any excuse to talk about his favourite topic. 'Mr Erskine's father was rector of the Academy during the war and afterwards. Daniel Erskine had to do his National Service after the war, and then came back here to teach at the Academy. He was a wonderful teacher. My father

57

wasn't keen on me spending so much time on music, but it was wonderful. And then we left.'

'Why did your father decide to leave Kilstane?'

'I don't know.' The resentment was still throbbing there. 'We just packed up and left. Said there was better work down in England. It wasn't all that much better, if you ask me.'

'And you went to school there?'

'In Leeds. And when I left, I got a job in a piano showroom. Tuning pianos, repairing, selling music. Until my mother and father died, and I heard there were these premises for sale, and I could come back to Kilstane and set up on my own.'

'You manage to make a living. Rather specialized, in a small community like this, isn't it?'

'I do regular piano tuning. Playing the piano or the organ at weddings and that sort of thing. Setting up amplification for local events. I could have expanded. I was offered a franchise for installing and maintaining and replacing jukeboxes and fruit machines in the pubs and cafés for ten miles around. But I didn't fancy that line.' The music from the speakers suddenly stopped. 'That was Erskine's *Selkie of Wastness*,' he said reverently.

Whatever it was that Lesley ought to be asking, she realized she was in danger of being deflected by the tide race of his enthusiasm.

'His music has obviously meant a lot to you,' she said, 'but—'

'Too much.'

The voice was very quiet, just as the footsteps down the stairs in the far corner of the shop had been quiet – inaudible, in fact. The woman in the shadows looked diffident, almost immediately sorry that she had come down and had spoken. Already she was starting on an apology.

'Sorry, Adam. I thought when I heard voices . . . this time of day, and being half-term, you'd need someone else down here.'

He went over and took her arm, leading her towards the others. 'My wife, Nora. Detective Inspector . . . er . . .'

'Gunn. And this is Sergeant Elliot.'

'It's half term, and the kids are home from school. They still function according to the break-time clock, and come out to wander round the shops. Lifting whatever takes their fancy. It needs two of us on the scene to keep our eyes open.'

Lesley looked at the larger instruments, trying to envisage a raiding party carrying off a guitar or a double bass.

'Not the big stuff,' said Lowther. 'Just clarinet reeds, violin strings, a violin mute, anything they can slip in their pocket.'

'Even though none of them would know how to play a note,' murmured Nora Lowther.

Sergeant Elliot had been silent for a long time. Nodding towards the now silent speakers, he decided to contribute. 'And they don't come in to listen to this Daniel Erskine's music?'

'There aren't many who care for it. Only Adam.'

It was said with a loyal but sly smile. Lesley sensed between the two of them something not bitter enough to be antagonism, but a sort of resignation – a marital weariness, just as when a husband or wife endures an incurable mannerism or a repetitive turn of phrase. You had to get used to it, but there was always a drag of disillusionment underneath.

She ventured: 'Since you're such an expert on Daniel Erskine, Mr Lowther, can you tell me whether, after he had left Kilstane, he came back from time to time? Or never?'

The shop door behind her squeaked open. Looking past her, Adam Lowther said: 'Here's someone who's just been visiting him. Perhaps you'd better ask Sir Nicholas.'

'Ask me what, Adam?'

The remembered voice sent prickles down the back of Lesley's neck and all the way down her spine. She could hardly bring herself to look round.

At first she thought he looked older, but then saw the lines in his lean, predatory face as those of tiredness. That patrician chin and those high cheeks were for once unshaven, and the sweep of dark brown hair back from his forehead was ruffled and unkempt. He had obviously just come from the car against the kerb outside, and was wiping his eyes after what must have been a long journey, blinking to adjust to the interior of the shop.

59

'Sir Nicholas.' She forced the words out.

'Detective Inspector Gunn. Or is it DCI Gunn by now?'

'No, it's not.'

'Oh, I thought . . . but anyway, I wasn't expecting to see you here again.'

She caught Adam Lowther glancing shrewdly from one to the other. He might not have had her training as a detective, and might have spent some years away from Kilstane before coming back, but he had that Kilstane look of heavy-lidded speculation. And she wasn't going to let there be any speculation about her and Nick. Sir Nicholas. She had nearly let herself drift in that direction once before, and she wasn't going to let herself drift into anything like it again.

6

Nick Torrance sat in the window seat of the first-floor hall in
Black Knowe while Adam Lowther recited the renewed
arrangements for The Gathering. Half slewed round on the seat,
he feasted his eyes on the prospect of sunlight on the gleaming
Leister Water and the braes and moors beyond. Over the last few
years the sturdiness of his tower house and the beauties of the
estate had become almost a physical part of himself. Or was he,
rather, becoming a part of *it*? He felt the rise and fall of the
hunched shoulders of the fells and the long groping arms reaching out towards the borders of Northumberland, where other
pele towers and bastles still stood in mute memory of forgotten
noise and bloodshed.

Adam Lowther was saying: 'Well, sir, we can now definitely
schedule the chamber concerts for the hall here?'

'I made that clear from the start. But there's no way we could
cram the full orchestra in here. Not if we wanted an audience as
well.'

'That's all right, sir. We've had safety clearance for the
Academy hall. There's only a minor subsidence on the tower
corner, and that section was sealed off anyway. The public
entrance is on the old playground side, the hall doors and
windows have been double-checked, and the stage is as sound
as a bell.'

'More than can be said for the bell tower, hm? Well, that seems

61

to cover everything. Song recital in the Tolbooth – all going smoothly? I mean, I gather your wife was a bit shaken up. If she's not up to it yet—'

'She'll be up to it.'

It sounded like an order rather than a reassurance.

'She has a charming voice. But I've always thought of her as rather shy. You must be quite a taskmaster, getting her to face up to a public ordeal.'

'We get along fine.'

'I'm sure you do. And your own lecture on Erskine's music – word perfect, I imagine?'

'I think I've got it in order.' After a significant pause, Adam said: 'And the main point, Sir Nicholas. Erskine himself. Still no word that he'll be coming?'

'None. Sorry, Adam, but I did tell you I couldn't hold out much hope. I think we go ahead on the assumption that we feature his music, but not the man himself.' To waken the devotee from what threatened to be a swift, gloomy withdrawal, he went on: 'Right, then. I'm sure you'll cope. The open-air installations, everything's on track?'

Adam came closer, and looked over Nick's shoulder, down on to the sparkling haugh where the rain-soaked grass was drying out.

'Isn't that Mr Kerr down there?'

Nick edged round a few more inches on the seat. 'Sorting out some problem with a generator, I think. Worried about it making too much of a noise. Wouldn't want to drown out the rap groups, would we? Maybe you'd better go down and have a word with him. If it's going to interfere with music in the marquee or on the platform, I've no objection to them running a cable from my ground floor.'

'I'll go and check on it. And I'll be back to you if there are any snags.'

'Strikes me you've got it all under control, Adam.'

As he was about to leave, Adam pulled a CD package from his pocket and offered it awkwardly to his host. 'Thought you might be interested in this. A new release. Very much in line with what we're trying to achieve.'

It was a two-disc set of Scottish orchestral music. Some of the usual things – McCunn's familiar *Land of the Mountain and the Flood*, then the more challenging Violin Concerto by Erik Chisholm, and James MacMillan's *The Trials of Isobel Goudie*, concluding with Erskine's suite, *The Lady of Lawers*. Nick grinned to himself. Adam was determined to convert him to the Erskine cause!

He slid the second disc into the player concealed behind a tartan drape, and selected the first Erskine track. The opening movement, *The Ash Tree*, started as he watched Lowther striding towards Kerr far below. Its opening bars were deceptive enough, but then some perverse force began to tangle with them. Nick fidgeted. There was an undertone of evil magic in the music. Not just like the silly superstitions around Paganini and *The Devil's Trill*, or the crap talked by Hitler and his zombies about the decadence of Mahler's music, but something deeper than that. A real decadence here, being struggled with by an elusive theme in a lilting, gypsyish rhythm. But all of it dominated by a throbbing as dangerous as a vibration that could crack a bone or shatter a building – a resonance threatening to shatter and pulverize the mind.

He supposed he ought to persevere but, just as on that drive up into the wilds of Sutherland, he wasn't in the mood. Opening the window to let the clear, tangy air in, he decided to clear his mind as well by sitting down at the keyboard and working his way into a Bach fugue. It never failed. Bach never let you down.

The second subject sparkled up like an undercurrent from the Leister Water, rippling over, mingling, clashing, and then separating and flowing blissfully away to make way for a mocking inversion. His fingers were beginning to move more and more supply, like the fingers of a man making love, when there was a discreet but incisive cough behind him.

Mrs Robson said: 'Sorry, sir, but that young policewoman's here to see you. If you'd like me to tell her you're not to be interrupted—'

'No. Show her up, Mrs Robson.'

He moved away from the piano and was waiting by the door as Lesley Gunn came in.

'I'm not guilty. I've got an alibi. I was nowhere near the place at the time. It all happened years before I came here.'

'I think we've already established that.'

He waved her towards a chair. 'It's lovely seeing you again,' he said. And meant it.

She looked around the room, her professional eye sizing up the tapestries he had bought from the sale of a Roxburghshire manor, and the two high-backed Orkney chairs facing the huge fireplace. Obviously she remembered the clarsach and the cabinet with its historic quaich under a glass cover. Equally obviously, she was aware of what was missing.

Looking at the Raeburn above the piano, she said: 'I see you've dismissed the Bareback Lass. Sent to the storeroom in disgrace?'

'I felt it would be tactless to leave it there. Local visitors might have some embarrassing memories.'

And Lesley Gunn herself, he thought, might be embarrassed by memories of the trouble she had helped to stir up.

'I hope your burglary precautions are better covered than they used to be. Window locks, and locked cabinets, that sort of thing.'

'And a loud burglar alarm to frighten any passing pheasant?' He couldn't help adding: 'There was a time when I hoped to rely on you covering all that sort of thing.'

'That's still my job. For the whole community.'

One thing seemed pretty certain from this matter-of-fact attitude of hers: she was still obsessed by her job, and whatever regrets she might have about turning down the position he had offered her, she was never going to admit it. Probably not even to herself.

She was such a contrast to the diaphanously clad horsewoman of that sensual painting. Although a plain clothes officer, she somehow presented the appearance of being enclosed in a strict uniform of her own – a crisp white blouse with a high neck, dark blue jacket and blue skirt, and darker blue stockings. Looking at the taut swell of cloth over her breasts, Nick felt an adolescent hunger to unbutton that jacket so that the shapes could flow soft and free, warm and inviting rather than armoured against any intrusive touch.

Once he had kidded himself that they were mutually telepathic. Now he was afraid, from the sudden sharp glance she gave him, that she could indeed read his mind. As if determined to chill his thoughts down, she said: 'I've just been to the mortuary again.'

'Ah. Any headway?'

'They haven't dared to make too rough an attack on the head yet. The parts of the body they've been able to get at . . . well, chipping away at that concrete casing is like chipping off bits of Kendal mint cake.'

Nick didn't find the concept very appetizing. 'And you don't want to remove bits of the corpse at the same time.'

'Exactly.'

'And you still haven't a clue who it is?'

'Not so far. It's not like a drowning or a bit of GBH. When a body's been immersed in water for any length of time, or violently beaten up and disfigured, it's possible with modern techniques for a forensic pathologist to do a theoretical reconstruction around the bone structure. But here the bones themselves have been crushed and distorted by the concrete setting. We don't know what we're going to be left with. They're considering calling equipment in for a laser scan before doing too much demolition.'

She was so cold, almost callous, which was not how he remembered her – or how he wished to remember her.

'Well,' he said, 'I'd be happy to help in any way I can, but I don't see there's much I can contribute to your investigations. It all happened long before I got here. I'm only an incomer.'

'You're the laird. People will talk to you – if you make them.'

'We don't have dungeons or thumbscrews on these premises any more.'

She was still staring at the Raeburn but no longer focusing on it. 'Would you know exactly when Daniel Erskine left Kilstane?'

'Before my time,' he emphasized again. He waved out of the window towards the two figures plodding across the grass as if pacing out a cricket pitch. 'Adam Lowther's the one. The all-time expert on Erskine. Ought to have been on *Mastermind*. Apparently he applied some years back when it was at its height, but they turned him down. Told him it wasn't a broad enough subject. He was pretty mad about that.'

'Yes, I've had a preliminary chat with him. But then there's the awkward question of his father.'

'What about him?'

'As far as I can make out, he seems to have left in a bit of a hurry. Not that there's necessarily any connection. Erskine leaves because he's making a name for himself as a composer, and can't devote himself to teaching at the Academy any more.'

'Plus he's been seriously injured by a man whose wife has been having it off with him.'

She was well and truly focused now. 'Is that how it was?'

'A man was sent to prison for smashing Erskine's hands. No more working at the piano. No more writing music down.'

'But I thought he went on composing. Still does. And Lowther's said there was some hope of him appearing at this festival of yours.'

Nick gave her a concise account of his trip to Altnalarach. Halfway through, she took out a notepad and jotted down a few figures, then frowned over them. When he had finished, she said: 'I'll have to compare these dates. When Erskine left Kilstane. When the Lowthers left. And when . . .' She brooded, pursed her lips again in a way that caught at his breath. 'When Erskine's attacker got out of prison, and when – *if* – he came back to Kilstane. And where he is now.'

Nick felt a twinge of unease. He would hate to find himself having to relate what Adam had told him to what Lesley seemed to be working towards. He could only hope that when she had sorted her dates out, they would prove to be incompatible.

There was a faint clash of voices from below, and then a determined stamping up the stairs and into the room.

Captain Scott-Fraser took three paces forward and snapped to attention.

'Afternoon, Sir Nicholas. Thought I'd show myself up. Know the way well enough by now, hey?' He jerked his head towards Lesley. 'Ah, our young policewoman, right'? Thought we'd run across one another sooner or later. Must have a confab, hey? I'm on the Police Committee, y'know. Ready to offer any support you need. A surly lot, some of the locals. You need advice, don't hesitate to come to me.'

Nick made a belated attempt to introduce them. 'Detective Inspector Gunn. Mr Scott-Fraser.'

'Captain Scott-Fraser, Sir Nicholas.'

'Of course. Captain Scott-Fraser.'

'Well, officer.' He looked Lesley up and down with a supposedly jovial, patronizing smile. 'Must be difficult, operating at full blast these days.' He switched his smirk to Nick. 'The Force isn't what it used to be, hey, Sir Nicholas? Needed to be at least five feet ten, and carry a damn big stick and stand no nonsense. Nowadays these kids . . . hooligans . . . drugs and God knows what . . .'

'Did you have some particular matter to discuss with me, Captain?'

'Ah, yes. Thought I'd better come to offer advice about crowd control and stopping gatecrashers and unruly elements. We know the sort of people who'll show up, don't we? Oh, we know damn well *those* sort.'

'I think we've got matters pretty well in hand.'

'And I'd be prepared to offer some administrative services in this festival,' Scott-Fraser stormed on. 'Just to make sure we get it right. Thought at one stage I might have been co-opted on to the committee.'

'We do already have the services of Mrs Scott-Fraser.'

'Surely, surely. The little woman's doing her best, so I hear. But I might contribute. Used to be a Military Resources Administrator once they'd shifted me out of uniform, y'know.'

Meaning, according to one of Nick's informants soon after he arrived in the community, that Scott-Fraser had been the civil service equivalent of a glorified corporal i/c stores. The same informant had slyly reported Scott-Fraser's remark about the arrival of the newly created Sir Nicholas Torrance in the community: 'Quite a fluke, a chap like that inheriting a title, eh?'

One thing was clear: in the captain's mind the dissemination of music couldn't be all that different from the orderly allocation of munitions or cap badges, and a bit of discipline would do all these longhairs a lot of good.

Before Nick could find some suitable comment, Scott-Fraser's attention was distracted by the sight of the piano keyboard with the lid open.

'Aha.' He swung smartly towards it, played a few bars of *Ain't Misbehavin'*, and glanced conspiratorially at his host in expectation of his approval. 'Don't write tunes like that any more, hey? Hey?'

They didn't even write it like that in the first place, thought Nick. He had been accustomed to playing the piece in Fats Waller's E-flat, but Scott-Fraser had managed his few bars entirely on the white keys.

'For a start, you and I ought to sit down together, Sir Nicholas,' he was booming on, 'to make sure that that committee doesn't squander all our resources and never get a squeak out of the orchestra or whatever. Pretty slipshod lot, wouldn't you agree?'

'We're not running a military band festival,' said Nick mildly.

'More's the pity.' When no further response was forthcoming, Scott-Fraser harrumphed twice and said: 'Well, I can see you're busy. Can't cope with two problems at a time, right? Won't keep you. Get together later, hey?'

When he had gone, Lesley began a long, slow, almost silent laugh, and gestured towards the piano. 'Not quite in the same class as what I heard on my way here. Under your window.'

'Oh. The Bach.'

'There was a vapour trail up in the sky. And then I thought I saw another one, nearly parallel with it. Crazy, but they seemed to match what you were playing – a curve like a rainbow, with an echo underneath that . . . well, it sort of turned itself upside-down. Oh dear, I'm talking rubbish, aren't I?'

'No.' He moved to the piano stool and began to play. 'Like this?'

'Yes, that was it.'

'The inversus' – his fingers moved over the keys with all the joys of a lively dance – 'and the rectus. And then the stretto – doubling up so that the second subject overlaps.' He stopped at the *dal segno* bar-line. 'You can hear what the old man is up to?'

'Weird. I don't just hear it. I can *see* it.'

Her eyes were no longer cool and calculating, but sparkling with enjoyment. Anxious to keep that expression in her face, he went on: 'You know so many tricks of the trade when it comes to works of art. Maybe it's time you moved into the musical world, and learned some composers' tricks.' He picked out four notes on the piano. 'Our recent friend. Bach. He used to like playing around with a fugue on the notes of his own name. B-A-C-H. In German, B stands for B-flat, while H is B-natural. Lots of composers played jokes with the letters of their own name, or of a beloved. Alban Berg played some complex tricks in his *Lyric Suite*: he introduced his own initials A and B along with F and H – that is, B natural in German – in contorted sequences. His wife never suspected they were paragraphs in a passionate love letter to his mistress, Hanna Fuchs-Robettin. Would a good detective have spotted the clue?'

'A musical detective.' The idea seemed to amuse her. But then she got up. 'This won't do. I've got a corpse on my mind, and I'd better go ahead with analysing local variations on *that* matter.'

'Better things? Do remember, like the man said, that all art constantly aspires towards the condition of music.'

It came out sounding absurdly solemn. But she was still smiling as she made for the door.

The movement of her hips and shoulders as she left were music in themselves. Not the wild inchoate music of someone like Mairi McLeod or the conflicts of a Daniel Erskine, but something as confident as a firmly grounded passacaglia above which lilting variations danced confidently onwards.

The sooner he got back to the keyboard and cleared his mind with a particularly austere piece by Bach, the better.

7

At the weekend DI Gunn drove home to spend a couple of days being plain Miss Lesley Gunn in her Kelso flat after days and nights of discomfort in the spartan flatlet behind Kilstane police station. She had brought no homework with her. She had every intention of spending some leisurely time in the bath, thinking of nothing whatsoever, and going for several walks along the river and round through the Knowes to the abbey grounds. It was a route which she had always found wonderfully soothing.

It proved difficult to keep her mind entirely blank. Sprawled out in the hot water, she found herself obsessively drawing imaginary lines between the corners of the white tiles on the bathroom wall, trying to make a complete diagonal from the top left-hand corner to the bottom right-hand corner. But the number of tiles was uneven, and she finished up on the first row from the bottom. To shut it all out, she closed her eyes. Immediately she had a blurred vision of that embedded corpse, with the echo of voices to accompany it – the voices of Buchanan, Kerr, Adam Lowther.

And Nick Torrance.

When she heaved about in the water, vigorously soaping herself and making an effort to muffle those voices, the only thing that worked was a memory of music. And that could prove even more exasperating. Bad enough to be haunted by some cheap popular tune that you couldn't drive out; but even more frustrating to find yourself grasping at a shred of something richer, just beyond your reach, luring you on, like a sliver of soap evading your clutches under the surface of the bathwater.

Instead of the promised walk along the river, on Saturday afternoon she went to the library. Vaguely she was looking for something about Bach. But the only music volumes they had on the shelves were a biography of Beethoven as heavy as the composer himself, the score of a Broadway musical, and a study of Schumann. She decided Schumann would have to do.

On the way home she sinfully bought a slice of millionaire's shortbread to go with the remains of breakfast coffee waiting to be heated up. Careful not to spray crumbs of chocolate or short-bread on the pages, she began reading at random.

The story of the composer's life was interesting enough in itself. But after half an hour, something leapt off one page at her.

She had been given piano lessons when she was little, but hadn't persevered. There was no piano here in the flat, but even after all this time she found she could still interpret the notes on the page and hear them in her head. In a cockeyed way she remembered that the rising and falling shapes of a theme over the lines of the stave were as captivating as the sounds them-selves. And, even with her eyes closed, she could still see them just as she had seen those provocative formations in the sky above Black Knowe.

Damn Nick Torrance. Why the hell should he have implanted this new irritant in her brain?

Among the musical examples in the biography was a stave on which the author demonstrated what he called one of the composer's 'motto themes'. Early on, Schumann had fallen in love with a girl from the town of Asch, and extracted from his own name those four letters which in German notation could be made into notes – A-S-C-H, playable as A-flat, E-flat, C and B.

It was the sort of puzzle you could find visually in Leonardo's sketches or a Poussin painting, but here in musical terms.

And Schumann was at it again in several variations round the 'Clara theme' of his wife's name, coming out as C-B-A-G#-A.

In the afternoon she tried listening to Radio 3 – *to improve my mind?* she mocked herself – but the concert was of what the announcer described in hushed tones as aleatory experiments, with so many gratuitous squeaks and thuds that she did not realize for a while that one of them was actually her phone ringing.

From his disgruntled voice one might guess that Superintendent Maitland was peeved at having his afternoon's golf interrupted, and intended everyone else to suffer as well.

'Took your time to answer the phone, didn't you? Sorry if I've dragged you off the bog.'

'I was listening to the radio, sir.'

'Really?' It was plain that he considered this as outrageous self-indulgence when compared with the austerities of golf. 'Well, anyway. First thing Monday morning, Gunn, I want you to present yourself at Blaikie and Lamont's, the auctioneers in Dalspie. There's a picture there for you to evaluate. Right up your street.'

'Which street would that be, sir?'

'You *are* our expert on paintings. That's what we pay you for, isn't it?'

'Yes, sir. This picture. . . ?'

'Apparently there's an auction scheduled for next Wednesday, but Arts and Antiques Squad have had a last-minute tip-off that one of the items could have been stolen from one of those stately homes you're so keen on wandering around. They can't spare one of their top boys, but they think you're qualified to handle it. The auctioneers are being told not to let that item into the sale until you've assessed it. They won't be best pleased to see you,' added the Super with malicious relish.

'But the Kilstane inquiry, sir?'

'Until forensic have dragged that stiff's tin overcoat off and chopped away its concrete underpants, there's not much you can do in Kilstane. Let Elliot have a watching brief. He's a good, competent lad.'

A different setting, but still up her street. No need for her to hang about Kilstane. *Take your time* . . . Wasn't that what he had said? Now it was *Get out of there when you're told.*

What might be called the first scout paid an exploratory visit on the Sunday afternoon. Jolted out of listening to a Shostakovitch quartet, Adam was called down to the shop door by a persistent jangling on the bell, to be greeted by a man in his early thirties with dreadlocks, a greasy black jacket, and what was not so much a beard as a tangled hedge sprouting out of control.

'You Adam Lowther?'

'That's right.'

'I'm Zak Runcorn. Drummer with the Hard Thrust group. Wanted to take a look at the site we'll be playing on, just to make sure it's fit for use.'

'If you'd got in touch and made an appointment, I could have had things ready for you to—'

'Look, man, we have one hell of a schedule. If you've booked us, you do things our way. OK? I don't have long. Just show me the pitch for the gig, and I'll know how to space the amplification.'

'We have all the facilities for setting up—'

'We do things *our* way. OK?'

There was nothing for it. Adam led the way down to the haughs below Black Knowe and showed Runcorn where Kerr had staked out the lines of power cables with small white markers like those for a flower bed.

Zak Runcorn stared around disapprovingly at the countryside as if there was far too much of it for comfort.

'And the stage?'

Adam indicated where it would stand, with its back to the tower house and facing down the slope.

'Huh. Look, man, you've got a guarantee of a good crowd?'

'We've done our best to publicize it. Selling plenty of tickets.'

'I don't want to show up here just for some crummy gig with only a few sheep-shaggers off the hills gawping at us. I *have* been on *Top of the Pops*, you know. *And* on *Desert Island Discs*.'

Yes, Adam did know. He had never been offered the chance of choosing the greatest Daniel Erskine pieces as his favourite listening, and explaining why. Runcorn's choices, he seemed to remember, had been all his own performances.

'I mean, this is going to make some impact. A great revival. And it'll put your little place on the map.'

In fact it was obvious that Runcorn's fame had been on the decline for quite a while, otherwise he would not have deigned to come to a way-out venue like this.

Struggling to be sociable, Adam said: 'Any special features we can look forward to? A few years ago, in Leeds, you were making quite a thing of reggae.'

'For Christ's sake, man. How ancient can you get? We've gone through hip-hop and gangsta rap since then. You'll hear where we're at now once we've got the gear set up. And hey, what's this about some dead meat being found in your school? Read something about it in some paper or other.'

'Rather an ancient mystery. The police are still investigating.'

'Could make a new number out of it. Dead bodies, living bodies – y'know, significant social comment.'

'Sounds a bit kinky.'

'Aim for their guts, that's what I say.' When Adam did not respond, he went on: 'Next thing, the question of accommodation, right? Let's get that settled before I go on my way.'

They began walking back towards the town. Adam tried to sound confident about the high quality of the digs which had been arranged for visiting players. One room in Kilstane's main hotel had been booked for the conductor of the Westermarch Orchestra, while the instrumentalists had been divided up for two nights among a number of bed-and-breakfast houses and a cluster of caravans on the site north of the town. The four Hard Thrust players were allocated to rooms in the *Buccleuch Arms*.

It wasn't in Zak Runcorn's nature to show approval or gratitude, but as they reached the pub he allowed himself a condescending grin. 'I had a kind of hunch we might finish up at this joint. That's why I left the wagon right here.' He patted the bull-bars on a rust-pocked Range Rover as they passed it and went into the pub.

In the quiet afternoon hours, Sid Carleton believed in what he called subdued lighting. Some of his customers called it downright dim, but there were usually so few of them in this lull between lunchtime and the early evening that Carleton saw no reason to pander to them. When his eyes had adjusted to the gloom, Adam saw that the one shape huddled on a stool against the bar was Deirdre.

'Sid, this is Zak Runcorn. Leader of the group who`ll be staying here. And maybe you can persuade him to join in one of the jazz sessions in the back there.'

'Jazz?' said Runcorn contemptuously. 'We don't play *jazz*. What century d'you think you're in?' His own eyes were getting used to his surroundings. He looked Deirdre appreciatively up and down. 'Well, could be this'll be a good place to stay. Like to show me where I can give the rooms the once-over?'

Sid Carleton lifted the flap and came out, leading the way to the door marked *Residents Only* at the end of the bar and the flight of stairs beyond. Runcorn swung his left arm casually as he followed, so that his hand brushed Deirdre's bottom.

Deirdre smirked. Then she dragged a stool closer to her own and patted it with much the same movement. 'Fancy seeing you out at this time of day, Adam. Nora not with you?'

'She's lying down. She often does on a Sunday afternoon.'

'All on her own? No Sunday afternoon love-ins?'

He had no intention of telling her how few of those there were nowadays. It wasn't that Nora ever pushed him away or mumbled some excuse; just that she didn't seem to mind one way or the other, and that blunted his own appetite. He had got used to it.

He tried his own challenge. 'Duncan not in drinking mood? That's unusual.'

'I think he's in *The Globe*.' It was the scruffiest bar in Kilstane, open at all hours and featuring regularly in sheriff's court appearances by patrons accused of various breaches of the peace. 'At least he can get pissed there without me watching him and making him feel guilty.'

'He holds it pretty well, considering the competition round here.'

'It's about the only thing he *can* get hold of nowadays. He's not up to anything else. Unless your Nora is getting her rations from him.'

'Don't talk rubbish, Deirdre.'

'Those sessions of sickly romantic music – don't you think they might start acting it out?'

'Come off it.'

That poky little Sunday School room where they practised behind the Episcopalian church, with its piano and spare cassocks, was hardly conducive to unbridled passion.

Adam realized that he had let Sid go off with the visitor without first getting a drink from him. He propped his elbows on the bar and studied the long line of malt whiskies on the top shelf.

Deirdre drained her own glass and banged it down as if to summon Sid. Her hand strayed along the counter towards his. 'It's a pretty lousy situation, isn't it? For both of us. I can think of better ways to pass a Sunday afternoon.'

'Me too. I was listening to some music when that character showed up.'

'You were? Oh, well . . . Not that Duncan's ever been really up to much anyway.'

'Why did you marry him, then?'

He knew right away that it was a question he shouldn't have risked asking. 'Because you weren't around, were you? He was the best of the bunch that was left. Well, the least grotty, anyway.'

'Oh, now, look. When I left I was only a kid.'

'Old enough to know what to do with me when you got the chance. And what I wanted you to do.'

Footsteps clumped down the stairs. Sid Carleton and Zak Runcorn came back into the bar. Runcorn wasted no time. 'Right, that's settled. Time for a drink, eh? And you, darlin' – what's *yours*?'

Deirdre didn't hesitate. 'A large vodka and Irn-Bru. Very kind of you.'

'And you, squire?'

It struck Adam that, in spite of his sneers at out-of-date forms of pop music, Zak Runcorn was still using a very clumsy out-of-date jargon. Definitely past it, on the skids. His real name was probably Charlie Slaithwaite.

'A pint, thanks.'

'A pint of what?'

'Sid knows my tipple.'

'And me,' said Runcorn, 'I'll have a quick half. Don't want to get done for drink-driving.'

He was staring greedily at Deirdre. She knew just the right response. There was no giggling, no looking away and playing coy or hard to get. She tipped her glass back very slowly and widened her eyes at him over the rim.

Adam felt an uncomfortable stirring in the pit of his stomach. And a bit lower down than that. All right, then, Deirdre was sexy. Yes, there might have been a time . . . once upon a time. But those times had gone by, and now, looking at her, you knew what living with her would be like. Always bristling, unable to let a day go by without at least some big scenes, big resentments, something to get her adrenaline flowing at top speed. Not what you wanted around when you were absorbed in music.

Runcorn knocked his half pint back, tapped Adam amiably on the shoulder, and let his hand stray in a leisurely sweep down Deirdre's back. 'This could turn out to be quite a gig,' he said.

When he had gone, Sid sauntered back to his office behind the bar. After a moment when Adam wondered what to say before making an excuse to leave, Deirdre abruptly took up where she had left off. 'And what happens? You come back with Nora. And don't tell me *she's* up to it. How the hell did you come to marry someone like that?'

'She was . . . well, I'd known her a long time. Her husband was a mate of mine. Worked together for the same firm. They were good to me after my father died. Sunday dinner, evenings

78

out together, that sort of thing. You know how it is.'

'Pathetic! And what happened to this husband of hers? Don't tell me you killed him in a jealous rage?'

'He died in an accident.'

No point in going through all the details. It was all something Deirdre wouldn't be able to grasp. The inevitability of it all. No way of getting out of it, and no real compulsion to do so.

George had been the driver of the store's delivery lorry, fitted out and padded for the transport of grand pianos, uprights, and the occasional harp or electronic keyboard. He had been crushed to death when a youngster on work experience had slipped while they were manoeuvring a grand piano up an awkwardly sloping driveway. The company turned out to be inadequately insured, and argued every inch of the way over the young widow's compensation. They were not best pleased with Adam when, as family friend, he stood by her and found a useful legal contact for her. Her parents were relieved: they didn't have a clue about such matters, and in any case were more devoted to their younger daughter, who had lived up to expectations by producing a grandson. It suited them even better when Adam drifted into marriage with Nora. That was how it had been: drifting with the current until it was too late to strike out for the safety of the bank.

The store management were even less pleased with the marriage. Adam Lowther was too good a worker to be fired, but from then on the atmosphere was never pleasant. When he saw an advertisement in a trade paper for the sale of premises in Kilstane, he knew it was time to go back home.

If Nora agreed.

He dreaded the idea of her refusing. But that wasn't her way. 'If that's what you want,' she said.

'Look, if you don't fancy the idea . . .'

'No, if that's what you want.'

That was how she always spoke when she didn't really fancy an idea but wasn't going to be difficult. She was never openly reproachful, preferring to give way with a wan grace.

And she never reproached him about her miscarriage three months after their move to Kilstane, when she was told she could never have another child. She never so much as hinted that the loss might have been due to the strain of moving to a place where she would always feel a foreigner.

As if plucking his own thoughts out of the haze, Deirdre said: 'Nora doesn't belong here, does she?'

'She's got plenty of interests.'

'Like hell she has. Adam, for crying out loud' – she stared desperately around in the gloom of the bar – 'they're both out of the way right now. Duncan's out, your wife's out to the wide, why don't we . . . there has to be *somewhere* we can go. Just for a quickie.'

The street door swung open.

'Oh, Mr Lowther. There you are.' It was Neil Galbraith, who ran the local printers and stationers in Union Street. 'Been looking all over for you. Can I be going ahead with printing those final detailed programme notes? Time's getting short.'

'I haven't seen a proof yet.'

'It's all laid out in my machine room. If you could just come along, maybe tomorrow, and give it clearance . . .'

'I'll come now, if you like.'

'I don't want to interrupt you on a Sunday, Mr Lowther.'

'You're not interrupting anything.'

As they went towards the street, Adam caught a harsh whisper from Deirdre. 'No, that's true. Not a bloody thing.'

Maitland had been right. DI Gunn's appearance on Monday morning at the offices of Blaikie & Lamont was not welcome. Apparently there was no longer either a Mr Blaikie or a Mr Lamont in the land of the living, but a Mr Finlay Sproat took it on himself to tighten his already thin lips and make it clear that the firm was not accustomed to the presence of a police officer on its premises. It would be appreciated if she would be good enough to conclude her business as swiftly as possible, apologize, and make herself scarce.

Lesley said: 'If you'd be kind enough to let me have a good look at this supposed Wilkie.'

'We have every reason,' said Sproat in a tone as reedy and thin as his lips, 'to *suppose* that it is a genuine Wilkie. A very fine example of his genre studies.'

With a bad grace he went through a ritual of unlocking a heavy door at the back of the main office and locking it behind them.

There were shelves on every wall, bearing a collection of china, gold and silver dishes, candelabra, japanned boxes, jade and marble figurines, and a miscellany of ornaments whose value Lesley recognized at once in spite of so many being appallingly ugly. On an easel in the centre of the room, under the full light of a crystal chandelier, was a large oil painting of a north-east coast family clustered at the head of precipitous steps leading up from the sea, waiting to haul in a fishing boat and help unload the catch.

Lesley stood contemplating it for a good three or four minutes, aware of Sproat fidgeting behind her, prepared to grab her arm if she dared to lay a finger on the canvas. He was waiting for her verdict; and she was happy to keep him waiting, even though she had no doubts whatsoever. The whole composition was so much in the style of *The Penny Wedding*.

At last she said: 'Of course it's a David Wilkie.'

'We never had any doubts on that score,' he said self-righteously.

'What can you tell me about the provenance?'

'One thing we have already made clear, officer, but I suppose I must make it clear again for your benefit. This item came into our hands after a house clearance by a reputable firm from Hawick. We did not check the provenance: we simply do not have time to do that with every item we put up for auction. It is specified in our conditions of sale that we cannot be held responsible for authenticating items put under the hammer.'

'But you must surely have had your suspicions that the appearance of a Wilkie in this condition was a bit too good to be true.'

'We had no reason to suppose any malpractice. But' – his manner became even more sanctimonious – 'the moment someone at our preview raised doubts and chose to contact your Arts and Antiques Squad, naturally we agreed to allow your inspection.'

'The firm in Hawick – you've spoken to them?'

'Of course. A company of impeccable pedigree. So far as they were concerned, it was a routine house clearance, and they were not professionally competent to assess each item individually. They simply passed on the major pieces to us, as they have frequently done in the past.'

'I think I'd better have a word with them.'

'I imagine they'll be expecting you.' He made it sound like a rebuke.

Lesley took another long look at the painting. The idea of it showing up in a routine house clearance was hard to accept. It must surely at some time have hung in some laird's family home. But how recently? How many hands might it have passed through before reaching this auction house?

'Is there anything further I can contribute?' asked Sproat without enthusiasm.

'Perhaps I may come back to you after I've tried tracing my way backwards.'

He was glad to unlock the door and show her out.

An early lunch wouldn't be a bad idea. Across the street was the old railway station, so small that it might almost have been part of a narrow-gauge preserved line; but the track bed led to a magnificent viaduct over a curve of river. In one end of the building was the local tourist office; in the other, a small café decorated in the style of an old-fashioned station buffet, with posters and framed timetables on the walls. Typical, thought Lesley. They destroy the line, damage the local economy, then get all nostalgic and do a mock-up of what used to be a living part of the community, plastering every available inch with old photographs of steam engines and trains stuck in snowdrifts.

As she slid a tray along the rail at the counter, an elderly middle-aged woman came alongside her, risking a nervous smile. Lesley smiled back just as uncertainly, then realized that she had seen the woman only a short time ago. She had been behind the desk in the auctioneer's outer office.

'You're the detective, miss?'

'I'm *a* detective, yes.'

There were three tables free, but when Lesley settled herself at one of them, the other woman edged closer and appeared to be waiting for an invitation to join her. Lesley smiled and nodded, and the woman immediately unloaded her tray, turned to put it on a rack, and seated herself in the chair opposite.

She glanced out of the window. 'My dad used to work on the trains, when there *were* trains here.' She sighed. 'Regular services there were, running between here and Kilstane, and over to Peebles. Before they all got shut down. When I was a wee lass, I used to be brought here for a day out when there was a rugger match on.'

'You're not a native of the town, then?' Lesley asked politely.

'Och, no. I'm from Kilstane originally. But I married away. I was a McCabe.' She announced it as something to be proud of. 'Janet McCabe. Only I've been Janet Gillespie for a gey long time.' She took a mouthful of Scotch pie and kept her eyes on Lesley as she chewed away. She was wearing a drab brown cardigan and faded tartan skirt, and a heavy cairngorm brooch twitched on her sagging left breast with each breath or word. 'We go back on the bus, now and then. Treats the other way round now I'm grown up, you might say – going back home for a treat.'

Any idea that Lesley might have had of this woman nipping across the road to whisper some secrets about the Wilkie painting vanished. She simply wanted to gossip about her birthplace, as if it were miles away in space and time.

'Aye,' said Mrs Gillespie, 'I've always insisted my man takes me back when there's something important on.' There was a provocative glint in her eyes as she added: 'We saw you there a few years back, during that Common Riding when everything went wrong.'

83

Lesley tried to smile while her mouth coped with a forkful of ham omelette, and managed a throttled 'Mm'.

'And noo there's this business o' somebody's body being found in the old Academy. Who'd ever have thought it? I went to the Academy myself, when it *was* the Academy. When Mr Erskine was in charge.' Mrs Gillespie rarely had a captive audience for her reminiscences, and was making the most of it. 'Though even then there were some tearaways. Including his own son.'

'Daniel Erskine?'

'Aye. Him and that mad foreign pal of his. Even in their teens, there was no holding those two.' She was almost smirking at some outrageous memory. Unexpectedly, for a woman so homespun and faded, she blurted out: 'Didnae have much in the way of gang rape in those days, but those two put the fear of God into the town.'

Fear . . . or shameful delight?

'The foreign friend,' Lesley prompted.

'Friends or rivals, you could never be quite sure. Sometimes chasing the same girl, and sometimes . . . well,' said Mrs Gillespie coyly, 'sharing them out, you might say. Or fighting over them. Erskine or McCabe, you never knew where you were, because maybe they didn't want you to know.'

'McCabe? That's not a foreign name. I thought you said—'

'Och, they all had to take Scottish names.'

'Because their own were unpronounceable in this country?'

'It wasnae that, no. The boy's father was flying with the Czechs in the RAF. They all had to have English or Scottish names on their documents, so that if they got shot down in enemy territory, or word leaked out about them, any relatives they'd got back home wouldn't be rounded up. Mind you, it was a bit of a cheek for them to call themselves McCabe. Ian McCabe, the lad was.'

'You don't know what their real name was?'

'Never did, no.' Mrs Gillespie looked up at the preserved station clock above the door to the deserted platform, and hurriedly champed on her last mouthful. Obviously her lunch break was limited to half an hour. 'But the father did get shot down, and quite a while after the war was over young Ian and his mother went back to wherever it was. And you know what happened to Danny Erskine.' Wistfully she wiped her lips with the paper napkin.

'He became a famous composer.'

'That's as may be. But he got his hands smashed in, did he not, for letting them stray too often?'

She pushed back her chair, looked as though she would love to say a few more words, but then glanced again at the clock and scurried for the door.

Lesley decided to relax over a coffee for a few moments before heading for Hawick and the house clearance firm. She was halfway through the cup when her mobile rang. An elderly man at the other side of the café glared. She huddled closer to the wall, like a woman hiding a shameful secret. Sergeant Elliot's voice said: 'Guv, I thought you'd like to know that they've got down to our stiff's right hand.'

'Oh. And. . . ?'

'It's badly smashed. Hard to tell at the moment whether the pressure of the concrete did it, or . . . well, you do begin to wonder, don't you?'

'Yes,' said Lesley. 'Yes, you do indeed.'

8

The sound of pipes from beyond the children's playground suggested that someone had been sent out of doors to practise by a wife with a bad headache. Through an open window above the market-place drifted the scraping of someone tuning a violin. And as Nick Torrance walked down the kirk wynd beside the Episcopalian church he could hear a thin but pleasant voice, accompanied by a rather clunking piano, beyond the stained glass of the Sunday School room. The figure in the central panel of the window was, as usual round here, that of St Andrew.

He realized the singer must be Adam Lowther's wife. He had met her only a few times, and it had been difficult to make conversation. She was quite pretty in a faded sort of way, too shy to be capable of relaxed conversation. The same could be said of her voice: light and quite engaging, though without any decisive characteristics, it suited very well the plaintive lullaby *Beloved Gregor*.

The morning sun slanted down between a jagged fence of chimneypots, striking brightness from the row of Georgian houses in Meikle Yett Street. All of them had contrasting colour washes to relieve the stony austerity of the frontages. The bright yellow of one of them bounced sunlight back, overpowering the terracotta wash and grey architraves of its neighbour. The Tolbooth at the far end, on the corner of the square, retained its untreated stonework, as befitted the grimness of a one-time jail. Above it all, the blue sky promised a gentle shift from late spring into early summer.

Two familiar voices resounded from the wynd beside the police station.

'They haven't heard the last of this. Dammit, are they totally ignorant of who I am?'

'Cuthbert, you're going to be late for your appointment.'

'Can't be bothered. Trouble with all of 'em nowadays. Simply can't be bothered. Some vicious little vandal slashes my tyres, and where are *they*? Where *are* they?'

'Sitting in their patrol cars by the loch,' said Mrs Scott-Fraser wearily. 'But if you don't—'

'Sitting there,' Captain Scott-Fraser ranted loudly enough for an echo to bounce back off the wall of the wynd, 'trying to catch someone doing five miles over the odds. Because it's more comfy that way. Less effort. But just let them wait for the next Police Committee meeting. Let them just wait.'

Nick stood well back in the shadow of a close as the Scott-Frasers emerged into the main street. 'I think they *will* have to wait, Cuthbert,' Mrs Scott-Fraser was snapping. 'And right now—'

'All this talk of zero tolerance. I'll give them zero bloody tolerance.'

'Have you remembered to ring the insurance company?'

'Sitting there in their cosy patrol cars while the hooligans run riot—'

'You haven't remembered, have you?'

They were walking perilously near to Nick. He wasn't going to be found cowering out of their way; but he didn't fancy stepping out and being drawn into conversation – or, rather, into the non-stop ranting which with Scott-Fraser passed for conversation.

Fortunately Cynthia Scott-Fraser seized her husband's arm and turned him forcibly round to face in the opposite direction. 'Cuthbert, you've got three minutes to get there for your eye test.'

'I won't let this rest. I'm not going to—'

'I'll pick you up outside the opticians at twelve-thirty. You've got that, now – twelve-thirty?'

When he was quite sure their voices had faded away and he was in no danger of having Mrs Scott-Fraser gladly thrusting a spare three-quarters of an hour of her company on him, Nick emerged and headed for the print shop.

There was no nonsense here about desktop publishing or the suave impersonality of monitor screens and laser printers. The main room was filled with a hot smell and the constant clatter of ageing machinery.

'Mr Lowther asked me to run my eye over that brochure for concerts in the marquee. Apparently he had to add a few paragraphs to balance the final page.'

'That's right, Sir Nicholas.' Neil Galbraith cleared a space on a cluttered table, and kept dodging to and fro while Nick checked the final two pages.

Adam Lowther had certainly made the most of that remaining half page. This year's Gathering had not yet taken place, and there were still a few imponderables to be faced, but glowing forecasts were set in clear black type about future splendours: a competitive festival to cover an impressive range of proactive disciplines – vocal, instrumental, composition and speech – and specialist classes for Scottish country dancing, folk groups, and Gaelic poetry. And of course the ongoing exploration of the entire Daniel Erskine œuvre.

Nick marked a couple of literals, and waited for Galbraith to stop pacing around him.

'Before you go, Sir Nicholas, I wonder if you can help me? About a bit of journalism. You know I do some freelance work on the side.'

Galbraith in fact doubled as reporter for two regional freesheets as well as printing a monthly one for Kilstane, and acted as a stringer for any national newspapers he could persuade to use his local stories. Today he looked very eager indeed.

'If you want a feature on the Gathering,' said Nick, 'you'd do better consulting Adam Lowther.'

'Not that, sir. It's all these new revelations about yon corpse in the Academy. Yesterday's *Express* had a short piece about one of the hands being smashed, but that was all. Don't know where they picked that up. Not from *me*,' said Galbraith resentfully. 'It would help if I could use my local knowhow to get the details right for them.' By which he presumably meant that it would help his own part-time income. 'Do you think there's anything in the idea of those injuries . . . well, sort of tying in with that business of Daniel Erskine's bashing, years back?'

Again Nick hastened to shift responsibility. 'You'll have to ask the police about that.'

'I've tried. Nae chance.' He evidently shared Scott-Fraser's view of the local police. 'The sergeant says he's not authorized to issue a statement, and the detective inspector in charge of the inquiry is away doing something somewhere else.'

Nick thought to himself that Sergeant Elliot was clearly a well disciplined young officer who knew better than to take responsibility for making statements to the press which could lead to embarrassing gaffes and repercussions.

As Galbraith ran a desultory but expert proof-corrector's eye down the last page of the brochure, Nick said: 'You'd do better making a story out of the Gathering. At least we're pretty clear on our facts there.'

Galbraith grimaced. 'You don't know the nationals, Sir Nicholas. They'd only be interested if there was some big scandal connected with the festival.'

'Which we can do without. Don't even think of it.'

Reluctant to let him slip away too easily, Galbraith said: 'It'd be interesting to have a picture of the face. The dead man's face, I mean.'

'I can just imagine it on the front page of the tabloids, yes.'

'You'd be knowing about the old superstition hereabouts.'

Nick sighed. 'Which one in particular?'

'The thrawn face. Thrawn – twisted and contorted, ye ken. It used to be said that if ye died with a thraw, either ye'd led an evil life or ye'd been murdered. And if murder was the way of it, then watch should be kept over the corpse until those death thraws smoothed themselves out ... and then it would denounce the murderer.'

'I'm sure Detective Inspector Gunn would be delighted with a little help like that,' said Nick as he left.

Walking up the slope towards the knoll on which Black Knowe stood, he recognized her car drawn up in the shadow of the tower.

Mrs Robson had primly shown her into the sparsely furnished reception room on the ground floor which, once upon a time, had been the emergency byre for livestock hustled urgently in when a reivers' raid was threatened. As Nick came in, she glanced at her wristwatch as if reproving him for keeping her waiting.

'Oh, so you're back,' was all he could think of to say.

'Only temporarily. I'm sorry to burst in on you at such short notice.'

'Rounding off that other business, whatever it was?'

She took out a polaroid photograph and handed it to him. 'This is a bit of a long shot, but does this ring any bells?'

He studied the scene of the family clustered in their plaids and bonnets at the head of those dizzying steps, with the thrash of sea and sky behind. And yes, it did strike a chord.

'Wilkie?'

'Yes, it's a Wilkie all right. I just felt I'd seen it listed somewhere, and it might have belonged to one of your friends.'

'Another of the landed gentry?' He grinned, but she merely looked embarrassed. 'Sorry. There are still a lot of them I'm supposed to know, but don't. But yes, somewhere or other ...'
He tilted the photograph, half hoping that a different light would provoke a memory of where he had last seen it.

'It showed up,' she said, 'after a house clearance. I've tracked it down to the old Glenlaggan estate. But the big house was given over to an agricultural college two and a half years ago, and the contents sold off to cover death duties.'

'That's right. That's where I saw it, just before old Hutchison died. But everything would have been catalogued. You don't

90

have a run-of-the-mill house clearance for a place of that calibre. That's for specialists.'

'Exactly. And all that the firm in Hawick can offer is that they never handled anything from the laird's house, but from the mains.'

'The home farm?'

'That and the estate cottages. Some sold off to the tenants, but several of them moved off for jobs elsewhere, and the contents of the mains were all cleared to make way for a folk museum.'

'And who was living in the farmhouse at the time?'

'That's what I have to find out. The heritage people dealt through a factor, but he's moved out as well – somewhere over in Argyll. But I just wanted to make absolutely sure: you do remember the painting?'

'I'm pretty sure I do. And this' – he handed the photograph back to her – 'is an original? Not just a copy?'

'It's the real thing. Up for auction until we stopped it.'

'I'd love to hear the full story when you've unravelled it.'

'The threads are still a bit tangled. Now I'd better get moving.'

'Back to Hawick? Or pacing round Glenlaggan?'

'Both. But first I've got to check with Sergeant Elliot how things have been going round here.'

'A very discreet young officer. But doesn't it make you a bit dizzy, juggling two cases in the air at the same time?'

'We often have nine or ten going on at the same time. And loose ends all over the place.'

Nick thought of Scott-Fraser's grumbles. 'But you don't let them get you down?' Rashly he added: 'You don't think the top brass are trying to hassle you?'

She froze, staring at him in what might almost have been hostility. 'Sometimes I do get that impression. But I won't get paranoid about it.'

'Why don't you pack it in? That job I offered you, we might still—'

'No,' she said fiercely. 'I'm not going to give in. I'm going to get both these things sorted out. No way do I give up.'

After she had gone, he sat at the piano for a while, improvising around a few snatches of half-formed themes, occasionally linking them up into a tune whose sentimentality surprised him. When the phone rang he half welcomed the interruption.

Lesley Gunn said: 'I thought you ought to know, before it's on the radio news or in the local rag. This Galbraith stringer is bouncing about all over the place, and he's bound to come to you for a comment.'

'A comment on what?'

'Our corpse. No identification yet, but it's a woman. And she was pregnant.'

Part 2
FALSE RELATIONS

1

He had arrived. Erskine had, after all, set foot once more in Kilstane. Adam Lowther didn't know the hows or whys. They didn't matter. Erskine had changed his mind, and was here. Adam faced a day of mounting practical problems, but faced it with jubilant music in his head – not just a swirling pot-pourri of Erskine's music but a great symphony of light and air, the sheer joy of being alive.

Nora gave him her usual peck of a kiss as he set out into the morning, leaving her in charge of the shop.

'Happy now? I've never seen you look so excited.' If there was a hint of a reproach, it was typical of Nora that her expression should imply she supposed she herself must be partly to blame.

'It's going to be a hell of a scramble,' he said jubilantly, 'reorganizing things to fit in around him.'

'Everything to be made worthy of him?' As he tucked his briefcase under his arm, she added: 'You're not afraid that . . . I mean, you're sure you won't be disappointed?' It didn't deserve an answer. He was on his way through the door when she said: 'Mind you're back for this afternoon. I've got a practice with Duncan. You'll have to look after the shop.'

Closing the shop door behind him, he wondered guiltily whether he really ought to have brought Nora here. She had been reluctant to come, had lost her baby, and didn't enjoy going out for walks while he reminisced about his childhood memories or talked of music. At most he got grudging politeness.

Would their marriage have been less edgy if they had stayed in Leeds?

Halfway down St Ninian Street he was stopped by Enoch Buchanan. 'Will that be true, then?'

'What, Mr Buchanan?'

'Ye'll be letting that blasphemer and defiler back into this town? I tell ye, we'll no' be having it. I've made my views plain enough at all oor meetings.'

'You made your views plain, yes, Mr Buchanan. But the majority agreed to offer an invitation to Erskine, and he has now agreed to attend.'

'Dinna say I didnae warn ye.' Buchanan glared up at the overhead bunting with its frivolity of crotchets and quavers in garish colours. 'That spawn of the Devil did an unco' amount of wickedness before. Lies and fornication. But not this time.'

Adam left Buchanan fuming by the grocer's window, obviously preparing to go in and rant at MacKenzie over the heads of waiting customers.

Next port of call was the police station. Arrangements had been agreed for extra duty officers to keep an eye on the Town Hall and the Tolbooth, sharing a display of musical instruments and scores, and of course the invaluable portraits of Kilstane worthies. There was little fear of vandals painting moustaches on these faces, since most of them already sported great tracts of facial hair; though there was no way of predicting the ingenuity of really determined troublemakers. Next he was told that a Drugs Squad officer would be at the station tomorrow and wanted a word with him about surveillance of the open air concerts and the pub bars.

In the last twenty-four hours a dispute had arisen over a concert by a small pipes ensemble advertised as taking place in the Tolbooth. Nobody had noticed until yesterday that this date clashed with the Incorporated Crafts Guilds of Kilstane's annual tournament for the MacLean trophy, instituted by the same benefactor who had funded the Academy tower. Despite the impressive resonances of some ancient tradition, the tournament was in fact a knock-out game of dominoes in memory of MacLean's passion for that game. The clash would have to be sorted out by this afternoon at the latest.

He would cope with that after lunch, after his inspection of the outdoor setup. He felt unstoppably cheerful under the jauntily fluttering bunting with crotchets and quavers on it – Galbraith's idea, and since he was providing it cost price, nobody had cared to criticize.

On the way round the town towards the Academy he stopped at Marshall & Corsock's garage and coach office to check on the timetable for bringing people in from the villages and getting them back again, allowing ample time before and after concerts. And had they liaised with William Kerr over the float for the combined marching and driving New Orleans band?

Everything seemed satisfactory until Sandy Corsock looked out of the office window on to the forecourt and groaned. 'Oh, God, *him* again. I wish he'd fill up back home in Rowanbie and let *them* subsidize him.'

Adam turned towards the window. Captain Scott-Fraser was pouring fuel into the tank of his Range Rover at the pump. He stood at an angle, propped against the side of the vehicle, his lips twitching as he watched the flickering digits of litres and money.

' "Put it on the bill." ' Corsock had Scott-Fraser's terrier-like bark off to perfection. 'That'll be the refrain. "Put it on the bill" – and then forget about it. Don't suppose you have any dealings with him, though?'

'I tune his piano.'

'Cash on the nail?'

'Sometimes he forgets, and I have to remind him next time.'

'Remind him? More like a long chase. Takes a long time to catch up. And then he gets hoity-toity and says it's the last time he's going to be insulted by us. So Rowanbie gets the benefit of his custom for a while – until he gets tired of insults over there, and goes the rounds until eventually he comes back here. You're lucky. I don't think there are any other piano tuners round here, are there? No payment, no keyboard capers.'

97

As Adam came out, Scott-Fraser was thrusting the gun back into its slot with the decisiveness of a dedicated officer shoving his revolver back in its holster after executing half a dozen deserters. He was delighted to have an audience.

'Look at them! Look at those prices! And that's just for litres. There was a time you could get a couple of gallons for the price of that. Outrageous, isn't it?' He came round and leaned on the massive bull-bars, an impressive fitment, though there were few bulls or kangaroos or anything of dangerous size hereabouts. 'Glad to have bumped into you. About this chap Erskine. He's arrived?'

'So I believe,' said Adam. 'He'll be staying with Sir Nicholas, of course.'

'Hmph. Well, I'm sure you'll see him before I do. Thought it might be an idea to invite him to next Thursday's Schiltron Circle luncheon. You'll be giving that talk of yours about him, won't you? Looking forward to it, Lowther. What better than having the man himself there in the *Pheasant*, putting you right, eh? Think you could have a word with him?'

'There might be some objections, sir.'

'Objections?'

'I think Mr Buchanan is a member of your society?'

'Miserable old fart. Drinks water all the time. Even for the loyal toast. And he grudges that anyway. But what's he got to do with it?'

'I've just been talking to him.' Or listening to him, thought Adam. 'He has always been opposed to Daniel Erskine showing his face in Kilstane again. And he's capable of making trouble. I think he would oppose any idea of Erskine himself being present.'

'Would he, indeed?' Scott-Fraser had made the suggestion a bit tentatively at first. This made him very positive. 'I'm Chairman of the Schiltrons, and I'm issuing an invitation. And that's that. Shall I leave it to you?'

'It's rather short notice, sir. And' – Adam wasn't sure how much ScottFraser knew, or wanted to know – 'there's the matter of. . . well, of injury to his hands. I think he might have some difficulty in eating a formal meal.'

'Very sharp of you, Lowther. Very tactful. Should have thought of that myself. No need for him to sit through all our ceremonies. Ask him along at the end. He can lift a glass, can't he? Give him a dram, ask him to chat for ten minutes or so, pick up where you leave off, sort of thing, and answer a few questions. Make a change from old Blaine's serial reminiscences about his holiday up the Norwegian fjords. I leave it in your capable hands, Lowther.' Scott-Fraser slapped his thigh and marched round to the driver's seat, waving up at the office window and bellowing as he went. 'On the bill, right?'

Outside the Academy, rubble had been tidied away. A lorry had been driven up to the main entrance, and two young men were carrying chairs into the building. In the hall itself, one door at the end of the passage into the tower had been sealed off, but an electrician was checking the EXIT and EMER-GENCY EXIT signs above the others. Two women were scrubbing the floor of the stage, while the two young men clattered to and fro across the auditorium, scraping and slamming chairs into rows.

He returned to the shop to make a couple of phone calls. Nora was not on her own. Deirdre and Duncan were arguing as he arrived, and all three of them turned on him, ready to throw another problem at him.

'We're supposed to be rehearsing this afternoon,' Duncan blustered. 'Nora and me, we have a lot to go through. But they'll not let us use the room.'

'Who won't?'

'One of the kirk elders says the choir has to have the Sunday School room for *their* practice.'

Adam opened his folder and skimmed yet again down the schedule of dates and times. There was no mention on it of the choir.

'The minister says it's important the choir is perfect for the service of fellowship on Sunday,' added Nora forlornly.

Adam leaned against the counter. To go and have a row. . . ? That wouldn't help the general atmosphere. In any case it was too late to rearrange this afternoon's bookings at this stage.

He said: 'You'll have to use the shop here. That piano's in better condition than the Sunday School one, anyway.'

Deirdre said: 'And you can give them some pointers?' It sounded suggestive, but none of them could imagine what she was suggesting.

'We'll have an early lunch, shut up shop for the afternoon, and I'll leave you to it. I've got plenty to do elsewhere. Too much, really.' He went to the door and swung the sign round to say CLOSED.

Nora looked at Deirdre without favour but asked: 'Would you like to join us? Jut a bit of cold meat and salad.'

Deirdre flashed a smile at Adam and was about to speak when her husband said: 'We'll have a snack in the pub. Back here at one-thirty sharp, right?'

'I'm fed up with that bloody pub,' said Deirdre. Coming from her, it might be true for just the moment, but on the whole it was not very convincing.

As the two of them left, Deirdre glanced back at Adam as if imploring him to rescue her from her husband's clutches. That, too, was only a momentary impulse.

Nora said: 'You're not really going to fall for her, are you?'

'Fall for Deirdre? Come off it.'

'She seems to have her eye on you.' Nora sounded almost sympathetic.

When they went upstairs for lunch, she slowed on the landing and for a moment he wondered if she fancied half an hour in bed rather than eating. But somehow the timing wasn't right, the mood wasn't right, and he didn't reach out for her. She quickened her pace and went on into the kitchen.

After lunch he dropped in at the booking office in the corner of the Tourist Information Office, staffed in Duncan's absence by a blonde girl whose father was the Marshall of Marshall & Corsock's coach business. She was very good at explaining smoothly to visitors why the coach timetables were frequently misleading, and why some services failed to run at all.

Adam checked with her that complimentary tickets had gone off to the three music critics who counted, and that someone was dealing with a demand from the most pompous of them for an ensuite room with a desk and laptop terminal in the *Pheasant*.

Then he set off towards the haughs below Black Knowe to make sure that the marquee was being set up for the Folk Revel. And there were still arguments about parking spaces nearby. A couple of farmers had offered facilities free in the scruffier of their less fertile fields. Others wanted to section off bits of land and charge above the odds, and also be guaranteed against damage and vandalism.

Neil Galbraith was there with his lumpy box of an open-reel tape recorder, greedily contemplating the soaring tower house rather than the men erecting the marquee. He greeted Adam as eagerly as Buchanan and Scott-Fraser had done earlier; which meant that, like them, he was interested not so much in Adam himself as in his possible usefulness.

He set about ingratiating himself. 'Had a word with my oppo at Border TV. All set to get the cameras and that long-legged interviewer here for the opening concert. I think you can count on a five-minute item in the local news programme.' He glanced again at the tower. 'Any chance of you fixing me an interview with this Erskine character?'

'He's only just got here. Might not be in the mood.'

'You're the one who's so keen on his work, if your shop window's anything to go by. And those leaflets I've printed for you. You must have some sort of leverage.'

Meaning, thought Adam, that one good turn deserves another. Galbraith would pad his local paper with compliment's for the Convener Depute and lean on his TV friends in return for an exclusive.

'Maybe we could be going up to the house together,' he went on. 'You being well in with the laird, like.'

Blatant. Crude flattery and insinuations. At the same time,

101

Adam wanted an excuse, any excuse, to catch just a glimpse of the great man.

Half reluctantly, half hopefully, he climbed the steep slope to the motte platform on which Black Knowe stood, with Galbraith humping the recorder and puffing beside him.

The distant chime of the bell far within brought Mrs Robson to the oaken door.

'Afternoon, Adam,' she said amiably. To Galbraith she offered only a raised eyebrow and: 'Young man.'

Adam said: 'Daniel Erskine is with Sir Nicholas?'

'He is.'

'Any chance of our seeing him?'

Mrs Robson studied Galbraith's small but heavy tape recorder doubtfully, unsure of it and of the request.

'I'll see.' She sounded far from optimistic.

She closed the door without inviting them to wait inside. Galbraith scowled. Adam, slightly dizzy with apprehension, looked back down the green slope ... What would Daniel Erskine make of this view, corning back after so long? Inhaling the breeze, the smell of grass, the faint tang of wood smoke from a cottage on the edge of the town?

The door creaked open. 'Sir Nicholas wants you to go up, Adam.' As Galbraith took a step forward, she said: 'Not you. The laird's guest isn't interested in having his name in the papers.'

Adam went up the broad stone stairs, breathless, and on into the hall. Sir Nicholas Torrance was on his feet, waiting to greet him with a friendly slap on the forearm. Another man sat in the window seat, a hunched silhouette against the brightness of the sky and the distant moors.

Adam had waited so many years for this moment.

Torrance said: 'Adam, this is Daniel Erskine. I fancy you know as much about his music as he knows himself. Mr Erskine ... Adam Lowther.'

A gloved hand was extended. Adam did not know whether to grip it or simply touch it. There was no strength within the glove: just a wad of something spongy.

'It's wonderful to see you again, sir.' It came out hoarse and crackly.

'Again?'

'I was in your music class at the Academy. For a little while.'

'And Mairi McLeod,' said Torrance.

Although he was sitting in the full brightness of the window, Erskine remained a dark, shrivelled figure. The woman seemed to have drawn all the brightness into herself. Shaking hands, Adam felt a shock run up his arm. Hearing of Erskine's amanuensis, he had visualized a spinsterish devotee with grey hair in a bun, and steel-framed glasses. This creature was a glowing vision with burnished golden hair on fire with sunshine, a long, creamy neck rising from her loose white shirt, and a scattering of freckles on her bare arms.

Erskine had hardly lifted his head when introduced. Mairi McLeod turned her head slowly from clear-cut profile to challenging full face, her tigerishly tawny eyes staring boldly into Adam's, lingering, appraising.

Breaking the spell, Torrance said: 'Right, Adam. Do sit down. And tell us how all your arrangements are going.'

He outlined the programme, waiting for Erskine to show some interest. Then, for the benefit of the Chairman of the Gathering, he brought him up to date on problems of accommodation and transport, and how they were being coped with. At the same time he tried to awaken Erskine's interest by enthusing about the programme for the opening concert, devoted mainly to Erskine's own music: two of the early tone poems, and the *Symphonic Variations* to round off the evening. 'And thanks to Sir Nicholas here, two of that wonderful violin and piano cycle will be performed in this very room.' All the time he was watching, from the corner of his eye, the huddled shape of the man who had shaped his whole love of music. But it was Mairi McLeod whose eyes met his again when he mentioned the duets.

Unexpectedly she changed the subject. 'When it comes to accommodation, in my day the whole lot used to roll up with sleeping bags and stretch out on the grass or under the trees.'

Torrance laughed. 'Not what the senior members of our committee would approve, Adam?' He did his own bit to try and stimulate their guest's attention. 'Thursday lunchtime, our friend here is going to give a talk about you to the Schiltron Circle. Right, Adam?'

'Right.' Abruptly he threw out the challenge. 'Captain Scott-Fraser of the Circle is wondering whether Mr Erskine could spare a few moments to address them towards the end of the meeting. You always get questions at the end of these talks. I think it would be a great honour if the answers could come directly from you, sir.'

At last the great leonine head with its mane of grey hair swung slowly round.

'What the hell is the Schiltron Circle?'

'A local group,' explained Torrance. 'We've got the usual cliques round here – Rotary, the Lions, Probus, the Incorporated Crafts. All earnestly doing good. And shoving their noses into everybody else's business.'

Adam was relieved that their host was doing the talking on this subject. He would never have dared even to imply that whiff of derision himself.

'Never heard of it in my day,' grunted Erskine.

'They'd be grateful for just a few words.'

'Not the sort of words I might give 'em, they wouldn't. Anyway, I never go to lunches or dinners. Never.'

Adam glanced at the gloved hands and winced silently. Seen this close, the enormity of what had been done to such a great composer was even more terrifying than reading about it on a two-dimensional printed page.

'I think that if you simply showed up at the end of my waffling, and answered a few questions . . .'

'They want me to answer questions? By God, that's asking for it.' It was difficult to tell whether he was chuckling or just grumbling to himself. But then his rheumy eyes grew suddenly bright below his straggling eyebrows and he was looking full at Adam. 'Lowther. I heard that right, did I? Lowther.'

'That's right, sir. Adam Lowther.'

'Yes, of course. I did know a family of that name. There was a Molly Lowther?'

'My mother. And my father was Jamie Lowther.'

'Yes. So he was.' Erskine edged himself forward on the window-seat. 'They're still here?'

'My father moved us away. My mother died – she was expecting a child, but it . . . well, she was taken ill, and she and the baby both died soon after we'd left.' Just like Nora and himself, he thought. The shock of an unwilling move, the loss of a baby. 'And when my father died quite some years later, I came back.'

Erskine was staring thoughtfully at him, more like a painter appraising a subject than a musician. With unexpected gentleness he said: 'I'm sorry. Yes, I do remember them. And you're Molly's lad. And I did teach you music. Not for long, though.'

'More's the pity, sir.'

'I wouldn't be too sure of that. But well, now' – this was even more unexpected – '*you* want me to address these Schiltron folk?'

'They would appreciate it.'

'I'll have to think about it.'

His brooding stare into Adam's face was crossed by Mairi McLeod's puzzled gaze. It was as if she had still not worked out what had changed his mind about coming to Kilstane.

2

Lady Flora Hutchison was a slim yet powerful woman in her early thirties with sleek ashen hair and the confident air of a hostess accustomed to organizing dinner parties, garden parties and the everyday routine of her twin brother who sat meekly beside her. But at the moment she was not at her most confident. Lesley Gunn had caught them unawares, and could see that Lady Flora was making an effort to show herself capable of coping even with this awkward piece of news.

'It really is rather embarrassing.' She was probably annoyed more by having to confess her embarrassment to a police officer than by the turn of events itself.

'Poor old Sinky,' contributed Sir Hamish.

'Sinky?'

'Our old housekeeper. Mrs Sinclair. Always called her Sinky.'

'Where does she come into this?'

Lady Flora sighed. 'When we disposed of the house' – she glanced around the lounge as if briefly contrasting it with the more palatial surroundings of their past – 'we made special arrangements for Mrs Sinclair. She'd worked for the family all those years, and her late husband had been my father-in-law's ghillie. One couldn't just leave her to find her own way in the world. We settled the west gatehouse on her for life.'

'Least we could do,' said her brother.

'But the picture. . . ?'

'She came originally from Caithness, and was always going

on about how she loved that painting. It so reminded her of the Whaligoe steps. So before clearing everything out we made her a present of it. And now one supposes she must have decided to sell it, presumably because she's finding it hard to make ends meet. Embarrassing,' said Lady Flora again. 'But she'll be very upset if she learns that we've heard about it. A bit disappointing, because she made such a thing about loving it, but we wouldn't dream of making her feel awkward. Do you have to pursue this any further?'

'I'm afraid so,' said Lesley. 'Just to tidy up the loose ends and make sure everything's above board.'

'She'll be very upset.'

Mrs Sinclair was indeed upset. For the first five minutes of the interview she was flustered and uncooperative. Even when shown the warrant card she had kept the visitor waiting until she had fetched her reading glass and peered at every word on the card. Then reluctantly she took Lesley through to a sitting-groom crammed with furniture from what must originally have been a much larger room.

She had a very red nose and a red face scoured by years of work, or fresh air, or perhaps too much drink in her declining years. Her hair was grey and wispy, with only a few straggling strands on top.

Lesley went straight to the point. 'I'm here about your missing picture.'

'My . . . oh, no. I mean, who's been saying I've . . . I mean, *what* picture?'

'The Wilkie painting of which you were so fond.'

'What has that got to do with the police?'

'Have you sold it?'

'Sold it?' Mrs Sinclair flared up. 'I'd never have done such a thing. Never.'

'Then where is it?'

Mrs Sinclair rubbed her nose even redder with her handkerchief: 'What her ladyship would say if she knew . . . what they'd think of me . . .'

'I'm afraid they do know. I had to approach them to establish the provenance of the picture and what happened to it. They were the ones who gave me your address.'

Mrs Sinclair seemed to be collapsing in on herself. 'I'm so ashamed. After all they did for me. I'll nae be able to face them again. What'll they be thinking of me?'

'They're not blaming you. Truly they're not. The picture was yours, if you wanted to sell it, then—'

'*Sell* it? I've told you, I'd never have sold it. It was taken.'

'You mean stolen? Burgled?'

'Aye.' Mrs Sinclair was busy now crumpling her handkerchief into a soggy ball. 'I wouldnae have dared tell them. I was so ashamed.'

'What exactly happened?'

'For a start, there were these people came to the door, only I wouldn't let them in. Didn't fancy the look of them. And soon after, there was this burglary, when I was out shopping.'

'Ah. Knockers.'

'I beg your pardon?'

Lesley realized that it had come out sounding to the old lady like a rude word. 'They come knocking at your door asking if you've got anything to sell. Promise to offer a good price for genuine stuff.'

'Aye, that's just the way it was. There were two of them. I didn't fancy the look of them,' said Mrs Sinclair again, more emphatically and self-righteously. 'Wouldn't let them in.'

Lesley glanced back through the half-open door to the tiny lobby. 'That console table – they probably offered you a couple of hundred for it?'

'So they did.' Mrs Sinclair shook her head, so that a few strands of hair glinted in the light from the window. 'It was never worth that.'

'No, it's only a modern copy.'

'So I knew they must be up to something.'

'If you'd said yes, they'd have had an excuse to come in and look round to see if there was anything really valuable.' Lesley looked up at a rectangular patch of wallpaper slightly less sun-bleached than the rest. She stood up, set her back to the open door, and confirmed at once that anyone looking into the room from the front door would have had a clear picture of the Wilkie. 'Knockers,' she repeated. 'If they can't make a smart deal on the spot, they size up the joint and then engage burglars to collect what's worth having. Didn't you report it to the police?'

'I was so ashamed. It would have got back to the ears of the family. After all they'd done for me . . .'

'The main point is that you can confirm that you did not sell the painting, which you were perfectly entitled to do, but that it was removed by burglars?'

'How many more times do I have to say it?'

'Mrs Sinclair, please don't be too upset.' Lesley spoke as gently as possible. 'We know where the picture is, and I think that in due course you will get it back.'

The old woman looked at her half sceptical, half longing to believe that promise.

Lesley drove back to Kilstane and made a phone call to the Arts and Antiques unit at New Scotland Yard. She was greeted with warm approval.

'Yes, we've had our eye on that firm for a little while now. The Hawick people are perfectly respectable, but that little lot in Dalspie are part of a larger consortium, tied in with a very presti-gious auction house right here on our own doorstep. Started out with small stuff – fiddling a lot of electric train sets through to the auctioneer's own son, hiding valuable pieces in a tin bath full of junk and tipping a friend off that he could offer a derisory bid and carry it off. Not enough to be worth prosecuting in the early stages, but gradually the stakes have been building up. We'd be glad to have something really meaty now. Fashionable contacts at this end, but with a lot of shadows we'd be interested in brushing away.'

'Shall I go back to Dalspie and—'

'Leave the next stage to us, and we'll get back to you. As representative of the local force, you'd like to make the arrest yourself, if it comes to that?'

And lose that poor Mrs Gillespie in Dalspie her job?

Right now Lesley decided it would be more fruitful to follow up the little matter of the dead woman and her unborn child.

From the start they had been banking on some traces of flesh, some shreds of clothing which in the end would lead to the identity of the corpse. Just a few fibres could be enough for modern forensic scientists. But the remains on the slab were in poor shape for analysis. A large part of the torso had been crushed by the setting concrete. The casing had been done in a bit of a hurry. and had sprung cracks here and there. Bacteria would have got in and rotted the flesh away completely over the years.

And there were no remains of clothes. The woman had been entombed naked.

'Only a few shreds of what looks like sacking,' said DS Elliot. 'Ordinary sacking. So all we really have to go on is bones.'

'Dental records?'

'I've started on that. But the local dentist is new to the district. Very modern, very with-it. No records left over from his predecessor. But I'm trawling through the school dental records, in case there's some abnormality or some special treatment that survived into the adult jaw.'

The pathologist pointed out that the bones in both the woman's hands were badly smashed. Could this have been deliberate, or just part of the general crushing? Anything to do with the way Daniel Erskine's hands had been crushed?

Back in the station, Lesley approached the desk sergeant. 'Do you still have any records of the time that Daniel Erskine's hands were smashed? And what became of the assailant after he got out of prison?'

'Before my time, but folk have long memories hereabouts. As I remember it, the man who did it was one of the Langs – the Roxburgh Street Langs.' It was as if this was enough in itself to explain any murder or mayhem which might occur in the town. 'He was an oil rig worker. The story went that he got back earlier than expected from one spell offshore, and found his wife in bed

110

with this Erskine fellow. Dragged him out into the yard and went at his hands with a sledgehammer they used for breaking up lumps of coal. Fixed him well and truly.'

'And afterwards?'

'Made no bones about it.' The sergeant snickered. 'If you see what I mean. Pleaded guilty and proud of it. Said that Erskine's hands wouldn't be wandering over his wife's body again, and wouldn't be much use on a piano keyboard. Got four years – or was it five?'

'I meant after he'd got out.'

'We never had any reason to follow that up.'

'I've asked around,' Elliot interrupted. 'Lang seems to have made himself scarce. His wife cleared off after he was put away, and there's talk of her divorcing him, but nobody's too sure. But how does this fit in with the time our corpse met her end? You don't think *she* might be. . . ?'

'What I do think,' said Lesley, 'is that it's high time we settled down to getting our dates sorted out. Who was where, and when.' She looked unfavourably round the bleak station walls, their only decoration a few lists of regulations, a don't-drink-and-drive poster, one of the timetables for The Gathering, and a photo of a missing schoolgirl, then raised an eyebrow at Elliot.

'Care for a coffee across the road?'

The Wee Bothy Tearoom sported lace curtains looped back to allow passers-by to see that trade was brisk, and plastic tartan tablecloths. Trade was in fact not all that brisk at this time of day. The only customers as Lesley and her companion entered were two elderly ladies at the window table. They could have been twins, in identical dark purple coats which they had not unbuttoned while eating. One of them was distinguished from the other by a large hairy mole on her right jaw. Her friend wore a large Victorian brooch which caught an occasional spark of light as a passing lorry's windscreen tossed a reflection into the tearoom. Propped against their chair legs were large plastic bags labelled MACKENZIE'S PROVISIONS: BONNIEST IN THE BORDERS.

The waitress was a thin girl with a whiny edge to her voice as she repeated their order for coffee and shortbread word for word, as if she would remember it better by rote than by the notes she had scribbled on her pad.

A few moments after she had disappeared through the kitchen door, there was a sudden blast of pop music from a speaker dangling above the serving counter. Lesley winced. The two women at the window table bristled. The moment the girl came back with the coffee and shortbread, the woman with the hairy mole snapped: 'Since when have ye had that dreary din?'

'It's all to do with the festival. And people expect to have that sort of music nowadays.'

'*We* don't expect it,' said the woman with the mole. 'And we'd not be wanting it. Perhaps ye'll see to turning it off.'

'I'll have to ask Mrs Craig.'

'Do that. Or send Mrs Craig out here.'

The girl shuffled off, banging her hip against one of the tables as she went.

'Always was a dismal dreep, that Reid lass.'

'Half Irish,' said the brooch dismissively. 'And there's a few saying the other half could have been a wee touch foreign as well. That so-called McCabe laddie who was here during the war, before he went back wherever he came from – there was talk of him and the McKechnie lass, and *her* son married that girl's mother from Larne, so . . .' She glanced at Lesley Gunn and Elliot as if noticing them for the first time, and leaned across the table to mumble confidences made even less intelligible by a mouthful of cake crumbs.

The music stopped in mid-bar. Mrs Craig was evidently in no mood for confrontation. When the girl came back, she steered clear of the window table before reaching Lesley and Sergeant Elliot.

'Well, now.' Lesley stirred her cappuccino. 'Who's top suspect?'

'It might narrow things down if we knew who the corpse was. A local girl, presumably. Somebody got her pregnant. And then tried to dispose of her. Daniel Erskine? But he doesn't seem to have been ashamed of his carryings-on. You've only got to listen to local gossip' – Elliot glanced at the silhouette of two women's heads close together against the window – 'to know that he didn't give a damn about the consequences. Why murder one of them in particular?'

Lesley, too, kept her voice down, not wanting to contribute any more fuel to the two old women's gossip. 'True. And in any case, do the dates fit? I fancy there's too big a gap.'

'Since Forensic are willing to estimate the time of death as around nine years ago, that would have been long after Erskine left the area.'

'He could have paid return visits. Openly, or surreptitiously.'

'That would take some establishing.'

'The other one – the Czech? The one they called McCabe. Another tearaway, by all accounts.'

'He went off behind the Iron Curtain. And when it was lifted, he doesn't seem to have reappeared.' Elliot meditatively crunched a corner of shortbread. 'But that possible date of death – that would be around the time that Adam Lowther's father took his wife and son away at very short notice.'

That idea had fidgeted off-and-on at the back of Lesley's mind. It was time to bring it to the forefront. 'Lowther senior may not have wanted to wreck his marriage. And working for a puritanical old bigot like Buchanan, there's a chance his job would have been at risk as well.'

'But Lowther only had an office job. Would he have been capable of getting a corpse up there on his own and sealing it up in a concrete overcoat? And if he had a helper . . . who would *that* have been?'

Lesley scraped froth off the sides of her cup with a spoon. Divination by tea-leaves had been an old custom: a pity there was no way that the patterns in cappuccino froth could provide any inspiration.

'Why do you suppose Erskine's come back after all this time? I understand he turned down an invitation to appear at The Gathering, but then changed his mind.'

113

'Changed it,' Elliot had no need to remind her, '*after* the news was published that our corpse was a woman. And pregnant.'

'Quite. It seems to me,' said Lesley, 'that we do have to interview Erskine. And Adam Lowther. And see about drawing up a calendar, complete with the usual paraphernalia of drawing pins and little stickers in pretty colours.' She finished her delving with the spoon. 'Erskine first, I think.'

'You do believe in tackling the tough ones first, guv.'

'Yes,' said Lesley, 'I do.'

3

Halfway through Thursday morning the pack began assembling. At first there was no apparent purpose. They emerged on to the streets one or two at a time, staring up at the streamers of flags with their semi-quaver emblem as if wondering how to whistle the notes, and then drifting vaguely together. It was common enough in the evenings to see groups of Kilstane teenagers lounging aimlessly about on street corners or huddled into shop doorways. But this wasn't an evening, and the men were not teenagers but middle-aged and older citizens of the town. They looked a bit baffled by their own aimless sauntering, waiting for a cue. Enoch Buchanan emerged from the alley beside the Tolbooth and stared across the marketplace like a sergeant-major planning manoeuvres on a parade ground. Instinctively the other men began to gather around him.

Adam Lowther, on his way back from the printer with another supply of leaflets for his shop, saw them, and beyond them saw two strangers dressed in calculatedly scruffy hobo costumes, carrying a concertina and a guitar. It was a day too soon for them to take on the role of strolling players, but they were in the mood to play, and seeing a potential audience waiting, they launched into a reel. There were as yet none of the police appointed to move them politely on.

Briefly distracted, neither Adam nor the cluster of men across the square saw two figures coming down the hill from the Academy. They could have been a couple of sightseeing tourists

115

at this time of year, simply taking in the buildings and atmosphere of the place, to be fitted into a pattern when they talked it
over later and riffled through their photographs. Neither of
them, though, was carrying a camera.

And they were no ordinary trippers. One was Duncan
Maxwell from the Tourist Information Office. The other was
Daniel Erskine.

Duncan must be guiding the visitor down familiar streets and
half-forgotten or lost memory lanes, explaining rebuilding and a
new one-way system which had been made since his day.

They all saw Erskine and all recognized him at the same
moment.

Without any apparent signal the men moved out on to the
square, splaying out to form an arc across the path of the two
men, its wings ready to close in and drive them into a narrow
cul-de-sac. Behind them a white van jolted to a halt and its horn
blared out. It was ignored. The concertina and guitar went on
grinding away at a less steady tempo.

Adam tensed, uncertain what move to make.

They were such an ordinary cluster of men. Nothing about
them to suggest a serious breach of the peace in the offing. But
among them were some who had marched, two years ago, to an
old croft outside the town where a paedophile newly released
from jail had been housed by the authorities, ransacked the
place, and beaten him up. They had been brought together today
by the reek of another prey.

Adam stepped out decisively and joined Duncan and Erskine.
'You can see what they're hoping, to do, sir. They want to drive
you into Souters Wynd and deal with you there.'

'Deal with me?' Erskine snorted. 'Scum. It was always the
scum that came to the top in this town, never the cream.'

'You'd better move. Can I join you?' Adam was trying to urge
them along the pavement without showing too obvious a panic.
'I never get tired of looking into places I knew when I was a kid.
You must have the same sort of feeling.'

'Sentimental crap. Only too glad to shake the dust of the place off my feet. Only it wasn't dust but shit.' But then, gruffly, Erskine said: 'No use thinking of the might-have-beens. Or even' – a mischievous, throaty chuckle – 'the things that really were.' Unexpectedly his padded right glove rested on Adam's arm. Adam felt that if there had been usable fingers inside that glove, they would have closed affectionately on his wrist.

The gang had decided to advance. 'Oot o' the way, young Maxwell. And you, Lowther – we've nothing against ye.'

Adam stood beside Erskine. 'Three of us are better than two,' he said optimistically.

The self-appointed vigilantes charged. Adam was knocked to one side. The leaflets he had been clutching went flying. Some went face down, others fluttered along the gutter with a photograph of a younger Daniel Erskine staring up at the sky.

Duncan grabbed Erskine's arm and rushed him towards the alley beside the Tolbooth.

By the time Adam had picked himself up, the mob had gone yelling in pursuit. Their voices faded, then raged out again from another direction. The pounding of feet ebbed and flowed, with a few murmuring intervals of frustration.

Three men came back to the square and began pushing their way into shops along High Street and hammering on house doors, like secret police determined to flush out a fugitive.

'Would ye be sheltering that Erskine scunner? Come on, Maisie, he's not worth it. Hand him. over.'

'Ye stupid gowk. Why would I be—'

'If it's not you, maybe it's Jessie next door, eh? We ken where your Wullie came from, don't we? And her Katrina . . . '

A vase of flowers snatched from the hall table was emptied over his head.

Adam gathered up as many leaflets as he could and headed for the police station. There was a woman in a dark blue cardigan at the desk in the outer office, but it was obviously not police issue. She was civilian staff.

'Where's the duty sergeant?' Adam demanded.

'The station's not fully manned on a Thursday morning.' She

spoke with prissy precision.

'Well, where's that woman detective, and her sidekick?'

'I believe they're away somewhere. And they don't come under our jurisdiction. In an emergency, Rowanbie station should be contacted.'

'Bloody hell, this *is* an emergency. There's a riot brewing out there.'

'If you'll give me the details, I'll phone through and see how they're fixed at Rowanbie.'

'Just give me the phone, and—'

'I'm sorry, but that's not allowed.'

'This is crazy.' As her face hardened with self-righteous dignity, he implored her: 'Look, please call Rowanbie, and tell them there's a vigilante mob on the loose, chasing Daniel Erskine.'

'And who might that be?'

'Erskine. The composer. And if you wait too long, there's a chance they could kill him.'

'Oh, really, sir!' She reached sceptically for the phone. 'May I tell them your name, so that we have a record of who is report-ing the alleged disturbance?'

Outside the station, Galbraith, his camera at the ready, was trying desperately to make out what distant noises might mean. 'Adam, is it true? They're after him? What's the story?'

Adam brushed past him and hurried back to the shop to make his own phone call. Through the window he saw a woman like an avenging fury, her hair wild, gesticulating with long, slender fingers as if to bring down incantations on somebody's head. Nora's head was bent before the storm.

A strident voice was added to the gesticulations as he opened the shop door. '*There* you are.' Mairi McLeod turned as if to accuse him of some monstrous crime. 'Where is he? Where's Daniel?'

'I don`t know. The last I saw of him. . . ' Adam faltered.

'I assumed he had come to see you.'

'Why me?'

'Well . . .' It was Mairi McLeod's turn to hesitate. Then she said unconvincingly: 'Oh, to arrange one of your concerts. Or just to talk.'

There was no way out of telling her the truth. 'He s been stravaiging, rambling round old haunts. Only I'm afraid one or two awkward customers seem likely to cut up rough.'

'I should never have let him out of my sight.' She took a long, shuddering breath. Her fingers clenched and slackened, clenched again, as if trying to strangle somebody. 'I want the police in on this before it's too late.'

'I've already been to the station.'

'And?'

He explained, and she exploded again.

'So he's out there on his own?'

'Duncan Maxwell's with him.'

Nora's little gasp of alarm didn't escape Marie McLeod. 'A reliable friend? Or not?'

'Duncan works part-time in the Tourist Office. He knows the place pretty well.' Adam hedged. 'Excellent guide.'

'But. . . ?

'He doesn't mind the odd dram or two,' said Nora dismally.

'That's all we need!' raged Mairi McLeod. 'A guide to anywhere you can get pissed.'

'He'll turn up.' On his way towards his own phone, Adam tried to sound reassuring.

The Schiltron Circle were assembling in the function room of the *Pheasant* as Adam hurried in from the saloon bar. He was only a guest speaker, not a member of the club, so had to wait deferentially by the wine racks while they went through their opening formalities. He had hoped to catch the Chairman before the ritual got under way and warn him that their most distinguished guest had unfortunately gone missing. but he dared not interrupt the preliminary rites.

Captain Scott-Fraser, his chest puffed out like a pigeon which could not possibly make room for anything further to eat this lunchtime, stood framed in the curve of the dining-room's bow window. and began a booming intonation.

'Let this month's chosen men-at-arms present themselves.'

Six members shuffled forwards along the narrow space between the wall and the tables. There were two accountants, one solicitor, a newsagent, a retired naval commander, and Enoch Buchanan.

Buchanan, breathing heavily, had only just made it on time. He glared at Adam in a way that suggested he was longing to pick a fight – which also suggested that they must have failed to get their hands on Erskine – but even Buchanan was not arrogant enough to break ranks at this point in the proceedings.

The Chairman stood to attention. The six men stood to attention. Upon his appointment, Scott-Fraser had wanted to adopt the title of Marischal, but the less grandiose title of Chairman had been established long before his appearance in the district.

'Form the schiltron.'

The six men huddled together in a tight hedgehog, each holding a skean-dhu at shoulder level, bristling outwards at an angle of forty-five degrees, symbolizing the tightly packed battle groups of Bruce's day.

Scott-Fraser cleared his throat and intoned: 'Now is the time . . .'

'Now is the hour,' responded the sextet.

The dirks were sheathed, and they took their allotted places at the table.

Scott-Fraser called upon an official known as a Pikeman to report on donations to local charities, and an appeal for more money to be allocated to Kilstane's home for the elderly to replace windows smashed by hooligans on the evening of a televised rugger match between England and Scotland. There was also an excess expenditure on the last Burns' Supper night, still unresolved from their last meeting. A small levy must be made at the end of today's luncheon in order to balance the books.

Adam could only be thankful that, as a guest, he was placed beside Scott-Fraser and ran no risk of being Buchanan's neighbour. On the other side of the Chairman was an empty place, waiting for the guest of honour to make his brief appearance at the end of the luncheon.

It was now his task to warn his host that Daniel Erskine might not, after all, show up.

'What? Why the blazes not?'

'There was some unpleasantness in the town earlier. Harassment by a group of ill-wishers.'

'Good God. Do you know who they were?'

'Yes.' Adam left it at that.

Scott-Fraser got the message. His glare down the table was met by Buchanan's even more blistering glare.

'Damn it. That is no fit behaviour for an officer serving in our ranks. Am I to understand that the fellow will now be too frightened to show up?'

'He may possibly not show up, no.'

'Most inconsiderate. No backbone, eh, these Bohemian types? But we can rely on you to come up to scratch, eh? Doing *your* bit, eh? You'd better fill me in before you get on your feet, so I know how to introduce you properly.'

Spending the hour of the meal making conversation with Scott-Fraser was almost as much an ordeal as sitting next to Buchanan would have been. It was made no easier by Scott-Fraser's heavy-handed attempt at a sympathetic joke. 'Don't like the way Buchanan's looking at you, eh? Looking you up and down – measuring you for one of his best oak and brass coffins.' But the moment came when the rhubarb fool and the cheese were whisked away, and Adam rose apprehensively to his feet.

He carefully did not look at Buchanan, but selected a meek-looking member halfway down the table on the left, whom he thought he recognized as a retired secretary of the bowls club. After a stumbling start, and the need to get rid of a frog in his throat, he forgot everything but the need to put across the real importance and beauty of Daniel Erskine's music.

'The major works fall into three periods. Rather as some painters have their spells known as cubist period, naturalist period, blue period and so on, Erskine's music shows three distinct phases. In the early compositions, when he was still living in Kilstane and teaching music at the Academy—'

'When he could spare the time from lechery,' snarled Buchanan.

Scott-Fraser reached for his gavel and thumped it against the edge of the table. 'Bowman Buchanan, I must insist on good order in the formation. It would be regrettable if I had to enforce a period of withdrawal.'

Buchanan growled, but subsided. As three members drank from tumblers of whisky, he ostentatiously waved for the water jug to be passed over to him.

'Those earlier pieces,' Adam continued, 'were what one might call a declaration of kinship with those working for the rebirth of Scottish folksong.'

'And the birth of several wee Scottish folk,' muttered MacKenzie.

'Then there comes that remarkable switch, after he had left Kilstane.' He was afraid to pause, offering Buchanan an opportunity to let fly about the reasons for Erskine leaving Kilstane – or being driven out. 'A sudden switch from, as it were, water-colours to oils.' He went on hurriedly: 'All at once there are violent textures, great bravura, great swings of sound. Searching rhythmic explorations that seem to stem from folk music without ever being folksy. At times there will be a Scotch snap, but almost at once it will be swallowed up in a sequence of syllabic tone-clusters which come from some other land altogether. If you come to the opening concert by the Westermarch Sinfonia on Sunday, you will hear a remarkable exploration of corrupt tonality and false relations, expressing beastliness and dissolution.' Buchanan grunted, but before he could decide whether or not to make a sarcastic comment, Adam ploughed on, hearing every note of Erskine's music in his head as he talked, so that he spoke faster and more ecstatically. 'What is so compelling is the way that he then resolves the conflict with a rhythmic insistence that almost physically wrenches the discords into a shape that refuses to be denied.'

One or two of his audience fidgeted on their chairs, and some-body knocked a coffee cup over.

There was one way, he was sure, to grab their attention. 'You will all be aware' – he made it an accusation against the entire community – 'that a brutal attack made upon Daniel Erskine by a deranged neighbour left him without the use of his hands. This was bound to affect his compositional techniques. After a few years of silence he was fortunate enough to acquire an amanuen-sis who worked intuitively with him, and managed to transfer his creative thoughts to the keyboard and to a written score. The limitations of such methods may in themselves have turned his mind to other concepts, though there is certainly no slackening of his intensity. At some stage during Miss Mairi McLeod's inter-pretative assistance he embarked on what we might call his third adventure, a quite different approach to the challenges of his creative career. In this third phase, we have another complete change of direction. Like Webern or later minimalists, he stripped music down to its very essence, but rather than aiming for cold abstraction he came up with something more recognizably Scottish, a pibroch rather than an alien strain, as if he were yearn-ing to come home. In *The Blacksmith's Wife of Yarrowfoot* there is a sensuous yet straightforwardly harmonic rather than contrapun-tal treatment of the theme of the witch who turns a young man into a stallion and rides him to a coven, but then is outwitted by him so that he rides her back as a mare. The symbolism—'

'Filth!' Buchanan could contain himself no longer. 'Typical filth. And if I get my hands on him, he'll soon learn what riding home has in store for him.'

'Bowman Buchanan, I must ask you to—'

'Och, I'll no' be sitting here listening to yon haivers a moment longer.'

Buchanan scraped his chair back and lumbered to his feet. Before he could extricate himself from the table and chair and squeeze past his neighbour, the door at the end of the room was pushed open. Daniel Erskine staggered in, half supported by Duncan Maxwell.

Adam's heart sank. To have let Duncan take charge of the great man ... a recipe for disaster. Though the disaster might have been worse. At least Duncan had found somewhere to keep Erskine from the mob. The back room of the *Buccleuch Arms*, by the look of the pair of them.

Adam said loudly: 'Mr Erskine, we had hoped to have the pleasure of your company a little earlier, so that you could answer a few questions about—'

'What did I tell ye?' Buchanan could not get his right leg disentangled from two closely set chairs. 'See for yourselves what kind o' man this self-styled genius has become – no better than ever he was. A drunkard and a lecher ...'

'Bowman Buchanan, for the last time—'

'And as for questions, there's a muckle deal o' those he's got to answer for.'

Erskine, swaying, tried to draw himself up and look dignified. When he spoke, his tone was less robust than Buchanan's, but much more savage and stabbing. The words were slurred, but came out with frightening venom.

'If that's the way you want it, then so be it. I've got plenty to say about this town and the people in it. Time somebody told the lot of you the truth. The truth.' He wiped his padded glove across the moistness of his lips.

'Mr Erskine.' Scott-Fraser got up and managed to stand to attention in spite of the back of his knees being cramped by his chair. 'Would you be fancying a dram with us?'

'Everything.' Erskine's bleary eyes scanned the whole assembly. 'Every damn thing. It's high time.' He emitted a shrill, shaky laugh. 'How about some truths about those weeds who couldn't father their own brats? And then had the nerve to get angry because I could do what they couldn't? And as for the women who said they'd been seduced – liars, hypocrites, begging for it. Never any need for rape in this town.'

Buchanan broke free. The man who pushed back his chair to block the way was Kerr. They confronted one another, chins jutting, as Erskine ranted on: 'And the music. Whatever tales this young man has been telling you about my music, isn't it high time to tell you the whole story of *that*? You'll hear the lot before I leave this town again, I'll make sure of that.'

He began to lean more and more heavily on Duncan. Someone from the end of the table made a move to help him, but he was too late. Erskine lurched forward a few paces, and collapsed face down into a plate of cheese and biscuits left behind by the waitress.

Buchanan managed at last to shoulder past Kerr. He drew himself up with the doom-laden wrath of an Old Testament prophet. 'All the daughters of music shall be brought low.'

That would have looked really encouraging on the programme notes, thought Adam glumly.

4

Strains of two electric guitars, shatteringly over-amplified, soared up from the haugh to the open first-floor window of Black Knowe like a vicious missile from some reiver intent on demoralizing the inmates before launching a full frontal attack on the tower.

Nick said: 'Remind you of the old days?'

He thought of her as he had first known her, when he was playing keyboards with a pop group at an Irish folk festival. There had been a lot of intermingling then – of performers with their instruments in impromptu groups during the public sessions, and performers shedding their instruments and much else in private after hours. Everything then had felt original, outrageous, all-embracing. Until, as you grew older, you discovered that everything had been done before, and probably better. Some groups grew louder and more outrageous. Others dissolved, and the instrumentalists went away to learn better music. But it had been hot and exhilarating while it lasted.

Standing beside him to look down at the platform and a guitarist struggling to produce a few chords without setting the amplifier into wilder hysterics, while others were erecting a large khaki marquee nearby, Mairi McLeod said: 'Some of them don't seem to have got much further than when they were thumping it out at their first gig.'

'Three-chord, three-string plonkers forever,' Nick agreed. 'Twelve bars, *da capo*, repeat, and go on repeating till you've

126

gone through two keys, a score of roadies, three marriages, three divorces, and a lot of alimony.'

He was aware of her studying him as they stood in the window embrasure, so high above the world. Mairi was wearing a dark green sleeveless dress which revealed all the olive smoothness of her throat and arms, bathed in the late afternoon sunshine so that they seemed to glow from within.

She said: 'At least you've managed to escape being married three times. Or even once – unless you've been holding out on me?'

'You could say I've been holding out on everyone. Or they've been holding out on me, more likely.'

'Come on now, Nick. I'd have thought a place like this would come complete with – what's the word? – a chatelaine.'

Visually, right here and now, thought Nick, he and Mairi must make just that conventional duo: the lord and his chatelaine, posed in the window of their great hall, serenely surveying their domains. Only Mairi did not have the makings of a lady of the manor. Even in a moment of stillness and contemplation like this, there was a tension in every sleek line of her body: she was never really at rest, a spring coiled and under tight control, but thrumming with the urge for release. She had always been a wild, fey girl, desperate for experience, greedy for life, committed enthusiastically to whatever she was absorbed in at the time.

She had been committed to Erskine for an unusually long time.

'Oughtn't there to be one of those boards outside?' She propped herself at an angle with her hands on the window-ledge. The sunlight was a blaze in the depths of her hair. 'Down there, a board with a painting of the castle when it was ten times bigger, with some fancy archaic lettering outlining the history of the place, and little vignettes of gallant knights and your bearded forebears?'

'It never was any larger than this. It's just a defensive family tower. And though my grandfather did have a beard, you would never have caught him on horseback tilting or charging. He was a railway engineer.'

127

The shrill noise outside became as grating as fingernails scratching in an enamel pan. As Mairi backed away, Nick closed the window and glanced at the clock.

'And there's another grandfather that doesn't belong,' said Mairi, settling herself on the settee. 'Didn't they have sundials in olden times?'

'Not indoors.'

She glanced at the door to the stairwell. 'I wonder when that old soak will come round.' There was none of the reverence which Nick had heard in her voice in Altnalarach.

He could not sit down. Least of all on the settee beside her. There was no longer any fire between them, fanned by the heady winds of past music; nor was there any likelihood of it being rekindled. He didn't want her to be under any misapprehensions – to do or say something impetuous, which he knew all too well she was capable of doing on an unexpected provocation or pang of emotional hunger.

He said: 'Just what did decide Erskine to come to Kilstane after all? Did you work on him on our behalf?'

'No, I did not. I knew it'd be a disaster.'

'Then why—'

'Our bloody fool of a wandering grocer came up with his delivery van, and a couple of sheets from the *Express* had got shoved between Daniel's usual case of Clynelish and our groceries. He doesn't usually want to know what goes on in the outside world, but he was in a hurry to get at a bottle and came across the story about your corpse being a woman.'

'Why should that interest him?'

'I wish I knew. Why he should want to come back here . . .' She changed the subject with unexpected ferocity. 'Do *you* ever want to go back to your old ways? Playing on the road, playing in studios, sitting at the mixing deck and trying to coax sense out of other people's musical ramblings . . . don't you ever fancy going back?'

'No. For quite a while I felt a bit uneasy at finding myself a baronet. Purely because a couple of the family had died in the wrong order. It seemed crazy. But I'm settling in.'

'Being the laird – Nick, knowing you, it must give you the giggles. Be honest.'

'For quite a while,' he repeated, 'I did feel as if. . . well, I was wearing somebody else's fancy dress. Somebody else's skin. Sooner or later they'd find me out.'

'But now?'

'I'm beginning to feel responsible for the people of Kilstane, and what goes on in the town.'

'Bloody hell.' Her brief savagery had turned to cynicism. 'Now you're wallowing in it. All set to become a real clan chief. But won't that take you back to London in the end? I mean, haven't they all made a habit of selling off their land, along with a few mountains, so they can acquire a plushy mansion in London and pick up a few non-executive directorships?'

There was a thud against the door. When it opened, Erskine held on to it until he was sure he could make it to the settee. Mairi made room for him, glaring.

'I think I could be fancying a wee dram.' He tried to chuckle, but the back of his throat must have been harsh, and the request came out as no more than a croak.

Nick expected Mairi to make some withering remark. But she shrugged, and indicated that Nick might as well open the drinks cabinet in the stone alcove beside the fireplace.

Erskine's half-closed eyes blinked towards the facing wall in bleary recognition as he downed the whisky. 'Like a bloody prison, isn't it? Stone walls and that sort of thing, they *do* a prison make, whatever the old versifier said. And I bet there used to be iron bars over that window.'

'Undoubtedly,' said Nick.

'Never invited to set foot in it when I was a lad.' He squinted, trying to get things in focus. 'Quite a little tour I had, during my spell of freedom. How did I get back here, though?'

'Adam Lowther rescued you from some other drunk.'

'Ah. That nice fellow. Nice and sociable. Duncan something, or something Duncan. That back bar . . . we had some good crack in there.'

'A dose of nostalgia?' Nick prompted.

'Nostalgia? Ha! The pub was the only place worth visiting. The rest of the town's just what it always was. Window curtains twitching. Snivelling about their wonderful Burns suppers. Pathetic. And their Schiltron odds and sods. None of it changed, none of it. Peely-wally old crocks on the street corners whispering over every step you take. And I bet that bloody chemist still has a harridan who makes it clear the shop is run for her benefit, not yours. Or maybe by now it's her daughter.' He burped.

Mairi grabbed his arm and wrenched him round to face her. 'Lowther said that when you made that scene at the lunch club, you were threatening all and sundry to tell the truth about them. Or about something or other. And you kept going on and on about it while he was steering you back here. Just what were you on about?'

Erskine peered into his empty glass. Mairi did not rise to the hint. She took the glass from him and set it firmly down on the small table beside the settee. Erskine let his head sag against the arm of the settee, and his eyelids drooped.

Trying to jolt him back to reality, Nick said: 'You *will* be at the opening concert on Sunday?'

'Oh, aye, I'll be there. You can count on that. Mm. Oh, yes. Maybe even give a speech, eh?'

Then he fell asleep.

Nick stared at the huddled shape. The air was still thick with beery breath. He said in an undertone: 'I still can't really understand why *you* of all people—'

'You wouldn't think he could be that good in bed, would you?' said Mairi out of the blue.

'At his age? You're not serious?'

'As good as you ever were. Truly.'

'But . . .' His imagination couldn't cope with the vision that was struggling to assemble itself. 'I mean, with no hands . . .'

It was an absurd thing to say, and Mairi made the most of it. 'Never mind the hands. He managed very happily with other parts of his anatomy.'

130

Erskine stirred. It was impossible to tell whether the sound he emitted was a faint snore or a knowing chuckle.

Mrs Robson tapped on the door and came in. She looked disdainfully at the man slumped against the arm of the settee. 'There's that Gunn lassie downstairs wanting to see ... *Mr* Erskine.'

'You mean Detective Inspector Gunn?' said Nick sharply.

'Well, aye, sir. It's just that, remembering her, I find it hard to think of her as-'

'Send the detective inspector up.'

Mairi shook Erskine awake.

Nick felt a tightening across his chest as Lesley Gunn came into the room. She glanced briefly from him to Mairi, and then apologized for the interruption.

'But I do have to take a statement from Mr Erskine to help us in our enquiries.'

Erskine looked her up and down, his eyes widening appreciatively. Nick was tempted to throw a jug of cold water over him. Or tell him to wipe that dirty grin off his face. There did seem to be a solid foundation for all those distasteful rumours about his character.

'What would be the nature of these enquiries, officer?' leered Erskine.

'We need to establish, sir, the dates when people concerned were still living here, or when they left, and whether they came back.'

' "People concerned"? Concerned with what?'

'With the circumstances surrounding the death of the woman who has been found in the Academy flue.'

'This is outrageous,' Mairi burst out. 'What possible connection could Mr Erskine have with some sordid murder, long after he left the town?'

Nick watched the slight tremor of Lesley's lips. She looked once more at him, then away again. 'What year *did* you leave Kilstane, Mr Erskine?'

'God knows. Somewhere in the late sixties.'

'You left on your own, after your . . . accident?'

'I didn't exactly have a devoted following.'

'Mr Buchanan has suggested in a roundabout way to one of my colleagues that his daughter—'

'That's enough,' snapped Mairi.

'Buchanan?' Erskine laughed. 'Like all staunch believers in Holy Writ, he's always been a great one for improbable yarns.'

'His daughter did not accompany you?'

Erskine seemed to be gloating over her – whether because she was so slim and attractive, or because he was enjoying tantalizing her, it was impossible to tell. 'Not that I recall, no.'

'You mean she definitely didn't?'

'I think I'd have remembered. She wasn't what you'd call desirable. Looked too much like her father.'

'And you didn't come back to Kilstane at any time, for a visit, or to—'

'I've never been back to this accursed place until now. And from what I remember of Buchanan's daughter, she was having it off with someone called Gallaher, or Gaffney, or something. An Irishman. One of Buchanan's labourers. Now I look back' – he rubbed his eyes with one leathered stump – 'I think the whole town knew it. Except Buchanan. Maybe the two of them cleared off to Ireland. And maybe her father would rather boast about her clearing off with a distinguished composer-to-be than an Irish brickie. Though in view of what he's said about me, that doesn't seem likely, does it?' He rasped another laugh, and produced another burp. 'I tell you one thing, though, Miss Sleuth. Never believe a word any of that lot tell you. They're too stupid to know the truth when it hits them in the face. Which it may well do when I get round to telling them. Oh, I could tell you a lot about the con-men in this town.'

'Please do,' said Lesley.

He rubbed his eyes again with his right glove as if daylight was hurting them. 'All in good time. My own good time.'

Nick was startled by Lesley's sudden change of tack. 'Did your boyhood friend McCabe ever come back?'

There was a long pause. Then Erskine's eyelids began to droop again. 'Don't see how he could. Poor old Jan.'

'I thought his name was Ian when you knew him.'

'Ian . . . Jan. Quite a lad. I ought never to have . . .' It faded into a mumble. Erskine's eyes finally closed and his head lolled back against the arm of the settee. Nick wondered if he was genuinely befuddled, or was contriving a tactical retreat; and wondered whether that had occurred to Lesley too.

He said: 'I'm sorry, he's not terribly clear about things this afternoon. You'd better come back another day.'

'If it's really essential,' said Mairi tartly. 'A complete waste of everybody's time, so far as I can see. It's all too vague, all in the past. You don't really know what questions to ask, do you? So it's just insinuations. A lot of nonsense.'

Lesley shrugged, defeated. 'From this weekend on, I'm off the case.'

Nick felt another tug across his chest. 'Giving it up?'

'A Sergeant Elliot will be tidying up the loose ends. But I'm ordered back to HQ.'

'Loose ends? And then it's being written off, this murder?'

'No case is ever written off,' said Lesley stiffly. 'It may have to go on the back burner, but the flame's only turned low, never turned off entirely. Not until the case is well and truly wrapped up.'

She looked regretfully at Erskine's sprawled body, clearly wishing she could have had a couple of definite dates, a couple of indisputable facts, to justify her visit.

'Well . . .'

Nick held out his hand. Her eyes met his in a moment of even worse puzzlement and uncertainty than she had shown towards Erskine.

'Remember' – Nick had let go of her hand, but was still trying to hold on to her in some way – 'if things don't work out, there's still that other opening we discussed.'

'Thank you. I don't think the question will arise.'

After Lesley had gone, Mairi said: 'Poor Nick.'

'Mm?'

'I knew you'd fall well and truly in love one day.'

'For goodness' sake . . . I rather like . . . I mean, I admire the girl, but it hasn't gone that far.'

'Oh, yes, it has. Too far to turn back now. It hurts, doesn't it? Me, I've always felt that a regular diet of uncomplicated lust is the healthier option.'

Through the window of his shop Lesley saw that Adam Lowther was busy. The town was filling up and visitors were picking up leaflets, studying some sheets of music, and reading the backs of CD cases. She hesitated. This was no moment for a final attempt to fill in blanks on a timetable of the past. She had been bluntly instructed to hand over to Elliot, write up her report, and deliver it to the Super when she got back. What awaited her in his office was still shrouded in mystery.

She couldn't help herself. As the customers drifted out, some with their purchases and some empty-handed, she let one of them hold the door open for her and went in.

'Ah. Inspector.' Lowther did not sound very welcoming.

She said: 'Just one point I'd like to clear up. Can you tell me the exact date your father left Kilstane?'

'What on earth. . . ? I know it was some time in 1981 . . . or was it '82? I could look it up, I suppose. But what's that got to do with anything?'

'I'm trying to establish everyone's movements around the time we believe that that unfortunate woman was killed.'

'Just a minute. Are you trying to imply . . .' He had been standing behind the glass-topped counter. Now he began to move round it, pale with anger. 'This is disgraceful. Bloody disgraceful. Why should my father—'

'I'm sorry, it's simply a matter of routine. If we can eliminate—'

'Eliminate? My father's been dead for years, but I don't see why his memory should be dirtied by your shifty insinuations.'

'Mr Lowther . . .'

134

Behind her the door opened and three young men came in, one of them heading for the display of guitar strings and two shuffling along the display of cassettes and CDs.

Adam Lowther was trying to keep them under observation while still glowering at her. 'If there's nothing else?' he said.

Nothing that could be said in front of other people. And he certainly wasn't going to shut up shop for her benefit and submit to her questioning. 'I could look it up, I suppose,' was the most she was going to get. She left.

When she had finished writing up her notes she could not sit still indoors. Questions kept hammering away in her mind. She resented being taken off the case in this offhanded way. Was she to be shunted into more menial jobs rather than the specialist work for which she was qualified?

Apply for a transfer? Approach someone in Edinburgh? Or make a clean break and see what her contacts in the Arts and Antiques group in London could come up with? Start afresh, instead of floundering, snared here in the past.

The past . . . A past inhabited by a younger Erskine, a shadowy McCabe, Adam Lowther's father now dead, a skeletal woman now dead. Music from the past, murder from the past.

She had to get out of this room. She walked round the town, across the square where the usual groups of teenagers lounged in resentful groups, waiting for someone to spur them on into some bout of vandalism, and down to the river. The evening sky was waking up rather than going to sleep. Faintly pink clouds, streaked with dark grey, acquired outlines of orange blood. The distant moors began to shiver with liquid fire like a lava flow, and against it stood the dark rocky silhouette of Black Knowe.

Old ghosts could come riding out of that backdrop. Reivers crossing the Border to steal more cattle and shed more blood. And the family feuds, generation after generation, lasting on into the world of the Buchanans and Kerrs. The past would never be dead.

Still the tangled net of it all was wrapped round her and the whole town like strands of a thickening cobweb in the dusk.

Erskine and that strange woman Mairi McLeod. A hunch that there must have been something between Mairi McLeod and Nick Torrance some way back. And what about herself and Nick Torrance? A past that had never resolved itself. And now never would. She told herself that as firmly as possible. It never would come to anything.

She tried to shake it off. To be rid of all of it.

Instead of all these smouldering fag-ends of the past, did nothing ever happen here and now, in the present, right in front of you where you could get at it?

In the morning, while it was only just becoming light, she was awoken by the mobile phone beside her bed. Sergeant Elliot started her day with the news that Daniel Erskine had been murdered.

5

Maitland's voice on the phone was incredulous and a shrill half octave higher than usual. 'Another death? Good God, I'm beginning to think there's a jinx on you, Gunn. I seem to remember another incident of murders taking place right under your nose while you were supposed to be investigating something else.'

'One can't predict these things, sir.'

'Too damn right one can't. What the hell happened?'

Lesley summed up, keeping her voice as brisk and neutral as possible. Daniel Erskine's body had been found at three o'clock in the morning halfway up a cobbled wynd in the centre of Kilstane. The side of his head had been severely battered and led to his death on the spot.

'Any trace of the murder weapon?'

'It was left near the body, sir. A large electric guitar.'

'A *what*?'

'A large guitar, sir. The sort used by pop groups. And we've got more than a few of those round here right now.'

'Any idea of which of 'em might have done it?'

'Not yet, sir.'

'Better stay where you are, then. For the time being. See what you can do about setting up an incident room ready for a full-scale inquiry.'

'Sir, there isn't a spare couple of square feet in the town. We've got a music festival just starting.'

'Festival? When the star turn's just been done in? Are they going ahead with the thing?'

'That's one thing we'll have to find out, sir. But in any event, people are still here. The place is crowded. And all the concert venues have been booked. The old school, the Town Hall, the Tolbooth. And every pub and B-and-B for miles around – all taken. And the nick here is too cramped.'

'Throw somebody out.'

'On what authority, sir?'

'Oh, for God's sake. All right. Get in touch with MacLeish at Wallace Street yard. I'll clear an incident caravan for you. Tell him exactly where you want it, and be ready to get it connected up, wherever that is.'

'And sir . . .'

'Yes, what is it now?'

'The festival itself. Ought we to recommend calling it off?'

There was a long pause. The answer, when it came, was peevish. 'You talk about authorization, Gunn. Where d'you think I could get authority for that, at short notice? The bloody people are already there, you've said yourself, swarming all over the place. If the organizers want to send them home, that's up to them. But unless they're likely to start a riot, what reason do *we* have for asking the Procurator Fiscal or the Sheriff to intervene?'

'They'd be more likely to get nasty if everything was cancelled,' Lesley agreed, 'than if it just goes ahead.'

'That's it, then. Just concentrate on the murder until I get a Senior Investigating Officer to take over. And keep me informed.'

'Sir.'

'I fancy I'll be sending DCI Rutherford as SIO. You've worked with him before. I'm sure you remember his methods.'

Oh, yes. DI Gunn remembered Rutherford and his methods all too well. And she could guess what the general tone of his greeting would be the moment he arrived.

Her prediction was accurate. 'Out of your depth again, Les? Fancy us being thrown together again like this. You should have got out while the going was good.'

'As I remember it,' she said, 'you were the one who told me to stay where I was because my promotion was as good as in the bag. Only it wasn't, was it?'

'You can't hold that against me. You know how these things go.'

'I do now, yes.'

'Let's get down to the real business, shall we? Where's the corpse?'

She took him to the tent which had been erected over the body. It completely blocked the narrow cobbled slope of Souters Wynd, one end of its roof fastened over the arch of a disused drinking fountain, its flaps twitching intermittently in faint puffs of breeze. Inside, the body of Daniel Erskine was crumpled over the stone bowl of the fountain, his bloodied head sagging into the niche in the wall. One man in white overalls straightened up, pulling off his gloves. Another had been edging round the corpse, taking photographs.

'Head staved in from the side,' Rutherford said after bending into the recess. 'And the weapon?'

The photographer nodded towards the side of the tent. A glow of late morning sunlight turned one wall of the tent golden, and glinted on something lying on the cobbles.

Rutherford grunted disbelief. 'A bloody guitar?'

'I think they have a fancy name for it,' said Lesley. 'Stratocruiser, or stratocaster, or something like that.'

'Some nut case drugged out of his mind, swinging out halfway through a chorus?'

A lot of the punk rockers and hip-hop weirdos would certainly have found Daniel Erskine's music and all he stood for old hat, corny, fuddy duddy, past its sell-by date; but surely not savagely enough to beat him to death?

A white van had been backing cautiously down the narrow wynd, stopping almost against the tent.

'I think we've finished here. We can move him to the morgue.'

'Hold it just a minute.' Rutherford lifted the flap and looked down the slope. A little knot of gawpers at the foot of the wynd moved away when he took a step out, not anxious to be asked awkward questions. He studied the rise of windowless walls on either side. 'Was he walking down the alley or upwards?'

'There's no doorway for anyone to hide in,' said Lesley. 'Easier for someone to catch him unawares coming from the top, rather than running uphill carrying that thing.'

'Mm. Or else he just blundered into someone drugged up to the eyeballs who lost his temper, and smashed him one or two.'

'And left the instrument here? They're pretty expensive.'

'It would have dawned on him that this was no place to be hanging around.' Rutherford waited for Lesley to accompany him slowly down to the marketplace. 'Are there a lot of these fancy banjo players in town at the moment?'

'Swarming with them.'

'Oh, great. But there ought to be enough fingerprints on that thing for us to identify one of them. After we've worked our way through the whole collection. But where the hell do we start?'

'Adam Lowther.'

'And who's he?'

'Runs the local music shop. A fanatical admirer of the deceased and his music. Had a lot to do with organizing this festival – and with calling it The Gathering.'

'Let's go see him.'

As they emerged from the narrow passage, Galbraith was waiting with his camera. 'Any chance of a statement, officer? Er . . . officers. Give me an exclusive, and I'll keep the rest of them off your back.'

The thought of this seedy little man withstanding the onslaught of determined Press hacks was enough to bring grins to both their faces. Rutherford did not even deign to answer, but waved him aside like a man swatting a fly.

They found the CLOSED sign in the glass of the music shop door. It took several rings at the door in the pend to bring Nora Lowther down. She nodded as if she had been expecting them, and silently led the way upstairs.

Adam Lowther was slumped in an armchair, his hands shaking but the rest of his body rigid in a trance of disbelief. He did not wait for the two detectives to introduce themselves, but said: 'I don't believe it.' Then he said it again; and again. And at last: 'It can't be true. *Can't* be.'

Nora Lowther indicated that they should sit down.

'Mr Lowther, do you know how Daniel Erskine was killed?'

'Someone says he was . . . beaten up. But who . . . it's insane. People in this town, after all these years . . .'

'His head was swiped from the side,' said Rutherford ruthlessly, 'like someone swinging a caber. Only this was one of those fancy electric guitars you sell. You *do* sell things like that, I believe?'

Adam stared at him, stupefied. He shook his head, then nodded. He was still in shock.

Lesley said: 'You wouldn't have sold one to any of the performers here during The Gathering?'

'No. They usually bring their own.' Adam forced a feeble, ghastly smile. 'I'd only manage to sell to one of them if he'd smashed his own instrument on stage. They do, you know – jump up and down and then smash their instruments just to drive the crowd wild.'

'So this couldn't have been one of yours?'

'No.'

'When you've got over the shock, Mr Lowther, perhaps we can come and talk to you again. We may have a few leads you'll be able to help us with.'

Rutherford showed signs of wanting to continue the questioning, but realized she was right. Only on a potentially guilty man was it worth leaning heavily at this stage, and Lowther was one of the least likely suspects.

As they headed for the stairs, Lowther burst out suddenly: 'If I could get my hands on him . . . if I knew what bastard did that, I'd . . . God, I'd. . .' Then he sank again into his petrified trance.

Back in the station, Rutherford said: 'Right. While we're waiting for our mobile home to roll up, fill me in with the details so far. Including that sad character Lowther.'

They had to sit on spindly steel chairs in the only available interview room in the station, which was as cramped as Lesley had assured Superintendent Maitland.

DCI Jack Rutherford had aged fast in the couple of years since they last met. His hair had only a few grey streaks, but it was stringier than she remembered, and his jacket was twisted up on his right shoulder as if he had got one of his jacket buttons in the wrong hole. At any rate those two things hadn't changed: the loop of his right eyebrow expressing permanent scepticism, and the way his shoulder hunched forward, like a man ready to throw a punch. Together they might intimidate a villain, or at least some young delinquent unsure of his ground.

'Do we know who found the body – first on the scene?'

'A young local. Name of Campbell. Blootered after hours on the half-and-halfs. Sergeant Elliot questioned him on the spot. Done twice in the sheriff court for smashing windows and vandalizing flower tubs, but not the murderous kind. That's left to the older generation.'

'Come again?'

She explained about Erskine being chased through the town. And Erskine threatening that he had 'plenty to tell' about someone or something unspecified. 'Which could have put the wind up some of the older folk who remembered him. They're an unforgiving crowd.'

'Les, do you think we might start at the beginning?'

'I think you'd better understand that the beginning, as I see it, was a long way back.'

'Keep it short.'

How was it possible to keep it short? She was sure that everything, including the two corpses, stemmed from events distorted yet by no means forgotten in Kilstane. Ready to fend off impatient interruptions, she launched into a historical summary.

In 1937 the Strepka family – husband Karel, wife Herma, and their seven-year-old son Jan – came from their native Czechoslovakia to Scotland. Karel Strepka, fluent in German and

English as well as his own tongue, had come to take up a position in the Glasgow branch of a joint Anglo–Czech machinery
import and export firm. As war threatened, Karel wanted to go
back to his own country to fight, but the firm insisted he stayed
on to co-operate with their world-wide contacts on moving
machine parts out of the way of the Nazis and the countries they
were threatening. He stayed until it was too late to go home –
and in any case unsafe. He enlisted in the RAF along with other
Czech and Polish expatriates, and was much valued for his
mechanical expertise; but at the outbreak of war he insisted on
being transferred to flying duties.

To protect their identities and avoid repercussions on relatives
left at home in occupied Europe, such people were encouraged
to change their names and documentation to Scottish ones –
Charles McCabe, Helen McCabe, and Ian McCabe. Combatants
were provided with similar identification in case they were shot
down and captured.

When 'Charles McCabe' was posted to a squadron at Wick, his
wife found a job in the kitchen of the local school, to be near him.
Early in 1941 he was killed in a bombing raid over Germany.

'Les, for Christ's sake.' The first interruption hadn't been long
in coming. 'Have you been watching too many war films on the
telly? What the hell has this got to do with—'

'Without the background,' she insisted, 'you'll never get to
grips with the foreground.'

She went on to explain that Helen/Herma would accept no
charity, but continued working in the school, where the family of
the dominie, Dr Kenneth Erskine, did all they tactfully could to
make things easy for Mrs McCabe and the little boy. Dr Erskine
was a keen musician, putting on school concerts and playing the
piano in concerts for the RAF base. The Erskines had a son,
Daniel, the same age as Ian, and during the war the two boys
became close friends, virtually brothers.

As the war was drawing to an end, Dr Erskine developed
arthritic problems and, needing to escape the Wick climate,
answered an advertisement for a vacancy as rector of Kilstane

Academy in the Borders. He and his wife agreed that they should take the 'McCabes' with them.

When the war ended, Mrs McCabe wanted to reclaim the name of Strepka and go back home in spite of the political turmoil and many problems left over from the German occupation. The Erskines persuaded her that it would be in Ian's best interests for him to stay here to finish his schooling, since he was now fluent in English and knew Czech only from the nostalgic tales his mother told him. In addition, there must be dreadful confusion in schools and the whole educational system in Czechoslovakia as it tried to emerge from the diktats of the Nazis, and she herself might find difficulties in settling back into her old way of life. Give it a few years, until they could both be confident in conditions back home. So Mrs McCabe stayed on reluctantly.

A few years after the war, when both boys were in their teens, word came that Herma's ageing mother in Prague was seriously ill. Herma left on a visit, saying that while she was there she would organize things so that very soon she could come back to Kilstane to collect Ian/Jan.

But after several months a letter smuggled out via Austria, to avoid censorship, said that the frontiers were closed, the Iron Curtain was down, she was not to be allowed back, and Jan must not come to Czechoslovakia. The new Communist regime was already making it clear that the families of Czechs who had served with the British forces were under a serious cloud in their own country. When Dr Erskine wrote back, there was no reply until someone who had escaped to the West phoned him and begged him not to pursue the matter. Mrs Strepkova was in enough trouble already, working in a factory as a virtual slave labourer because of her supposed Westernized contamination.

The Erskines shielded Ian from knowledge of this, though what he read in the papers made it pretty clear what was going on in his homeland. But he was a very self-centred teenager, and too comfortable with the Erskines to kick up any fuss. He had become pretty well an essential part of the family by now,

144

having known no other, and was later remembered in the town as quite a sly manipulator, calculating how to use people, looking melancholy and bereaved when it suited him, and aggressive or bloody awkward at other times, knowing just what he could get away with. To some extent Dr and Mrs Erskine must have worried about the influence he was having on their son Daniel; but they were too decent and vague to take any strong steps.

Under Dr Erskine's influence, both boys had become accomplished pianists, though Ian also had a gift for the violin and, as time went on, became more and more interested in the folk music of the homeland he had never really known. Daniel Erskine did his two years' National Service, and was tempted to stay on, having made his mark as a musician and being offered a course at Kneller Hall. It was either that or teachers' training in civvy street. His father was growing feebler, and needed his help in running the Academy. Daniel returned as deputy head, specializing in teaching music. Some of his own compositions were published and performed – but none of them created any great stir.

'Les, we've had the history of the war. Do we have to go through a course on music?'

'This is where the whole subject of Daniel Erskine begins to take off.'

'Don't get me too excited.'

By now the two young men both wanted to study composition, but found that in the Royal Scottish Academy of Music and Drama in Glasgow at that time the subject was 'not offered'. Stuck in Kilstane, they were both in danger of turning into local tearaways. No one was ever quite sure whether their exploits with local girls and married women were in collaboration or in rivalry.

Then the restless Ian met a violinist in the string section of a Czech orchestra visiting Edinburgh, rigorously supervised by a party functionary. He was assured that he could make a better living in Czechoslovakia than he could here. So, in spite of his mother's earlier warnings, he went to the Czech Embassy, boasted of his musical talents and, with his usual glib self-confidence, expressed his willingness to work for the state. No doubt he was confident that he would soon learn how to play it clever and use the system instead of being used by it. He went over. And didn't come back. And the Erskines could get no answer as to his whereabouts or wellbeing.

When his father died, Daniel Erskine quit teaching and took on any freelance jobs that were going. He played as an accompanist, took summer jobs in holiday resort orchestras, and got a few broadcasting sessions presenting his own works – accomplished but flimsy. He performed at various local music festivals all over Britain, including a number of folk festivals.

Then a jealous Kilstane husband smashed Erskine's hands, to make sure they wouldn't ever touch his wife again – or play the piano again, or be able to write music down. Daniel, like his old pal Ian, virtually disappeared from the Kilstane scene. Unable to play or to work out his own compositions at the keyboard, and unwilling to face the sneers of Kilstane folk, he shut himself away somewhere.

'Hold it right there a moment,' said Rutherford. 'This character who did the crippling – they caught him?'

'He was an oil rig worker. Away a lot. Just went berserk, smashed Erskine up, and gave his wife a bit of a pasting. She went to the police. But they didn't have any trouble. He just sat at home waiting for them to show up. Got five years. One year's remission.'

'And did he come back here? A forgiving little wife waiting for him – or don't we know?'

'Sergeant Elliot did some checking on that. Local talk has it that his wife cleared off soon after he was put inside. Nobody's bothered to ask where she went. The husband may have joined her when he got out, or he may just have gone off on his own.'

'The wife was never seen again?'

She could tell which way his mind was going. 'If it was

146

Erskine who put her in the family way . . . Or,' she suggested, 'another old enemy, another cuckolded father? Bringing us to our Academy skeleton.'

'It would help to know what that "plenty to tell" remark amounts to.'

'We might just possibly get a lead on that from Mairi McLeod. His amanuensis.'

'His what?'

'After his hands were smashed up so he couldn't play, or write – or get his hands on any of the womenfolk round here – he needed someone who could transcribe his ideas. I don't know where or when they met, but she seems to have moved in and interpreted all his ideas for him. Like Eric Fenby and Delius, you know.'

'Oddly enough, Les, I don't.'

'Maybe he whistled some of his themes, or dictated them note by note and then discussed the harmony. She must have had a pretty deep insight into his mind to get it right.'

'And did she get it right?'

'Judging by the amount of stuff that got published and played, it must have been a pretty good partnership.'

'OK, then. Let's start with this McLeod woman. Where was she when he got done in? If she's supposed to be his . . . whatever you called it . . . his nursemaid, companion, whatever . . . how did he get away from her?'

'We'd better ask her.'

Lesley felt the familiar breathlessness as Nick's voice answered the phone in Black Knowe.

6

Nick Torrance was waiting at the head of the stairs. 'Detective Inspector Gunn – still with us? I was surprised by your call. I thought that—'

'The new development,' Lesley said curtly.

'They're putting you in charge of murder number two?'

'Not quite.' Lesley glanced at Rutherford, who grinned.

'She's a wonderful Girl Friday,' he said. 'Sir Nicholas, I think we met a few years ago.'

'I think we did. In the same company.' He was still studying Lesley. 'But as I told you on the phone, I'm not entirely happy about you interviewing Miss McLeod so soon. She's had a terrible shock. And she's blaming herself, quite wrongly.'

'We appreciate her distress.' Rutherford's tone was that of a man who had used stock platitudes so often that they had become meaningless. 'But we do need to know all the circumstances just as quickly and clearly as possible. And she was the last person to see Erskine alive, wasn't she?'

'We can't be sure of that. He went off on his own, on some impulse. Might have gone anywhere, seen anyone.'

'Bumped into Mr Buchanan?' said Lesley.

'That thought had occurred to me.'

It was Rutherford's turn to stare at Lesley. 'Is this a suspect I ought to have heard about?'

'One of the angry old men I mentioned. But until we know the direction the victim took, we don't know whether they could have met up again.'

The door opened and Mairi McLeod walked across a pool of sunlight rippling on the floor.

Rutherford made no attempt to conceal the way he looked her up and down. Lesley remembered that silent whistle of his. Dressed in a clinging black dress, the woman looked even more provocative than if she had been dressed in blazing scarlet. But Lesley saw the change in her features – drained, stone cold. She looked almost as if she had suffered a stroke.

Before Rutherford could start his usual insensitive drone, Lesley said: 'You know why we're here, Miss McLeod?'

She nodded.

'I wonder if you can tell us exactly what happened last night. Where did you last see Mr Erskine, and at what time?'

Mairi moved across the room as a dark sybil. Or a brooding witch. She sank very slowly and silently into the window seat close to Nick's armchair.

'We went out for a stroll around ten o'clock. To see what was going on in the streets. Listening to all kinds of music coming out of every window.'

'A sort of sentimental stroll round his old haunts?'

Mairi uttered a strangled laugh. 'The only sentiment he felt towards Kilstane was hatred. Hated the place and all its residents. Loud and clear.'

Rutherford was impatient to force the pace. 'So why did he come back?'

'I could never really get it out of him. One minute he had no intention of showing up for the festival, but then . . . oh, I don't know. Something he read in the papers.'

'The dead woman,' said Nick, ignoring her reproachful glance. 'Somehow he was curious about her?'

'As if he knew something. Or wanted to settle something. But I never did get it straight.'

'Since we still don't know who she is—'

'But maybe *he* knew.'

149

'If so,' said Nick, 'he certainly isn't going to tell us now.'

'We should never have come here. I ought to have talked him out of it, somehow.'

Lesley was happy to leave the questioning now to Rutherford while she discreetly studied Mairi's face, trying to detect any hint of suppressed knowledge.

'Anyway,' said Rutherford, 'let's concentrate on last night. Miss McLeod, you say you went out together. Didn't you come back here together?'

'No. He went off on his own.'

'And you let him do that?'

Nick said sharply: 'Miss McLeod was Mr Erskine's musical assistant. Not his keeper.'

'Nevertheless, after what I'm told happened on a previous occasion . . .' Rutherford looked from one to the other, waiting for a response.

It came reluctantly from Mairi, a black silhouette against the window. 'Daniel said he wanted to see somebody. Someone he said he'd got to talk to.'

'Who would that have been?'

'I thought it might be Adam Lowther.'

'Why?'

'I don't know. There seemed to be something that Daniel wanted to know. He was drawn towards the young man.'

'Adam is probably his greatest fan,' added Nick.

'Daniel hated people making a fuss of him,' said Mairi. 'But in this one case . . . no, I don't know, I just got the impression that that was where he might have gone.'

'At that time of night?'

'I've told you, I simply don't know.'

'What do you suppose he meant by that remark about having plenty to tell?' said Lesley. 'Tell about who, or what?'

Mairi appeared to have gone off into numbness again. Then she shook her head. 'That's something else I've wondered about.'

'He never told you? Not even *you*?'

'No. There were times when he shut himself away – even from himself, you might say.'

As they left Black Knowe, Rutherford said: 'Our friend Lowther never said anything about Erskine going to see him.'

'Maybe he didn't. Or set out to go there and was waylaid.'

'I think we'd better eliminate him before we start looking around elsewhere.'

Nora Lowther let them in again, just as impassively as before.

'No,' said Adam. 'Of course he didn't come here. Why would he have done, at that time of night?'

'Just what we were asking ourselves.'

'I can't help. Look, why are you wasting your time with me? Oughtn't you to be out looking for whoever—'

'Mr Lowther.' A sudden urge possessed Lesley. 'Mr Lowther, have you got round yet to checking the date your father left Kilstane and took you to Leeds?'

Rutherford opened his mouth, startled; then closed it again, leaving it to her.

'Do you think I've nothing better to do, right now?' Adam protested. 'Have you any idea how much work is involved in co-ordinating all these recitals, and then having this dreadful blow on top of everything?' He wiped the back of his hand across his eyes. 'Do you know how I *feel*?'

He put out a hand vaguely towards his wife, as if clutching for support. She seemed still mulling over the earlier question. Expressionless, she said in a monotone like an incantation: 'If you think back – think how long your dad worked for Parrotts before you got *your* job along with my Harry, and then when *we* got married, it has to have been around the mid eighties.'

'In Leeds,' said Lesley, 'your father worked for this firm called – what was it, Parrotts? Are they still going?'

'What's that got to do with me? I packed it in and came back here to work on my own account, didn't I? Never saw much of old Mr Parrott, and he'll be dead by now, I should think. But what that's got to do with what's been happening here in Kilstane, I don't see.' He was growing more and more prickly.

151

'All that stuff's in the past, it can't have anything to do with the present.'

On the way back to the station, Rutherford expressed agreement. 'I wasn't going to drop you in it, Les, but I didn't get your drift. You sure you're not still bogged down too much in things more complicated than they need be?'

'It's all part of the same story. I know it in my bones.'

'Didn't know they played the bones in a symphony orchestra. Which is where you seem to be, half the time.'

At the station they were greeted by Sergeant Elliot with the news that a young man had just arrived to report a theft – the theft of an electric guitar.

He was a tall, lank specimen with a greasy leather jacket and moleskin trousers. His hands were twitching convulsively and his eyes were red and weepy. The most conspicuous item in his attire was a hangover. Lesley could smell him from several feet away. His name was Dave – 'Dave Barton of the Riverboat Cardsharps,' he explained, hoping they would recognize the name at once.

'Riverboat?' said Rutherford. 'Which river?'

'Well, actually we're from Mablethorpe, but—'

'Where was this instrument lost?'

'Somewhere near that place with a clock tower.' Dave's voice was slurred, and he reached for a grubby tissue to wipe one eye. 'I'd been with the lads, playing in one of those pubs, but . . . oh, I dunno, we went on drinking, and we got separated, and . . . oh, I dunno.'

'You went out for a breath of fresh air?' said Rutherford sceptically.

'Yeah. Only then I thought it was time to walk back and go to bed.'

'Where are you staying?'

'It's . . . oh, I dunno. Somewhere. A Mrs Mc-something-or-other, only she's sort of . . . oh, I dunno, y'see.'

'Sergeant, will you fetch the exhibit?'

Elliot left the interview room. Dave tried to keep the two

detectives in focus, but was growing more and bewildered. 'Look, I was hoping someone might have found it, but I didn't know there was going to be all this fuss.'

'How did you come to lose it?'

Dave looked sheepish. 'Well, I must have had a skinful, y'see, and I sort of sat down in the road and put my head back against the wall. And I must have gone off for a few minutes. And when I woke up, my guitar was gone.'

Elliot returned with the long-necked guitar shrouded in a polythene bag.

'Would this be your property, sir?'

'That's it, yeah. Where did you . . .' Dave faltered, staring through the plastic. 'Who the hell did that? It's all dented.' He stooped closer. 'And there's a hell of a lot of shit on it.'

'Not shit,' said Rutherford. 'Blood.'

'Blood? What's been going on?'

'You're sure you went off to sleep, Mr Barton? You didn't just wander around in a stupor and pick a fight with an elderly gentleman?'

'What elderly gentleman?'

'An ageing square, one might say, who sneered at your instrument and your kind of music.'

'No. I'd have remembered that. Look, I want out of here. I want—'

'And *we* want to find a murderer.'

'A what? Look, I don't know about any murder.'

'Perhaps you wouldn't mind staying here until you've sobered up. The sergeant will arrange for you to get a cup of tea. And then you may remember more than you've told us so far, and be able to make a statement.'

'I'm not having that. Not staying here. I haven't done anything wrong.'

'Sergeant Elliot, perhaps you'll discuss with Mr Barton the difference between helping the police with their inquiries on a voluntary basis, and being formally charged. Inspector Gunn can sit in when you show some signs of getting somewhere.'

Answering Lesley's unspoken question, he added: 'And me? I'm off to the morgue. I want another look at the late Daniel Erskine. A long, cool look. And it should be cool enough in those surroundings.'

Lesley said: 'And while you're there, take another look at our lady friend. I tell you, there's a connection.'

A few minutes after Rutherford had left, she settled down at the phone and got on to West Yorkshire police to ask them to trace the whereabouts of the Parrotts, if any of them were still alive and still in business. In spite of Rutherford's doubts, she was going to follow her own hunch.

On Sunday morning the caravan arrived and was manoeuvred in close to the bottle bank near the supermarket delivery bay. It was not a very satisfactory location, but by hiving off one side of the supermarket car park they could at least guarantee easy access for police cars and other vehicles when necessary.

Once linked up, the first call that came through was from West Yorkshire police.

Old Mr Parrott was far from dead. He had proved only too happy to answer questions and had volunteered to come along to his local station and talk. 'Too damned ready to talk,' grumbled the sergeant from the other end. 'Can't shut him up. Just loves the thought of being involved in anything to do with the police: crime, dangerous driving, petty theft, you name it. We could have him along here an hour from now, if that would suit.'

The only snag was that by the time the phone interview was ready to proceed, Rutherford was back and eager to take charge in the mobile incident room. He refrained from saying that he had given DI Gunn no permission to follow up her interest in the Leeds connections of the Lowthers; but made it clear that from now on he would be in charge of the proceedings.

Mr Parrott had been told that he could have a solicitor or a friend sitting in with him if he wished.

'Nay, why should I need that? I've got nothing to hide.'

He was only too ready to talk. The difficulty might be in stopping him.

'Pity we've not yet got direct visual links as a matter of course,' said Lesley in an aside to Rutherford.

He grunted. Technology was already getting ahead of him. 'I like to have 'em right in front of me. In the flesh. So I can see when they twitch, and watch them beginning to sweat.'

She was growing more sympathetic towards Rutherford. He was only middle-aged, yet was already one of the older brigade, further along the unending road of his profession than she was, and not looking forward to the next few thousand footslogging miles.

'Now, officers, how can I help you? I've done my share of backing our local police, as they'll tell thee. Wouldn't be reet not to extend the hand of fellowship across the Border, would it?'

Mr Parrott relished the sound of his own voice. He would need to be controlled.

'We won't keep you long, Mr Parrott,' said Rutherford.

'Take as long as it takes. Unless our local coppers can't afford the phone bill, eh?'

'The main thing is, do you remember a man from Kilstane in Scotland working for you in the . . . eighties, wouldn't it be?'

'Aye, it would be that. Of course I remember Jamie Lowther. A good worker. And there was that lad of his, now – young Adam. Remember him well, too. Helped to get him started.'

'Mr Lowther came to you with good references?'

'He did that. Very good. From a Mr Enoch Buchanan, that would be?' His memory was sharp enough, and he was proud of the fact.

Lesley leaned forward. 'Even though he left Mr Buchanan in a bit of a hurry?'

'I know nowt about that. His references were good, and he kept his wife and young lad in good style. Not strapped for cash. I paid him well enough. Never been tight-fisted if I get the service I want. But he always seemed to have that bit extra. Used to send his missus on shopping trips to Grassington every now and then. Very smart. But never put on no airs. Knew his place.'

In spite of his reservations, Rutherford was beginning to get interested. 'You think he came to you with a generous pay-off from his previous employer – Mr Buchanan?'

'Tha' doesn't go round asking questions like that.'

But Lesley was silently asking questions. A dour skinflint like Buchanan, who had said that Lowther had left of his own free will, with precious little notice given, actually handing over some money to help him on his way? And if not, how had Lowther managed to be so comfortable?

'It's how the man works, that's all you ought to be concerned with,' Mr Parrott was continuing. 'You wouldn't catch me nosing into what he'd done before. Unless it was criminal, of course, and that wasn't the way of Jamie Lowther.'

When Lesley and Rutherford left the caravan, the churches and chapels were letting out their congregations. As the women went home to attend to the food, some of the men with an hour's grace drifted into the *Buccleuch Arms* and the *Pheasant*. There was no such drift on the part of the few dark-suited men emerging from the austere little shack of the Wee Frees. Enoch Buchanan was holding forth to the group as if the morning's lamentations had not been enough to satisfy his appetite.

When he caught sight of the two detectives he tried to draw himself up even higher and puff himself out even further.

'Well, now.' His voice boomed across the street. 'Did I not warn the guardians of the peace that there would be a divine vengeance upon the sinner if he returned to the scenes of his debauchery?'

Rutherford crossed the street, with Lesley a pace behind. 'I understand you have indeed said that, Mr Buchanan. Several times. May I take it that you were not personally instrumental in the vengeance which has fallen upon Mr Erskine?'

'Mind your tongue, man. I am the voice of truth, not its weapon.'

But the pleasure in that florid, self-righteous face struck Lesley as being that of a potential weapon of the Lord who would not flinch if given the opportunity he might have been craving for years.

'Mr Buchanan,' said Rutherford very quietly, 'we'd welcome your help. Rather than embarrass you in front of your friends, might I ask you to come to the incident room with us and offer what assistance you can? In confidence.'

There was a moment of hesitation during which Buchanan could have swung either way – loud indignation, or pompous acceptance of a role as consultant. He chose the second. As the three of them walked away, he made a point of turning his head from side to side, addressing each of them with a serious lowering of the head, putting on an act of gravitas, suggesting to any onlooker that he was lecturing the police rather than being interrogated by them. He strode towards the caravan and up the two steps with a swing of his burly shoulders. Offered one of the only two vacant chairs, he preferred to stand with one hand on the video bench, looking down on them like a preacher in a pulpit.

'Would you fancy a cup of tea, sir? Or coffee?'

'I'll not be touching either of those. But' – he accepted grudgingly – 'I wouldnae be saying no to a glass of water. I've been reading a lesson, and I favour pure water to ease my throat.'

'Thank you for coming, Mr Buchanan. Of course this is an informal interview, simply trying to establish the whereabouts of key people in Kilstane at relevant times.'

'The times being what?'

'Can you account for your movements between midnight last night and three o'clock this morning?'

'I was at home, where every Godfearing citizen ought to be at such a time.'

'Can you confirm that?'

'I live alone since the death of my guid wife. But my word is enough for any man or woman in this town.'

'You didn't go out at all last night?'

'I went at around nine o'clock to a prayer meeting of our community.'

157

'And after that?'

'I went straight home.'

'Mr Buchanan, I have a crucial matter to put to you. If you would like your solicitor to be present—'

'I'll nae be paying for one o' those to profit from sleekit quibbles.'

One of the two uniformed women constables who had been fastening a map of the town below the three narrow window lights at the top of the main wall of the van, with a supply of coloured magnetized pins in a holder at one side, placed a glass of water on the bench close to Buchanan.

'Do remember that you are free to leave at any time, or free to consult a solicitor.' Rutherford kept it very mild and correct. 'Right? Now, I must put it to you that, according to what I have learned, you felt a strong antagonism towards the deceased.'

'Aye, I'm no' ashamed to confirm that. All decent bodies despised him and his sinful ways. But ye'd be wise not to listen to malicious gossip in these pairts.'

While answering Rutherford, Buchanan was looking so accusingly at Lesley that she lost her cool. She said: 'As a matter of interest, Mr Buchanan, why did Jamie Lowther leave your employ so abruptly?'

'Men do when the mood takes them.'

'You felt let down by him walking out like that?'

'I've answered all this before. He went, and that was that.'

'You gave him a good reference. Did you give him anything else?'

'And what else would ye have in mind?'

'You didn't give him any money? A large sum in severance pay, for example? A very generous sum?'

'No mair than the wages due to him.'

'Apparently he was not too badly off when he reached Leeds. There wouldn't have been any money missing from your accounts? He did do the book-keeping, didn't he?'

'And what might all this have to do with that man who's gone to the devil at last? *There's* the man ye should have questioned while he was around to be questioned.'

'Mr Buchanan, you've had a long-standing grudge against Daniel Erskine. Isn't that so?'

'I've already questioned Mr Buchanan on that matter,' Rutherford pointed out.

'I thought he might have been having some second thoughts about the consequences of—'

'I never need second thoughts,' said Buchanan. 'Never doubted what was right and what was wrong. What should be praised, and what condemned in the eyes of the Lord. The man was an abomination. Many's the girl he defiled in this town. Aye, and the shameless married hussies. My daughter went off with him, but he threw her aside.'

'Would you be surprised to know that, while he was alive, Mr Erskine denied that?'

'Nay, it wouldnae surprise me. Lying, deceitful creature that he was. Threw her aside,' he ranted again, 'after he had brought her down to his own level. She was beyond shame by then. Found somebody else, but never came back here. Never saw her again. Or wanted to.'

'But when Erskine himself came back as an honoured guest for this festival of his music, you hadn't forgotten him. Or forgiven.'

Buchanan's florid face was turning a mottled pink and purple, accentuating the hairy mole on his right jaw. He took a long gulp from the glass of water and slammed it down on the bench. 'Would you be trying to accuse me of ... och, no, I'll no' be listening to any more o' this.' He pushed past her, and past Rutherford's raised right arm. 'You left it too late to ask questions of the one who had such a lot to answer for. Only now' – he fired a parting shot over his shoulder – 'he'll be answering to a higher authority. And the sentence will be to burn in hellfire for eternity. And that's all I'll be saying.'

'Nice Christian character,' Rutherford observed after the door of the caravan had stopped vibrating.

Lesley said: 'He's holding something back. A lot, I'd say. All

159

of it churned up in a stockpot of hatred, distorting everything. And believing that whatever he says or does, he's always in the right.'

'That woman's corpse. I've been wondering...' Abruptly Rutherford swung round and snapped at the constable who was about to remove Buchanan's glass. 'Whatever you do, don't wash that. Bag it and put it away safely in that cupboard.'

When he and Lesley were outside, she said: 'Why are you so keen on keeping that glass?'

'I'm arranging with the pathologist for DNA tests on both our stiffs. And I'll be finding a way of getting samples from Miss McLeod and Lowther. A bit tricky, unless they give their permission – or unless we charge one of them.'

'With what?'

'That's the problem.' Rutherford sought reassurance from the welcoming sign beside the door of the *Pheasant*. 'Fancy a dram, Les?'

'Oughtn't we to be—'

'A dram, and then you can have your lunch, and then we'll retrace a few steps up that wynd.'

A few heads turned and there was a spate of muttering as they crossed to a corner table where a curve of the wall made it almost an alcove. Probably the public thought they ought to be out non-stop with sniffer dogs tracking killers down throughout the streets and alleys of the town.

Rutherford's dram turned out to be a pint of eighty-shilling and a large Lagavulin. Lesley settled for a lager.

'With lime?'

'Decidedly not.'

'Glad to hear it.'

When they were settled and Rutherford had sighed approvingly over his first long gulp of the beer, Lesley leaned across the table, aware of several groups of men lowering their voices and carefully not watching her. She lowered her own voice.

'What are you really hoping for from DNA testing?'

'Can't we have five minutes without feeding our headaches?'

160

Rutherford downed another long swig, then peered at her across the top of his glass: 'All right, what did *you* hope for when you started on this case?'

'I'd hoped some shreds of clothing round that first corpse would have helped us identify her. But she was naked. And the bacteria didn't leave much of her. What we'd thought might be shreds of skin lifted from the bone turned out to be sacking fibres. The body must have been wrapped in a sack.'

'For ease of handling, you might say?'

'You might.'

'You think there's a possibility that this Adam Lowther's father murdered the woman and then cleared off quickly?'

'It was about the right time, but I can't see a motive. More likely story, Erskine wanting to get her out of the way. And that doesn't fit in with our calendar. Erskine had been long gone. And we don't have any evidence that he came back around the probable date of that woman's murder, do we?'

'No. And still no idea about her identity. But you still think Erskine was somehow involved – and that's why he came back for a sniff round? I'd have thought he'd have preferred to stay away.'

Lesley summoned up all her courage. 'I'm still convinced this is all wrapped up with the music business, somehow.'

Rutherford groaned. 'I thought paintings and pretty knick-knacks were your line, Les. Since when have you been doing the old tonic sol-fa?'

'Music is an art form, too.'

'Not the sort my kids blast out, it's not.'

'I'm sure there's something in all this – Erkine's music, even that disappearing Czech friend of his, Adam Lowther's passion for music, that McLeod woman. . . it all has to come together somehow. Like a perfect cadence at the end.'

'For crying out loud . . .'

'The McLeod woman will be at the concert this evening. It'll be a memorial concert now. Interesting to see how some folk will react.'

'Oh, I get you. You want to go out for the evening.'

'One of us ought to be there.'

'Soft lights and sweet music? Probably send you to sleep.'

'No. It's the discords I'll be listening for.'

'Christ. Give me a butch policewoman who spends her spare time on a touchline rather than this.' Rutherford drained his glass. 'Just for ruining the taste of that last pint, you can buy me another.' When she got back, he said: 'All right. Go to that concert, and keep your eyes open. They'll all be there, won't they – everybody who's anybody in this grand opera?'

'That's the point I was making.'

'OK. But don't enjoy yourself. I'm not giving you a briefing to enjoy yourself.'

That evening the streets ran with rippling streams of people flowing towards the Academy, chattering like water over rocks. Some of the men remained silent, dragged by their womenfolk to a function they had no wish to attend.

Inside the entrance lobby, Mrs Scott-Fraser presided at a table, flanked by two timid women who kept glancing at her for approval or instructions. All three of them waited for Lesley to produce a ticket. Before she had uttered three or four words to say that she hadn't had time to book, Mrs Scott-Fraser shook her head regally.

'No sales at the door, I'm afraid. A late sell-out of tickets. Once the news of this dreadful business got out.' She looked Lesley up and down with increasing disdain. 'Really, people's ghoulish tastes are deplorable.'

Lesley produced her warrant card.

'Ah. On duty, officer?'

'Well, not exactly. I—'

'We have covered all safety aspects, and we have a paramedic in attendance in case of over-excitement anywhere. What do we need the police for? My husband's on the Police Committee, you know, and we're not aware of our having made any request for a plain clothes officer to be present. Since you appear to be here

162

in a civilian capacity, I'm afraid I must repeat that there are no seats available. I'm so sorry.'

Which she clearly was not.

7

A fat man and two fluttering women with turquoise silk wraps over their shoulders pushed past Lesley. The man thrust a clutch of tickets under Mrs Scott-Fraser's nose and tried to walk on. Mrs Scott-Fraser said: 'Just a moment, please, just a moment, I didn't see them properly.' The man snorted and tried to press on, but his way into the hall was blocked by Sir Nicholas Torrance coming out.

Nick said: 'Any problems, Mrs Scott-Fraser?'

'Nothing that I can't handle, Sir Nicholas.'

Grumpily the man turned back to the table and jabbed his tickets under her nose. After separating them and inspecting each one suspiciously, Mrs Scott-Fraser at last gave him a lofty nod.

Nick took Lesley's arm and drew her back against the wall. 'Coming here to pick up any false notes in the orchestra?'

'I thought I'd relax for a couple of hours,' she hedged. 'But I might have known the place would be booked solid.'

'Only because of the extra bit of drama. Word soon got round. Sudden rush of bookings from ghouls rather than concertgoers.'

He was still holding her arm. She was in no hurry to make him let go. She let herself be steered through the doorway into the hall. There was a constant squeaking and scraping of chairs as new arrivals squinted down at the ends of rows and then pushed their way along past the knees of those already in place.

164

'Where are we going?' Lesley asked as she was led to the fourth row.

'We reserved some seats for music critics. One has just notified us that he can't make it. Probably calculates that he'll get more free booze in Wexford than he's likely to get here. So there's an empty seat.'

His hand released her as he pointed along the row. It was Lesley's turn to edge past feet and knees, mumbling apologies until she reached the empty chair.

The Westermarch Sinfonia was assembling on the platform, and the repeated A from the oboe was sounding.

Her neighbour was a man with improbably flaxen curls and pouting lips, who eyed her with unashamed curiosity that had nothing sexual in it. He introduced himself at once. 'Colin Baird from the *Scottish Musical Quarterly*. What paper are *you* from? Don't recollect seeing you before.'

She wondered whether to say something about being just one of the audience, but then said: 'I'm a police officer.'

'Gracious me. Waiting for the orchestra to murder the music?'

It showed signs of being the running gag of the evening.

'Not at this very moment,' she said. 'I've just come to listen.'

'For your own pleasure? Goodness. I *have* to listen, of course. But frankly, if you folk do catch up with Daniel Erskine's murderer, I think you ought to shove a bouquet into his hands rather than put the cuffs on him. No more of those dreadful Erskine outpourings, Never could stand the man.'

'But you've come, just the same?'

'That's what I'm *paid* for, my dear.'

The orchestra fell silent as Sir Nicholas Torrance came on stage. The audience muttered and whispered until a few louder voices said: 'Shh. Shh.'

Nick's voice was clear and decisive. Lesley could see that he had no intention of meandering on. 'There is very little we can say this evening. What should have been a great musical tribute to our outstanding local composer is now unfortunately a memorial concert. But that will not detract from the musical

165

achievement. Saddened as we may be by the tragic death of Daniel Erskine, we can best pay our respects by celebrating what he achieved while he was alive.'

'Celebrating?' muttered Baird. 'Well, that's one word for it.'

There was a spattering of respectful applause as Nick walked off the stage. The orchestra resumed its tuning-up.

Lesley had a quick glance round at the audience. At the last minute, Mrs Scott-Fraser was fussing at the end of a row, making it clear that she was on the committee and everything might fall apart if she did not continue checking on every last little detail before edging her way past a long selection of knees to her place in the centre.

Mairi McLeod had a place of honour at the front. Would she stand up to the strain without dissolving in tears? It might have been better not to expose her so prominently.

The first violin took his place. Louder applause greeted the conductor. He was a tall young Glaswegian already developing a shiny bald patch in the middle of straggly, sandy hair. There was just enough of that hair to be tossed as he swung his head towards the orchestra and raised his baton.

Within five minutes Colin Baird was scribbling notes in the margins of his programme.

The first piece was a tone poem, *The Eildon Tree*. It told the story of Thomas the Rhymer, presented with a faery harp and the gift of telling the truth though, like Cassandra, he was rarely believed. Throughout the three linked sections the 'truth' theme was played by the harp, but subjected to a repeated counterpoint of attacks distorting it and trying to pull it apart.

Lesley concentrated not so much on the music as on what it might tell her about the man behind it, Daniel Erskine. She made an effort not to be distracted by the fidgetings of a couple in the second row, nodding complacently at each other every few minutes in order to display their critical acuity.

As soon as the last bars faded and the applause began, Baird was ready to pontificate. 'The *scordatura* in the second movement was fairly predictable. Tuning up the strings just to make a heightened impression. Old tricks, wouldn't one say?' He pouted condescendingly, sure she wouldn't understand a word, but enjoying the resonance of his own opinions. 'I'll grant you, though, that the configurations in the last piece have a certain provocative charm. Those clusters of repeated notes, unaccentuated. In the context of the title, one would have thought the rhythm is meant to be that of a Scotch snap – semiquaver first, then dotted quaver. Of course one does also find it in some Eastern European music, but in Erskine's muddled way he seems to have combined it with the repeated curves of demotic speech patterns one finds in Janáček's music. Derived from Moravian dialect, of course.'

She was saved from having to contrive some response by the return of the conductor, the obligatory bow, and the clearing of throats as players and audience waited again for the rise of the baton.

In the next piece, *Fantasia on Three Hebridean Melodies*, Lesley found she didn't need to concentrate. The music itself was seizing her attention. One insistent theme began to beat in her head, shouldering its way through the harmonic complexities. She could see other members of the audience, but they were shapes from a dream, transparent against a startling reality. Colin Baird's lips twitched in self-satisfied derision. In the middle of her row, Mrs Scott-Fraser was jabbing an elbow into her husband's side as he threatened to fall asleep against the shoulder of his other neighbour. And all the time a repetitive pattern struggled to shape itself between Lesley's eyes and those irrelevant shapes.

At the end, just before the interval, Baird said: 'A pretty dismal theme for that final fugue, wouldn't you say?'

'I was trying to work it out. It did start on C, didn't it?'

'Aha! You evidently have a well-tuned ear.' It might have been a sneer or just a condescending encouragement.

'But then . . . well, another C, and . . . would it have been an A?'

'Nice work, officer. And then a B-flat, and . . . but really, how can anyone be expected to develop anything from a tone row that just wobbles to and fro around semitones? It was almost as dreary as that tune Frederick the Great handed over to poor old Bach. Only Bach was at least a genius.'

Chairs were scraping and clashing again as people drifted towards the bar in the cramped room next door which had once been the staff common room and then a stores office.

'You fancy a drink?' said Baird.

'Thank you, but no. I'll just catch a breath of fresh air.'

'Mustn't drink on duty, what?'

Lesley headed for the exit. At the table in the entrance, Mrs Scott-Fraser had buttonholed Nick Torrance and was holding forth. Nick greeted Lesley's appearance with relief, striding towards her on the pretence of something important having just occurred to him.

She said: 'I've heard something in that music. I can't quite believe it.'

'Some of it's pretty congested.'

'What I mean is, there's a message there. Or a joke. A sort of nudge-nudge, wink-wink. Could we go out in the yard for a moment?'

A few other concertgoers were strolling around the edge of the yard. One or two took the opportunity of staring over the fencing at the tidily heaped remains of what had been the school tower. From a far corner, Captain Scott-Fraser's voice rose in protest. 'Not a bloody tune anywhere. What sort of music d'ye call that?'

'Well?' said Nick. 'What's this sudden revelation?'

'There's this recurring theme.' She tried to produce a subdued whistle. When Nick bent towards her, she did it again, more boldly. 'What are those notes?'

'Assuming you have perfect pitch, which does seem to be the case, they would be . . .' He whistled faintly to himself. 'C . . . C . . . A . . . B . . . or is that B-flat? You wavered a bit over that semi-tone. And then it's E, or could be E-flat.' He closed his eyes. 'Actually, in the piece itself, I remember getting the theme in the major and then in the minor.'

168

Lesley said: 'So it spells CCABE. If there were an M . . . only is there a note represented by M?'

'Afraid not.'

The crowd was drawing back respectfully to allow Mairi McLeod to approach, in her black dress looking tragic and sumptuous at the same time.

'Later,' murmured Nick. 'We'll talk later.'

Back in the hall, Lesley found her head still buzzing with that theme. It made it impossible for her to detect anything else in the pseudo-classical suite which followed. At the end of the performance she hung about near the exit, jostled by people exchanging opinions which suggested they were glad the evening was over. Her pulse quickened as Nick elbowed his way towards her.

'M,' he said. 'The German for a minor key is *moll*. And the theme was continually working its back through various modulations into the minor.'

'The theme of McCabe,' she said.

The crush was again edging back to provide a channel through itself for Mairi McLeod to approach Nick as if seeking his protection.

'You'd better come and see me tomorrow morning,' he said quickly.

On the Monday morning, Lesley hurried to Black Knowe first thing, before Rutherford returned from a visit to the pathologist to discuss the ramifications of DNA testing.

A lot of noise was audible several hundred yards away from the tower. A group was rehearsing on the platform. Captain Scott-Fraser, also up and about early, came marching past Lesley towards the side of the stage. He groped under it and pulled a plug. A final squeal from one of the speakers left a few thin voices dying on the morning air.

'Damn racket. And damn bad taste, when a chap's just been killed. Even if he *is* no great loss.'

'What the hell d'you think you're up to, grandpa?'

169

'Can't sing without those boosters, hey? Go on, let's hear you. Pathetic little squeaks without 'em, hey?'

They showed every sign of assaulting him until Lesley quickened her pace and confronted them.

'Well, now, and where do you fit into this, gorgeous?'

She showed her warrant card.

'God, that's terrifying. We're awestruck. Isn't our awe mightily struck, fellers? You going to arrest us?'

'If you make it necessary, yes.'

The young man stared at her, then grinned quite agreeably, 'Whatever you say, officer.' He jerked a thumb at Scott-Fraser. 'Count yourself lucky. And clear off.'

'I'm not in the habit of being spoken to by—'

'Captain Scott-Fraser,' said Lesley, 'I think it would save an unpleasant incident if you were to leave.'

He went off, muttering about collapse of discipline, police siding with vandals, and raising the matter with the Police Committee. 'A dose of conscription would do 'em all a world of good . . . a world of good . . .'

Lesley went into the tower.

Nick was at the keyboard, and after standing up to greet her was eager to get back to it.

'He's worked wonders with that motto theme.' He picked out the notes that had been burning in her brain. 'Now listen to this.' Again his fingers stabbed and ran.

'Upside down?' she hazarded.

'A mirror inversion, yes. And then' – he bent over the keyboard – 'retrograde. And then he alters the pace, spreads it out – augmentation.'

He sat back, beaming at her.

'Somebody's been playing very complicated games,' she said. 'But where do they lead?'

'I've been doing a bit of telephoning before you got here. Would you like to come to London with me?'

'Whatever for?'

'My parents were first-rate musicians. Even in the bad old

170

Communist days they were welcome behind the Iron Curtain, provided they just played and didn't go around fomenting revolution.'

'What's that got to do with anything?'

'Jan Strepka,' said Nick. 'Ian McCabe to you. Decided to go back to Czechoslovakia, and that was the last anyone heard of him. Or was it? The Cultural Attaché at the Czech Embassy was a minor functionary under the old regime. Handled my parents' concert bookings and accommodation – under strict supervision. But he was a nice bloke. Kept his head down, and now he's been promoted. He's digging out some files for me by tomorrow. I think you ought to be there.'

'I don't see the DCI getting very enthusiastic over that.'

She was right. Rutherford said: 'Not again! Les, you're getting punch-drunk on this music. It's affecting your brain.'

'Yes, it is. But not the way you mean.'

'What the hell do you expect to find in London?'

'I'm not sure. But there's something waiting there. Erskine and the vanishing Czech, and these hidden messages in Erskine's compositions. Was there a corresponding code at the other end? And somehow there has to be a link with all the grudges that folk around here hold – grudges that last the way Border blood feuds used to last.'

'You're really hooked on this, aren't you?'

'You used to boast to me about your hunches. Why shouldn't I have a few hunches every now and then?'

'There are times when your memory's too damn sharp.' His right eyebrow and right shoulder twitched in unison. 'Oh, all right. Elliot and I have a lot of calls to deal with. A lot of folk have started ringing in. We can weed out the sensation seekers from the useful witnesses, if any. And then I want another session with Forensics. So clear off in the morning.'

'You won't regret it.'

'Huh. But it's strictly off the record. We don't want the Met to complain about us treading on their sensitive toecaps. So this will count as your statutory day off. If the worst comes to the worst, I'll report that you've been under stress and needed some time off.'

'I'm not under stress. I—'

'Don't bloody argue, Les. I'm looking the other way. Until' – he grinned his typical greedy Rutherford grin – 'you come up with the goods. And then I'll say we worked it out between us and we share the credit, right?'

8

Nora Lowther took a final glance at her face in the oval glass at the foot of the stairs, and made a gentle curve of her right index finger to flick a strand of eyelash upwards. She had to open the door into the pend before Adam could step down the last two stairs to stand beside her.

He kissed her a dry kiss.

'You do understand?' he said.

'Of course I do.'

'I hope it all goes well.'

She managed a thin smile. 'You haven't pulled the shop blinds down just so that Deirdre can sneak in for the afternoon?'

'Deirdre? Oh, not again. Anyway, she'll be at your recital to hear you and her husband, won't she?'

'She says she's not interested in that sort of thing. We do know the sort of thing she *is* interested in, don't we? And anyway, *you're* not coming to hear your wife sing, either.'

'But that . . . well, you know it's different. You do realize, after what's happened, I'm just not in the mood for . . . You do understand?' he said again.

'Yes, I do. It's all right, I understand all right.'

He stood in the doorway until she had reached the street, in case she turned round to wave. She did not turn. In the distance, the open back door of the *Buccleuch Arms* gushed a brassy blast of folksy blues from what advertised itself in Adam's window as The Unbeatable Band from the Debatable Land. He shut the sound out and went through the inner door into his shop.

173

It was in deep twilight. The heavy blinds which he rarely used, except for the occasional summer afternoon when the sun on his window display was so intense that he had to lower them halfway, were now fully down. The face of Daniel Erskine frowning out of a poster was no more than a dark ghost – really a ghost, now.

There might be a profitable trade if he kept the place open today and for the rest of the week, as planned. After last night's memorial concert, there might well be a number of people wanting to buy discs of Erskine's music, or the booklet produced by Lowther and Galbraith, or even a cassette of the Unbeatable Band. But he hadn't the heart to open for business and the breathless chatter that would go with it. Or the heart to go and listen to the recital of trivial ballads by his wife, to the accompaniment of Duncan Maxwell's thumping. Not after Erskine.

He tidied a few things that didn't need tidying, knocked his shin against a stack of cassettes, shifted them to one side, and shuffled round the edge of the screen to lift the lid of the piano, only to let it fall again.

Somebody tried the shop door. Then rattled the knob impatiently. 'Adam, I've got to talk to you.'

He slid down on to the piano stool and kept very still.

'Adam, I know you're in there. I know how you must feel. Do let me in.'

Deirdre rattled the door again, and he could see enough of her shadow through the blind to see that she was trying to peer round the edge of it. He didn't make a move; and at last she swore and went away.

Giving her a good five minutes in case she was still hanging about, waiting for a move, he got up at last and wondered whether to go and make himself a cup of coffee. There was nothing useful he could do in the shop, yet there was even less upstairs. He might just as well have gone to listen to Nora singing. But that was unthinkable.

In his head he went over and over an eight-bar phrase from Erskine's ballad, *Canobie Dick*. It clung to him with all the tenacity of a popular song, refusing to be dislodged.

Another rattle at the shop door. He froze.

'Adam? Adam Lowther?'

It was the husky voice of Mairi McLeod.

He called: 'Sorry, I'm not opening today.'

'I've brought you something. A very special souvenir. Please let me in.'

He opened the door.

She was dressed in a black sheath of a dress. Her arms and legs were bare, and there were dark crimson sandals on her feet. When he closed the door behind her, she walked into an even darker darkness, but she was no shadow: he was conscious of her whole being, the heat she was giving out even when she stood quite still.

'Could we have some light on the scene?'

He didn't fancy putting all the shop lights on. He went back round the screen to the piano, and switched on the tall anglepoise tilted beside it.

She held out a stiff card folder. 'I want you to have this. Daniel would be glad for me to give it you. He was so glad to have met you. And his music does mean so much to you, doesn't it?'

Adam opened the folder. Inside were sheets of music. An original manuscript score. He recognized immediately the solo line and harmonies of *The Mormaer's Strathspey and Reel for Fiddle and Piano*. It had always appealed to him that Erskine should have specified 'fiddle' rather than 'violin'.

He found it difficult to speak. 'This is your transcription, isn't it?'

'Yes.'

'It's . . .' His eyes wandered down the page, marvelling at the time it must have taken her to work out Erskine's intentions, play them over to him, revise them, and finally get it all down on the staves. 'You and Sir Nicholas are performing this on Friday evening, right?'

'I don't know. Maybe that's one recital that'll have to be cancelled.'

'You don't feel up to it?'

'Not without more incentive. Nick can be pretty good, but he's got so many things on his plate right now. And we ought to be rehearsing right now, but he's gone off somewhere for the day. And Daniel's music isn't really in his blood. I was wondering if you . . . do you think you could play it?'

He knew it off by heart. He opened the piano, set the handwritten score in place, and adjusted the anglepoise lamp.

Mairi prowled through the twilight of the shop and opened the glass cabinet with two violins, bows and sets of strings in it. Tuning had to be perfunctory. She was all at once in a hurry. She came and stood behind Adam, and just the sensation of her being there was like an embrace.

'Right,' she said. 'Let's see what you're made of.'

He had tried playing the piano part before, from one of the printed copies he kept for sale. So far he had sold only one copy in the past three years, in spite of pointing out its beauties to customers.

They started raggedly, and he tried to mumble an apology for a spate of wrong notes; but Mairi McLeod was laughing, and scraping through an out-of-tune passage as if it were the greatest joke in the world. She was adapting to the strings' faults in the way a gipsy fiddler adapts, plucking the sagging flat note up into something that became more than the original written notation could ever have hoped to be. Halfway down the first page they were not separate performers but a duo. The music came alive under their fingers. The rhythm drove them both. With the woman setting the tempo and urging them on, Adam realized for the first time that the so-called reel had more the elements of a polka. Then the steady, middle tempo swing of it began to quicken. Mairi's attack on the strings became more incisive and insistent. She said nothing, but her bowing urged them into a new fury, and he could hear her breathing wildly.

When they finished, he stared at the last few bars without any longer seeing them. Getting up from the piano stool would mean their performance was at an end. He didn't want to repeat that piece – but wanted something to continue it, carry it along into another wild duet.

Mairi spoke in little more than a whisper. 'You really do feel it, don't you? It's in your blood.'

He forced himself to stand up and turn round.

'You,' he said. 'You and Erskine. In that music, the two of you—'

'Ah, the two of us.' She ran her fingers through her tangled hair. 'Me and Daniel. Oh, you're on the right track. But still only halfway along it.' She carefully put the violin aside. 'The way you played that piece, you knew what it was all about. The pulse of it – you *knew*. You recognized me, didn't you?'

'He certainly captured you in it, yes.'

'Nobody ever captured me. I'm the one who does the capturing.'

She put her arms round his neck. Her breath was as warm and fierce as her music had been. Her lips and tongue were greedy, but not for talking.

When she stepped back, it was only to stoop and lift the hem of her dress. She had got it only just above her hips when Adam was helping her, and she was laughing and making a grab at his shirt buttons.

Naked, they impatiently turned the piano stool towards the wall, and Mairi first straddled it, taunting him, fending him off, until at last he had his hands on her shoulders and forced her round, splayed across the prickly tapestry of the stool. The pulse of the music was still beating through his body – in the blood, as she had said. And as he pounded the rhythm of it into her, her convulsions answered with jolting spasms in the same rhythm. At her writhing climax, his left arm thrashed wildly and his elbow struck a discordant cluster of notes from the keyboard, and Mairi shrieked in harsh ecstasy.

When it was over they were silent apart from their breathing – Adam's gasping, Mairi's slow and satisfied, almost a purr.

She pulled her dress back on. 'I needed that. God, how I needed it.' As her head emerged through the dress, she ran her

177

tongue along her lower lip. 'We really must have another rehearsal tomorrow afternoon, before the recital.'

'A rehearsal?' He was laughing uncontrollably. 'If that was a rehearsal . . .'

'There's another longer piece in the programme. We'll have to tackle it before we go on stage. Too much to hope that you already know *Variations in a Dorian Mode*?'

'I've gone through them over and over again. I've got the music in that top drawer over there. I'll spend the rest of the day going through it.'

'Another session tomorrow morning, then?'

For the first time he thought of Nora, and said awkwardly: 'Here?'

'Nick'll probably be back sometime tomorrow. He can play the chaperon, I'm afraid. But he'll be relieved not to have to accompany me. He was never really at ease with those pieces.'

Adam showed her out through the side door. As she was about to step out into the pend, she said: 'You're nearly as good as your father.'

Before he could ask her what on earth she meant, she was gone.

And as she vanished from the daylit arch at the end of the passage, he saw a woman on the far side of the street. She stared a moment, then she too had moved away.

He felt an uneasy certainty that it had been Deirdre Maxwell.

9

The Cultural Attaché turned over the top sheets from a bulging folder on the desk before him. 'Strepka, yes. We do indeed have records of his movements. My predecessors kept a very substantial dossier on Jan Strepka.' He managed something between a rueful smile and an apology. 'We have not yet got round to examining all the documents we inherited from the old régime, and deciding which to discard.'

Dr Ladislav Hykisch had put on weight since Nick had last met him while travelling with his parents, and had acquired the status of Dr instead of plain Mr. There was a glint of gold in one of his teeth, and a gold pen lay in a Bohemian cut glass tray. The major change was in his attitude. In the past he had been very reserved, literally keeping his head down, but now he was enjoying the privileged comforts of his Embassy office, and looked one straight in the eye. Also he no longer spoke broken English, as if then it had been politic to deny any suspicious fluency, but now one could be openly at ease with the language.

Nick said: 'What exactly happened to McCabe – Strepka, that is – when he returned to Czechoslovakia?'

'The same thing that unfortunately happened to many people connected with wartime allies. Airmen who had risked their lives in the RAF battling against the Nazis were regarded by my superiors as outcasts – contaminated by their time in the West. Their children also. Many were sent to work in the mines in

Silesia. No academic or administrative post was open to them. Excuses were found to send many to prison.'

'Strepka went to prison?'

'For two years, yes. Because he had been caught smuggling records of decadent Western music into the country. Even worse, he tried to compose music and have it performed in public. It was music not to the taste of the authorities. Far too adventurous. Contaminated by the West,' Hykisch repeated.

'So he stopped composing?'

'No. One might say that he learned to change his tune.'

'Churning out proletarian anthems?' said Lesley.

'Not even that. In any case that would have been regarded with suspicion. One had to be a devoted party member to be trusted with commissions of that kind. No, he ingratiated himself by writing uncontroversial musical comedies and soundtracks for films of no consequence. A few less humorous, but still based on subjects supposedly from Slav history. Moscow insisted that we were all one great big Slav family. Strepka made a tolerable living by dressing up folklorist legends in tinkling little melodies, with much bucolic humour and sturdy peasants singing of life on the land. He was skilful. He could capture the essence of a genuine old melody, transform it, make it acceptable. Oh, and he had a great popular success with a banal theatre piece set in the Little Quarter of Prague.'

'Yet all the time,' said Nick, 'if he'd had any integrity whatsoever, he must have longed to write music worthy of him. Music for its own sake. But you don't think he ever composed any serious music again?'

'Not that we know of. Or knew of officially.'

'Just a minute, sir,' said Lesley. 'Was there any chance of him smuggling his *real* music out and having it played abroad?'

Hykisch's smile became almost demure. 'That thought has occurred to me from time to time.'

'And?'

'It could not have been done openly. That would have been

180

too risky. Our people in Prague could have been very severe about that.'

'But performed,' Lesley persisted, 'in some guise or other. Under another composer's name?'

Nick could not take his eyes off her tilted half-profile and the creamy beauty of her neck. The tight sweep of hair over her ear was entrancing. For the last few minutes she had been still and thoughtful, but now her lips had parted and she was a sleek animal poised for the kill.

'He never sneaked back to Britain every now and then?'

'There is no record of it. And' – Hykisch was grimly sardonic – 'there would certainly have been a record.'

'So he and Erskine never met again.'

'Not in England, no. Or Scotland.'

'Just a minute. Are you saying—'

'Sir Nicholas will remember that it was possible for Westerners to visit our country under certain conditions. His father and mother, for example, were allowed to attend musical events – the Prague Spring festival, the Hodonin folk song and dance festivals, and so on. More people were allowed in,' he added dryly, 'than were allowed out.'

'And Erskine visited?'

Hykisch turned over another sheet of paper. From where he sat, Nick could see the purple blotches of official stamps at the top of each page.

'More than once. When he was still active, he conducted one of his compositions at the Dvořák Hall.'

'Not too adventurous for the authorities?'

'An innocuous piece, as I recall.'

Lesley was unstoppable. 'And did Mairi McLeod ever accompany him?'

'It would have been before that business about his hands,' said Nick. 'The two of them couldn't have met by then.'

Hykisch detached a sheet of notes from the clip inside the folder. 'We know, of course, about Erskine's misfortune. But he did visit a number of times after that. And we have records of

181

visa applications from a young Miss Mairi McLeod. She appears to have been a violinist. What I believe is called folk pop. Performing at folk festivals. Our cultural chaperons were very keen on folklorist occasions.'

Lesley said: 'I didn't know that she—'

'That's her, all right,' said Nick. 'That's how she started. She must have been very young then. That's how I met her, when I was supervising recordings. Once at Glastonbury, and then . . .' He tried to dismiss the sudden surge of memories. 'Before I became . . . well . . .'

'Sir Nicholas Torrance.'

'Exactly. Quite a while before.'

He wished he could avoid Lesley's questioning appraisal. But her real prey was elsewhere. She swung back to her inquisition.

'But once the Communists had been overthrown, and the borders were open, why didn't he revisit Scotland openly?'

'Because he was dead.'

'He died . . . over there?'

'He died,' said Hykisch, 'trying to get out.'

'You mean he made a run for it?'

'He was working on a musical film in the vineyards of Valtice. Right on the Austrian border. He managed to cut through the first fence and hoped to make a dash for it. But it is not so easy.'

'The first fence? How many. . . ?'

'In your spy films, you are always shown the hero somehow turning off the electricity, cutting his way through the wire, or flying over it on a motorcycle, or something absurd. But beyond the first fence was always a narrow minefield. And then another electrified fence. And even beyond that, the open fields were not . . . well, not open. A half kilometre was still Czech territory, always under surveillance from the watchtowers. Very deceptive.'

'How far did he get?'

'Only into the minefield.'

'And got blown up?'

'No. The guards in the watchtowers were waiting. He was seen, and shot.'

'When was this?'

'In May 1989.'

'If only he'd waited another six months or so, he could have walked out without any hassle?'

'Exactly. The Velvet Revolution opened us up to the world once more.'

'When you said the guards were waiting for him . . . had somebody tipped them off?'

Hykisch lowered his head and shuffled a few more papers. 'At the time I was in no official position to know the details of these things. But it was rumoured, yes. Always there were rumours in those days. It was best not to ask questions.' He decided to change the subject by picking up a booklet from the side of his desk. Nick recognized it as a programme for the Kilstane Gathering. 'After you telephoned, Sir Nicholas, I sent out for this from the concert booking office beside Leicester Square. I see that you are, as I believe you say in this country, following in your father's footsteps. You and Miss McLeod are performing this . . . ah . . . *Mormaer's Strathspey and Reel* and also—'

'Change of programme, I think. Or change of a performer, anyway. For a time I thought Miss McLeod would be too upset to play, but she has decided to go ahead. And she is approaching a better partner on the piano. A very talented musician, steeped in Erskine's music.'

'I have heard of a reel. But a strathspey, that is new to me.'

'It's a Scottish dance, slower than the reel, mainly in a sort of lilting rhythm of dotted quavers and semiquavers.'

Hykisch nodded politely but was clearly none the wiser.

'Is there anything else you wish to ask?'

'Thank you, but I think you've answered one of our main questions.'

'I shall be interested in any conclusions you draw.'

Did he know something, or was beginning to guess something? His expression was that of a man who had still not quite shaken off the deadpan stolidity of his predecessors.

On the way out, he led them across a reception hall with crystal chandeliers, tall windows with polished shutters drawn back, and a grand piano looking lonely in the middle of the floor. As they passed, Nick couldn't help fingering a few bars from memory.

Hyndisch stopped in his tracks. 'What was that?'

'The main theme of an Erskine piece. The *Mormaer's Strathspey*. Which I was originally programmed to perform with Miss McLeod, as you remarked.'

'How strange. How very strange.'

'The rhythm is odd, yes. Not a true strathspey.'

'No, what I meant was that the tune is familiar. Or almost familiar. And the rhythm also. They remind one of an old traditional air, *The Court Dance of Prince Mohimir*.'

'Prince who?'

'Mohimir was a powerful Celtic prince of Moravia in the eighth century. A great legendary figure.'

'Mohimir?' said Lesley. 'And the Mormaer. A prince . . . and mormaer, a high steward.'

'It is a remarkable coincidence.'

Lesley said: 'As I was saying to DCI Rutherford, somebody's been playing games with us.'

'And with audiences,' said Nick.

He was about to take this further, but Lesley shot him a warning glance. They made their formal farewells, and walked up Kensington Palace Gardens in silence for a few minutes. As they emerged on to Kensington High Street, Nick took her arm. She tensed, gave him a quick glance; but then smiled into the turmoil of traffic.

He said: 'Fancy a disgusting meal in the plane on the way back?'

'I'm a bit churned up. I've got other things to digest.'

'I'll arrange a large malt for you, for starters. I'm driving at the other end.'

It was not until ten minutes after takeoff that she turned towards him, resting her cheek against the seat, and said: 'Well?

Are you thinking what I'm thinking?'

'Probably. Erskine and Strepka. Erskine could have brought Strepka's serious compositions out with him. According to my father and mother, outgoing visitors' luggage was hardly ever examined at Ruzyne. Not if you were a visitor of any standing. And even if they did give Erskine a going-over, what was so suspicious about him carrying a batch of music with him?'

'He'd been performing, he'd brought his own music in with him and he was taking it home again.'

'Exactly. And later, travelling with Mairi as his amanuensis, companion, call it what you like . . .' The quizzical smile provoked by his stumbling phrase threw him for a moment, but at that same moment the plane banked and made a tight turn, and by the time it levelled out he went on: 'Either or both of them could have carried things like that.'

'McCabe . . . Strepka . . . he would rather have his music performed under another man's name, so long as it was performed – and *heard*.'

'But what about Erskine? Even if Strepka was that idealistic and that self-effacing, were he and his old schoolmate so close that Erskine didn't mind having Strepka's music mixed in with his own?'

As the stewardess came along with drinks and the promise of food, Lesley stared out of the window as if conjuring up themes and theories out of the pallid clouds, while Nick thought of Mairi McLeod and found himself resenting her as some kind of traitor, a mocking cheat who had slipped through his grasp.

With the glass of Glenmorangie in her hand, Lesley returned from contemplating the heavens. 'Suppose . . . just suppose . . . that Erskine never *did* write any truly substantial music of his own. The early stuff was pretty trivial. There never was any such thing as a real Erskine style.'

'According to Adam Lowther, there were in fact three different styles. Three successive periods. The first very simple, then a second much richer, and then a final quite different phase.'

'Simple stuff, of no great merit? That's what I mean. And then all at once he blossoms and begins to acquire a fine critical reputation. Only it's Strepka's work which is making Erskine's reputation for him.'

'But when Strepka is killed. . . ?'

Lesley's sudden hoarseness might have been due to the bite of the Glenmorangie at the back of her throat. 'The supply has dried up. Yet Erskine's compositions still keep appearing. And his reputation grows.'

'Only now the works are in yet another different style. Perhaps he has found his own voice, with the help of Mairi McLeod?'

'His own voice?' Lesley drained her drink as the food trays were handed out. Or another useful voice?'

'I don't get you.'

They ate for a while in silence. Nick broke it with: 'But who killed Erskine? And why?'

'And how does that tie in with our first corpse, in the Academy tower? Or are we just unlucky, with two unconnected murders on our hands?'

'The only possible connection, and it's a pretty tenuous one, is that once it was publicized that the remains had been identified as those of a woman, Erskine changed his mind and came down to Kilstane. Why?'

'I do think,' said Lesley, 'that we must turn our official attention to Miss McLeod.'

'You can't seriously think—'

'Wasn't there a lot of talk about Erskine revealing some awkward truths? He was going to speak out about something. All in his own good time – he said something like that to me.'

'I do remember that. And I believe he gave quite a drunken rant to the Schiltron Circle on the same subject. Threatening all sorts of unspecified revelations.'

'Maybe about his collaborations? Guilt over Strepka? Or the part played by Miss McLeod? She might not have been in favour of that.'

'Why on earth would she want to kill him? He was her livelihood.'

'If he was about to blow the gaff on her doing all the actual work—'

'But wouldn't she be more likely to *want* him to do that at last? She would always have longed to be taken seriously as a composer in her own right, but for years she had been using him ... or he had been using her. It would be wonderful to be accepted in her own right.'

Thinking of that brief session in the house at Altnalarach, Nick remembered Mairi talking about the second strain which struck away from the main melody of a folk song.

A second strain – and now, somehow, a third?

Lesley was saying: 'And do we really think there's a chance that it was Strepka's old friend – and possible collaborator – who betrayed Strepka, making sure he never got out and would never receive his due as a composer?'

It was almost dark when they touched down at Edinburgh. In the car, heading south towards the Borders, they found only the same questions to talk about, and the same non-answers to offer. After a while they relapsed into silence. Nick glanced from time to time at that profile.

Even in silence, the subject was still the same. Music. Mairi McLeod had been wild, unpredictable music. Lesley was Mozart. Such an immaculate surface, but pulsating with deep, lasting passion underneath.

When they stopped outside her door in Kilstane, he said: 'I think I'd better have a quiet word with Mairi.'

'Please don't. We don't want her alerted. I certainly intend to see her myself. And it may not be so quiet.'

He got out and walked round to hold the passenger door open for her. As they brushed close together, with one hand still on the door he put his other arm round her and kissed her. For a moment her lips remained tightly, obstinately shut. Then they softened, and opened. Until her weight pushed the door half shut, and she stepped back.

Nick said: 'Lesley, this is ridiculous. I—'

'Yes,' she said breathlessly. 'And we mustn't *let* it get ridiculous.'

10

He had been half expecting an outburst and was braced ready for it. But Nora had never been one to explode in anger. She simply withdrew into herself with a weary shrug. This morning she sat at the kitchen table with her head down as she folded and refolded half a dozen napkins.

'No.' Her voice was barely audible. 'No, I don't believe it. You don't have to lie to me.'

'But it's true. Sir Nicholas is too busy trying to keep an eye on the whole Gathering. And he missed a crucial rehearsal because he was off somewhere else. He doesn't *know* the music the way I know it.'

'There's more to it than that.'

'Please don't spoil things, Nora. This music means a lot to me.'

'Don't I just know it.'

'Why don't you come along and hear us play?'

'You didn't come when Duncan and I were playing. Why should you expect me to come to yours?' It was not bitter: just dull and resigned.

He had wanted to slip into the conversation as casually as possible that Mairi had invited him, later, to drive up with her to Sutherland so they could go through Erskine's scores and papers together. There were things on which she particularly wanted his opinion. It would be a wonderful privilege. But every word he said about it here and now would be misinterpreted.

189

No, it wouldn't. That was the trouble. It would be interpreted all too accurately. His excitement at the thought of being away from here, being deep into Erskine's home and music and deep into Mairi's tempestuous body would have shone too blatantly through every word he uttered.

He looked at his watch. 'Must be off. There are some tricky passages we have to get right.'

'I'm sure you'll work wonderfully together.'

Undoubtedly it was Deirdre Maxwell he had seen on the other side of the street. And Deirdre wasn't one to keep her mouth shut.

Deirdre Maxwell said: 'You know who's been having it off with Erskine's tart ever since they got here?'

Although the shallow slit windows just below the ceiling of the caravan were open, the sun striking the roof made the interior hot and sticky. Lesley and Rutherford were in shirtsleeves, but tried to maintain a stiff upright appearance. Deirdre was wearing a flimsy dress of orange and yellow diagonal stripes which looked cool and summery, but there was a smear of sweat along her upper lip.

'I hate doing this,' she went on, 'but I felt it was my duty to come and offer what help I could to the police.'

There was an outbreak of crashing and splintering as somebody unloaded empty bottles into the nearby bottle bank.

'Very public-spirited of you,' said Rutherford without a muscle in his face twitching.

'They had it off in the shop, with the blinds drawn. While his sad little wife and my husband were doing their bit for the festival by playing duets up the hill. And this morning he's off round to the laird's place. Right under his nose. I saw them go in.'

'They're rehearsing for this evening's recital,' said Lesley. 'And Sir Nicholas is at home.'

'Rehearsing? Oh, yes, I'll bet. Right under his nose,' said Deirdre again. 'Why don't you ask Adam Lowther where he was the night that Erskine got murdered? Ask him why the two of

190

them wanted the poor old sod out of the way.'

'Have you any concrete evidence to support that accusation?'

'Evidence? Isn't that your job, collecting it? All I'm telling you is what's behind it.'

As she left, Rutherford watched the sway of her bottom through the skimpy material. 'I seem to sense a hint of sexual jealousy there.'

'Even so, that doesn't stop it being true. Maybe. Just maybe.'

'We'll have to pick our way cautiously round that one. Is there any way it ties in with what you picked up on your London jaunt?'

Lesley summed up the main points of the visit. Rutherford let out a shuddering sigh when she embarked on musical theory, but perked up when she detailed the probable meetings of Erskine, Strepka, and Mairi McLeod.

'Two of them dead, and one still with us. And looks as if she could have been exploiting both of them.'

'Or helping both of them.'

'Either way, it was for her own ends. Look, you said there was a hint that Erskine betrayed his old mate because he didn't want him showing up and claiming to be the real composer of all that stuff. Couldn't it have been the McLeod woman who did the grassing? And later, when it came to Erskine—'

'You can't suspect her of killing Erskine – her bread and butter?'

'Perhaps all those threats of his about letting the whole town know something or other were a signal he was going to let it all out. Everything about their relationship, and the phoniness of his own music. If your hunch on that is right.'

'Guilty feelings? Mm.'

'He'd maybe had enough of the whole bloody charade. And she killed him because she didn't want the world to know the truth about the music not being his. It had been nagging at him, until he was ready to confess. We've come across that sort before, haven't we?'

'But you'd think she'd be glad. Especially if she was doing

191

most of the composing herself. Wouldn't she want to be recognized in her own right?'

'Bloody musicians. Weird gowks. Why can't they have their fights and killings out in the open, like ordinary villains?'

'Or could she have been in love with Strepka during their meetings behind the Iron Curtain? And later she discovered that Erskine had been the one – he told her, or boasted about it when he was drunk – that he'd been the one responsible for shopping his old mate. And she killed him in a rage.'

'They did leave the house together that evening, didn't they? And that story of hers about thinking he was going off to see Lowther could have been just another bit of double talk. Maybe Erskine did actually *mean* to go to Lowther's place.'

'He seemed to be getting quite fond of him.'

'But the McLeod woman made sure he didn't get there.' Rutherford mopped his brow. A stain was appearing on the shirt under his right armpit. 'You reckon she'd be strong enough to swipe him hard enough with that guitar?'

'I'd imagine she has a good strong bowing arm.'

'We do need to get some more out of that woman. And some more from Lowther.'

'I've got an idea. But you won't like it.'

'Try me, Les.'

'The two of them will be performing this evening.'

He leered. 'Performing?'

'They'll be giving the recital in Black Knowe that Deirdre Maxwell was on about. I've been offered a ticket.'

'I'll bet you have.'

'I could watch them during the recital. The two of them, together.' She found it impossible to believe even fleetingly in the idea of Adam Lowther, with his love of the old man's music, being in any way involved with the murder or with the woman who might be a suspect. But she said: 'Body language, that sort of thing.'

'While they're fiddling and pounding away? A different sort of language, I'd think. Difficult to interpret.'

'In between movements. And afterwards.'

'Movements?' Rutherford allowed himself a coarse snigger. 'Body movements? All right, Les, let your imagination run riot.'

'It's on, then?'

'As long as you don't claim overtime for enjoying yourself.'

'I might be able to wangle a seat for you as well, if you like.'

He grimaced. 'Thanks a million. I'm prepared to leave pleasures like that to you. In the meantime, can we consider the possibility of other murderers?'

'Such as?'

'Mr Enoch Buchanan, for one. He seems to have gone around uttering some pretty hefty threats. And he might well have been the one to stir up that crowd you told me about on Erskine's heels.'

'You want me to go and see him?'

'I think that's one pleasure I can cope with personally. I'll take young Elliot along. But you and Constable Blair here could spend a few hours on the phone trying to find out where that numpty who smashed Erskine's hands went when he got out of chokey. There must have been a probationary follow-up, some employment centre somewhere, a rehabilitation course or something. And anything about his wife.'

Lesley and the young woman at the switchboard spent a fruitless afternoon chasing a man who, so far as anyone could recall, had never returned to Kilstane after serving his sentence. Not that any of those who remembered him thought any the worse of him for his crippling attack on Daniel Erskine. He would have faced no public shame if he had come home. But neither he nor his wife had ever been seen in the neighbourhood again.

The early evening was mercifully cooler than the day. Lesley had brought no great choice of clothes with her, but picked out a grey skirt and pale blue blouse with a high collar, and a darker blue jacket with silver braid woven into the lapels. It was just mild enough for her to walk at a leisurely pace through the town, accompanied by the sounds of some pseudo-Caribbean jangle from an open window, Even the *Pheasant*, as she passed it, had capitulated to the presence of a fairly restrained jazz trio. Leaning against the door of the public bar was Zak Runcorn, wearing a baseball cap backwards and letting his left arm droop nonchalantly to display the tattoo of an Aztec head.

As she crossed the haugh towards Black Knowe, the sun was far from setting, but had sunk just far enough behind the clump of Scots pine along the crest of the crag to make skeletal patterns against the flush of the sky. The platform for tomorrow's final Folk Revel threw a long shadow up the slope.

Nick was greeting arrivals at the foot of the tower stairway, and trying to persuade Mrs Scott-Fraser that he could cope perfectly well without her assuming the persona of a regimental sergeant-major. When Lesley came through, he touched. her arm in greeting. She was glad not to be wearing a short-sleeved blouse or shirt. The touch of his fingers on her flesh would have taken her mind off what lay ahead.

Carpets and furniture had been removed from the first-floor hall, and a number of seats brought in from the Academy. Galbraith was scurrying around taking photographs of the assembling audience from various angles. Finally he reached the curtained opening into the ante-room from which the performers would appear. As they emerged, he took two flash shots and then nodded obediently as Nick waved him away.

'Not during the performance.'

'Of course not, Sir Nicholas.'

There was a spattering of applause as Adam Lowther seated himself at the piano and Mairi McLeod bowed towards the front row of seats. Adam looked uncomfortable in a dark suit that did not quite succeed in being formal dress, and his black bow tie was way out of character. Mairi had shed her mourning black in favour of a flaming red dress with a low-cut neckline and bare arms. She looked both haughty and sensual.

A last-minute tuning up was followed by the ritual pause while the players took a deep breath, looked at each other, and waited for someone in the audience to stop coughing.

Once the two of them had started, they ceased to be two separate people. Lesley had difficulty restraining a gasp as the violin plunged into its strident opening phrase, while Adam Lowther at the piano piled up a rush of chords from low in the bass, urging his partner on, sustaining her until ready to push her upwards yet again, ever upwards. Mairi McLeod swayed in a rhythm coming not just from the music but from deep inside her. Her wide hips, too strong for any Sunday newspaper fashion supplement, started a conflicting syncopation of their own,

Through the clashing harmonies and discords, and a fierce passage of double-stopping, Lesley was sure she could detect a voice calling from far across Europe. She tried to shake herself out of what could only be a self-induced fantasy, dragging her eyes away from the two instrumentalists and glancing from side to side to regain her balance.

Her gaze met Nick's. He was staring at her with an intensity which matched the lust from the woman savaging her violin strings.

It doesn't worry you that your old flame has been having it off with Lowther, maybe even under your own roof?

Afraid of what he might read in her eyes, Lesley looked away.

During the interval some of the audience clattered downstairs to a makeshift bar, or for a few minutes out in the fresh air. Lesley stayed where she was. She was in no mood to talk to anyone or listen to anyone – not even Nick Torrance.

The second half began in more subdued mood, as if the fire between the two had been tamped down. But as the cross-rhythms of *Variations in a Dorian Mode* began to wrestle, the embers burned up again. And, like someone sitting in front of a fire and watching the flames dance, Lesley saw the flicker of repetitive phrases which became more and more transparent as each bar swirled by.

Applause at the end was half admiring, half relieved that it was all over. Nobody would have welcomed an encore. After a respectful pause, chairs were scraped back or sideways, and the audience made for the staircase.

Lesley summoned up her courage and walked towards the group at the piano: Nick, Adam Lowther, and Mairi McLeod.

'Well, Inspector Gunn,' said Nick. 'Detect any counterfeit notes?'

'Far from it. A superb performance.' She was looking at Mairi. 'But when it comes to detection, I was fascinated by some themes within both pieces. Particularly the last one. There was a lot of Moravian influence in the third and fourth variations, wasn't there?'

Mairi's stillness was in complete contrast to the swinging passion with which she had been playing. 'I'd no idea you were so interested in musical theory.'

'I'm quite fascinated by the use of motto themes. You know, like Shostakovitch's personal motto of D, E-flat, C and B.'

'Yes, I do know.'

Adam Lowther was staring from one woman to the other, puzzled. 'Moravian?'

'Just a minute.' Nick's expression had changed to one of disapproval. 'These two have just: finished a gruelling perform-ance. A splendid one. But damned exhausting. I don't think this is quite the moment to—'

He was interrupted by the effusive falsetto of the critic, Colin Baird. A most intoxicating performance, Miss McLeod. Mr – um – Lowther.' He gave Lesley a perfunctory nod. His pushy enthu-siasm was remote from the sneers he had communicated to her at the orchestral concert. 'True bravura.'

'Thank you,' said Mairi indifferently.

'How interesting those false relations in the fifth variation! Such daring polyphony on the composer's part, juxtaposing the diatonic notes with such a sequence of chromatics. Not at all what I had hitherto associated with the late lamented Erskine.'

Lesley made ready to move away, pausing for a moment close to Mairi McLeod. 'We'd be grateful for your help with some more questions, Miss McLeod. Perhaps I might call here tomorrow morning? You'll still be here?'

'Sooner or later I'll have to go back home to tidy up Daniel's papers, and my own. And decide what to do . . . now that he's gone.'

Lesley had the impression that she was carefully not looking at Adam Lowther. But when he headed for the stairs, Mairi followed as if still attached to him by the thread of their music, not wanting to break the spell yet.

'You *will* let me know before you leave the district?' Lesley called after her.

Neither of them even glanced back.

'Take it easy,' said Nick. 'Don't rush it and alarm her.'

'Tactics I've learned from DCI Rutherford, I'm afraid.'

'It's not as though we know anything definite yet.'

'Oh, but I think we do. What was it that pontificating poseur called it in musical terms?'

'Hm? Oh, you mean false relations. Or cross relations.'

'Yes, false relations. So very appropriate. Let's try and disen-tangle those relationships tomorrow morning. Say nine o'clock?'

'Have a heart. Let her lie in until nearer ten.'

The music was still reverberating in her own head. She trem-bled with it as Nick went to the door and turned the key in the lock.

'No,' she said, in such a whisper that she wasn't even sure herself of what she meant.

He put his left hand on her shoulder to draw her closer, and kissed her. Her lips opened to his. His right hand began an impa-tient exploration down from the high collar of her blouse, down demandingly to the waistband of her skirt. Of its own shameless accord her hand, too, wandered until he gasped, and laughed, and their mouths were laughing into each other. When their clothes had been tossed at random on to the chairs where the audience had so recently sat, his hands became fiercer, clasping her bottom and pressing it closer as if he wanted to drive straight through her.

'Lesley.' He cried it as if it were a burst of agony rather than a name. And in the end, when they were curled up on the cold floor, it was just a last, drained gasp. 'Lesley.'

The music in her head faded gently, drifting far away until only the faintest lilting beat of it remained.

11

A piercing screech set a flurry of rooks up out of the windbreak of larches and echoed off the stones of Black Knowe. One of the men setting up equipment for the final folk rave of the festival on the open-air platform dashed across the stage to the controls and reduced the noise down a long sliding wail to extinction.

Nick Torrance moved away from the window and automatically looked towards the longcase clock left behind by his grandfather. Only of course it had been removed like so many other features of the hall, before the previous evening's recital.

He glanced at his watch. Half past nine, and still no sign of Mairi. Sleeping off the emotional strain of that inflammatory performance of hers. But he had no doubt that Lesley Gunn would arrive on the very dot of ten. As if nothing had happened last night, she would be herself, punctual and impersonal.

But that was impossible. After last night, after today, everything had to change. Get all this business out of the way, and then there had to be a future, a real future.

If Mairi had not shown up by a quarter to ten, he would have to go to her room, which he had not done in the time she had been here. Once or twice her raised eyebrow had suggested what it had frequently suggested in years gone by and been suitably acknowledged in those years, but even for old times' sake he hadn't felt tempted. When she had taunted him about Lesley

Gunn, she had been too painfully close to the mark. Now Lesley was real, and nothing else was.

Mrs Robson tapped on the door and came in with the post and the morning paper. Another howl blasted in through the window and then was choked off.

'Good morning, sir. It's a fine day the day. And it'll be gey finer when we have an end to that skreiching, would ye no' say?'

'It brings in the punters, Mrs Robson.' He flipped through the envelopes and found nothing interesting. 'Oh, I wonder if you'd go and knock on Miss McLeod's door. We're expecting a visitor at ten.'

Mrs Robson hurried off with that fussy little shuffle of hers. Nick opened a few envelopes and looked round for somewhere to throw them and their useless contents. The waste paper basket with its embroidered tapestry surround, inherited from his mother, was another item not yet restored to its proper place.

Mrs Robson came back at an even more agitated pace. 'Sir Nicholas, she's nae there.'

'She's been down for breakfast and gone out for a walk?'

'Not that I've noticed, sir. And ye ken well I'd have noticed.'

He did ken that very well.

'And her bed's nae been slept in.' She was half alarmed, half eager for scandal about a guest she had never approved of in the first place. 'I'd be thinking she's awa'.'

Nick felt a chill in spite of the warm breeze from the open window. She hadn't been stupid enough to do a bunk? Maybe Lesley had spoken too soon, too clumsily, and set her off. He didn't want to fuel his housekeeper's speculations by asking whether the car in which Erskine and Mairi had arrived was still in the barmekin. After she had gone, her appetite still unsatisfied, he went downstairs at as leisurely a pace as possible, and did a slow stroll round his premises.

The Volvo was still there.

He wondered whether to phone Adam Lowther, but what exactly could he ask? Unlikely that she would have gone round to his place, still ablaze with a lust which Nick had every reason to remember in that music. Nora Lowther would have been unlikely to make her welcome and offer her a bed – least of all her own husband's bed.

He hoped Mairi had not had too devastating an effect on Lowther. Early middle-aged he might be, but Adam was still not quite grown up. Idealistic, naive, as passionate about music and particularly Erskine's music as some kids might be about model railways, he might too easily be shaken out of the stodginess of his everyday life with a dutiful, dull wife by the delights which Mairi could provide.

He heard the swish of wheels on the hard standing beside the tower, and hurried round to show the police upstairs. Lesley Gunn was not alone. DCI Rutherford had come with her. Nick was unsure whether to feel relieved or frustrated. One thing was sure: whichever way the inquisition went today, it was unlikely to be a discreet, low key operation if Rutherford was in charge. But without a target, what would the inquisitors be able to solve?

'Do sit down.'

'Thank you, Sir Nicholas.'

Nick realized that the only comfortable chair in the room was his own. The others had been removed, and the remnants of the recital were stacked one on top of the other against the north wall. Mrs Robson must have organized that first thing this morning, before he was awake. He dragged a couple off the top of a stack and nudged them forward. 'Sorry about this. Back to normal soon, I hope.'

'We all hope that, Sir Nicholas. Though in our profession, normality doesn't come high on the list. Now, I gather that you know a fair amount about the background of this inquiry.'

'Inspector Gunn and I did come across some interesting corre- lations, as I'm sure she's told you.'

'Aye. And we'd like to think that Miss McLeod can sort a few of them out for us. She knows we're here?'

There was no point in stalling. 'Miss McLeod doesn't appear to be here.'

201

Nick saw Lesley's eyes widen. Her lips moved faintly. She might have been saying 'Oh, no' to herself – just as she had whispered, disbelievingly, last night.

Rutherford's already craggy face had hardened. 'Not here?'

'She may have gone out for a stroll, or—'

'She knew what time we were due?'

'Not exactly. I' – he avoided Lesley's gaze – 'didn't have the opportunity to settle anything definite. After the exertions of her recital last night, she may have wanted to relax.'

'She's done a runner, hasn't she?'

'Not so far as I'm aware. Her car is still outside. I think you're jumping to conclusions, Chief Inspector.'

'Then prove me wrong. Where *is* she?'

Lesley said: 'She spent the night here?'

It was a question Nick had been dreading. 'My housekeeper thinks that possibly her bed hasn't been slept in.'

'Possibly?'

'I'm sorry. I can't be responsible for all my guests' movements. This is a home, not a gaol.'

'Of course, sir. Of course.' Rutherford sounded far from respectful. 'But since she was a guest in your home' – he laid sarcastic emphasis on the word – 'and, I gather, an old friend, you might have some idea of her way of life, her likely behaviour in a crisis?' When Nick could find no immediate answer, Rutherford suddenly rasped: 'Sir Nicholas, this is serious. This is a murder inquiry. Where *is* she?' He turned to Lesley. 'Looks as if there could be something in what that sneaking little tart was telling us.'

A babble of voices floated up from the platform on the haugh below. It could have been a rehearsal of some cataclysmic number with the volume turned up full. But it wasn't. They were hollering blue murder – which was exactly what it was.

On the grass under the stage was the naked, crumpled body of Mairi McLeod.

Part 3
DEADLY DISCORD

1

Detective Inspector Lesley Gunn was relieved that this time it was Detective Chief Inspector Jack Rutherford who had to deal with the phone call to Superintendent Maitland. Three murders, and two of them within the last ten days: it was not a sequence likely to please the Super.

Lesley tactfully stayed out of the caravan while Rutherford made the call, but fled back inside when she spotted Galbraith heading eagerly towards her with his reporter's notebook at the ready. From the top step she said, 'We'll be issuing a statement shortly,' and closed the door.

Rutherford was just putting the phone down. 'We're not in what you'd call good odour with the heidyins right now.' He mopped his brow and breathed in shakily through his teeth. 'Forensics ought to be nearly finished by now. Let's go take another look at her ladyship.'

The familiar van was drawn up as it had been drawn up near Erskine's corpse, this time with its open doors pinned back against the edge of the platform.

The photographer was still prowling round the body, going down every now and then on his knees to get a close shot of Mairi's neck or face twisted to one side. Lesley found it hard to be dispassionate, looking down at that beautiful but inert body. One of her arms was flung out in what could have been a last attempt to push herself up from the ground – or the abandonment of a woman greedy for her lover, impatient for him to add his weight to hers and press her into the damp grass until shreds of it clung to her head and shoulders and wide, flaunting hips. Only the head offered no welcome. It was wrenched aside, strangled and twisted. Clothes had been thrown aside, but not as if they had been ripped off. Hurriedly discarded, yes; but not torn brutally off in a struggle. She must have thrown them aside herself, opening herself, expectant.

When the photographer was finished, a man in a white overall stooped to examine the marks on Mairi's neck.

'You were at that recital last night,' said Rutherford. 'Supposed to be keeping your eyes and ears open. What do *you* make of it? What went on?'

'They were playing, the two of them, like folk possessed. Carried away by the music.'

'And ready to go on performing? Did she and Lowther go off together afterwards?'

'I . . . don't know.'

Rutherford fixed her with a beady stare. 'Otherwise occupied, Les?'

She longed not to blush, but knew she was failing.

'I left,' she said as firmly as possible, 'after I'd made the appointment for us to show up for our interview this morning.'

'It didn't occur to you to follow them?'

'No, it didn't. If they were going to . . . well . . .'

'Have it off together? Quite a lot of that in the air last night, was there?'

'There was nothing to suggest that anything like this—'

'Strikes me we'd better go and see friend Lowther.'

'I don't see him as a suspect. He was obsessed with the woman.'

'Love and hate? Not getting his own way with her?'

'From what Deirdre Maxwell had to tell us,' she reminded him, 'he was undoubtedly getting his own way with her.'

A second man was examining the dead woman's nails and carefully extracting minute flecks to see if there were traces of skin she might have clawed off her attacker, if she had put up a struggle. 'I think we can get a more thorough inspection once we've carted it off to the morgue, sir.'

Mairi McLeod was now an 'it', no longer a 'she' or 'her'.

'I still think we have to start with Lowther. The way things were going, he could have been the last person to see her alive. We see him, find out what there is to find, and then play it by ear.'

A crowd was gathering, held back by two uniformed officers. There were whispers and nudges. Women who had been in the audience last night were looking back over their shoulders at friends who had not been so lucky, telling them what they had noticed about the way the violinist used her arms, and how you could see how tempestuous she was, and what strange suggestiveness there had been in some of the music. They could almost have predicted that something would happen.

Galbraith lunged towards Rutherford and Lesley Gunn. Rutherford raised an arm which looked threatening but was merely brushing the reporter away. 'There has been an unfortunate occurrence. One of the festival performers has been found dead. When we have more details, you'll be notified.' Rutherford stamped on, with Lesley hurrying to catch up and not be intercepted by the reporter.

As they went into the town past the garage, Rutherford said: 'The same killer, d'you think? First Erskine, then Erskine's floozie?'

'Which lets Lowther out, surely? He worshipped Erskine. And was besotted with Mairi McLeod.'

'Who else, then? A serial killer? I mean, can we add that woman in the tower? Someone with a lasting grudge over more than one generation? Three in a row. Or perm any two from three.' He stared at a coach that was loading up musical instruments and some bleary-eyed ravers. 'Wonder if we ought to pull them in until we've completed our inquiries?'

'It's an internal thing,' said Lesley. 'Very local. Maybe a connection between one and two. Or two and three. But nothing to do with the visitors.'

'If it's one and two, then that lets Lowther out. Only a kid at the time that woman was done in. But running in the family? Father left in a bit of a hurry. Tied in with the murder? And somehow there's been something inbred, something going on into the present.'

'The killings could be related,' Lesley agreed. 'But not necessarily the same killer. An awful lot of the threads seem to be tangled up with one another, but not necessarily in a straight-forward pattern. Like a musical composition: you don't simply repeat the first tune, or leave it to one soloist, you make a logical progression from one to—'

'Oh, for Christ's sake, Les. You've put me off music for life.'

'Who do we know was here at the time of any two of the three murders? Or the right age to cover all of them? And with a motive for each of them?'

Before she could pursue this, there was a shout of 'Guv' across the street. DS Elliot was waving from the opposite pavement, eyeing a gap between a brewer's delivery lorry and an impatiently lurching, speeding and slowing Range Rover with an apoplectic Captain Scott-Fraser at the wheel. In the end Elliot opted for safety, and waited until the two vehicles had separated near the Tolbooth.

He was waving a green folder. 'Some DNA results through at last. And some fingerprints and an interesting bloodstain. I think you ought to see them.'

'Right now we're on our way to see young Lowther about our latest cadaver.'

'Guv, maybe there's somebody you ought to see first. Catch him when he's not expecting it.'

'What the hell are you on about, Elliot?'

But Rutherford let the sergeant steer them towards the caravan and lay out the new details on the table. After less than five minutes he agreed that priorities had shifted.

'Shall we bring him in?' said Elliot.

'No. I think the inspector and myself will go pay a call. Catch him when he's not expecting it, as you so rightly put it, laddie.'

2

The gates of the builder's yard were pulled right back to allow a large delivery truck to back in from the street. As Jack Rutherford and Lesley Gunn edged their way round it, two men began unloading rolls of plastic sheeting. Glaring down from the murky window of his office on the unloading process, ready to be critical if anything was dropped or grazed, Enoch Buchanan looked even less amiable when he recognized the two detectives. As they climbed the rickety steps, he moved to the doorway as if to deny them entry.

'Mr Buchanan.' Rutherford was at his politest, most non-committal.

'This is a busy morning for me.'

'And for us.' Rutherford mounted the last step so that Buchanan had either to make way for him or push him off. 'You'll have heard the news?'

Buchanan stood aside. 'If ye're meaning—'

'I think you know what I mean, sir. We have a few questions on which you may be able to help us.'

'That I doubt.'

Lesley followed Rutherford into the office with its smell of dust and something metallic, presumably from the battered kettle standing on a gas ring at the far end of the shack.

'You'll have heard, then, of another murder.'

'Aye. The harlot has followed him into perdition.'

'She didn't exactly follow. Not of her own accord, anyway. She was the victim of a deliberate killer. Knowing your strong feelings on the matter, we were hoping you could throw some light on it.'

'I'm no' in the mood to listen to this sort of thing.'

'We'll be only too pleased to listen to *you*, sir.'

Buchanan glanced at the clerk hunched up at the bench, pretending not to hear a word. 'Angus, get down there and keep an eye on those gowks. Any shortages or any damage, and I'll be wanting a report. You know what they're like.'

When the young man had gone, Rutherford leaned against the bench and pushed the vacant chair towards Lesley with his foot.

'Now, Mr Buchanan.'

'All I know is what I've been told this very morning. And there's nae doubt everyone else in the toon will hae heard it the noo. Why would the two of ye be coming to tell me, specially?'

'Because there are one or two very special things. Very personal matters.'

'Ye'd oblige me by not taking too long over this. My time is money.'

Lesley could see that Buchanan's blustering attitude was exasperating the always quick-tempered Rutherford. Instead of leading up to things gradually, laying some subtle verbal traps, he came out with it: 'Mr Buchanan, your fingerprints are on that guitar – the Daniel Erskine murder weapon.'

'Man, you're cracket.'

'There were lots of other prints. The guitarist's own, naturally. And those of one or two of his mates. Not surprising. But it was surprising to find yours there, Mr Buchanan.'

'And how would ye be guessing they're mine?'

'No guesswork, sir. We made a comparison with those you left on the glass when we interviewed you.'

'Snooping, is that the size of it? Nothing better to do.'

'Fingerprints, and bloodstains.'

'Erskine's blood, nae doot.' Buchanan relished the idea.

'And a trace of your own. Did you cut yourself on one of the strings when you swung the guitar at him?'

210

'And how would you be guessing at these other bloodstains?'

'No guesswork,' said Rutherford again. 'DNA tests.'

'And what would those be?'

Overriding Rutherford's impatient snort, Lesley said in her best imitation of a schoolmarm: 'The nucleus of living cells contains a genetic code unique to individual human beings. Even when they've been dead for many years – hundreds of years, even – family genes can be identified down through the generations. The faintest fragment of tissue, a hair follicle, cells from saliva . . . they're an infallible guide.'

Rutherford shouldered his way back in. 'You picked up that guitar and smashed it over Daniel Erskine's head. You left your calling cards all over it.'

Buchanan stared out of the window. The prospect offered him no comfort. 'Och, I'll grant ye I picked the filthy thing up. But that's all I did.'

'You never got round to telling us that.'

'Because I knew ye'd be making something twisted out of it.'

'Why would you have picked up something you detested so much?'

'There he was, that lout, that good-for-nothing. Drunk in the gutter. And that abominable thing beside him. So aye, I did pick it up. Gey stupid of me.' A hint of a whine crept into Buchanan's voice. 'I'll admit that, officer. I was no' in my senses. I . . . I picked it up and . . . och aye, I threw it as far as I could. Somebody else must hae got their hands on it later.'

'Somebody else?'

'There's plenty o' folk in this toon who had good cause to want that spawn o' Satan oot o' this world.'

'But you had a particular grudge, didn't you? Your belief – or misapprehension – that Erskine had defiled your daughter.'

'It was no misapprehension. It was him. Taking her away, and then throwing her back like a . . . like . . .'

'You're still sure it was him?'

'Who else would it have been?'

'We don't know, but we know it wasn't Erskine.'

211

'Man, how could ye be knowing any such thing?'

Rutherford nodded to Lesley that it was her turn. 'Again it's a matter of DNA, Mr Buchanan,' she said. 'The baby your daughter was expecting was definitely not Erskine's. We've made the comparisons between the two corpses, and what little remains of the unborn baby, and Erskine was not the father.'

Buchanan's sagging face would have been a pitiable sight if a hardened police officer was ever in the mood to pity a killer. 'My daughter. . . ?'

Rutherford said: 'Enoch Buchanan, I am charging you with the murder of Susanna Buchanan, Daniel Erskine, and Mairi McLeod.'

'That harlot? That was nothing to do with me. I was never—'

'You do not have to say anything, but it may harm your defence if you do not mention, when questioned, something which you later rely on in court. Anything you do say may be given in evidence.'

'Cracket,' said Buchanan again. 'All of ye, cracket.'

'We'd better continue this down at the station. Inspector, will you phone for a car?'

Buchanan was struggling to regain his dignity. 'I'm perfectly capable of walking.'

'If you're thinking of making a run for it—'

'Have no fear, man. I'll nae be one o' your shilpit runaways. I'll stand for what I believe, and the Good Lord will be my guide.'

Striding between them through the streets, he looked as he had looked that previous time – upright, offering the police mature advice rather than kowtowing before their questions.

In the interview room, Rutherford said: 'May I remind you that you are still under caution. If you wish your solicitor to be present—'

'I'll no' be seeing good money put into yon Wilson's pocket.'

'If you change your mind at any time, we'll suspend the interview until you have arranged to be represented.'

'Would you care for a drink of water?' suggested Lesley.

'So that ye can contrive further lees?'

She set the tape recorder, and Rutherford repeated the charge.

'I've told ye, I know nothing about the McLeod whore.'

'But the others? You do know something about both of them? Especially as one of them was your daughter?'

'No daughter o' mine.'

Lesley spread out a blueprint and two sheets of paper she had collected from the caravan.

'Mr Buchanan, you will recollect that in 1979 you spoke out very strongly in the Community Council against the proposal to build a new housing estate on the Monigour Moss.'

'What has that got to do with it? Why dig that up?'

Rutherford grinned. 'Digging up has a lot to do with it.'

'You opposed the idea on grounds of health, land subsidence, and other factors,' Lesley went on. 'Yet when you were overridden, you showed great determination in taking on the job of building contractor for the project. Double standards, Mr Buchanan?'

'Certainly not. If something had to be done, better it was in the hands of somebody competent than have a puir job made worse.'

'And you wanted to make sure you had control over the site. In a hurry to remove the body you had buried there. You'd buried it in a sack, and then had to dig it up again and find another way of disposing of it, hadn't you?'

'I dinna have to listen to this.'

'No, but if you're unwilling to answer questions here,' said Rutherford, 'I can keep you in custody while you consider the matter, and if necessary the superintendent will grant an extension and then consider applying to a magistrate for a further extension while our inquiries continue.' He waited a few moments, then smiled at Lesley. 'Inspector. I think we have permission to continue.'

She had the story at her fingertips. DS Elliot's researches had confirmed so much background guesswork, and she could see that Rutherford was happy to defer to her because she knew all the people by now, knew every nuance, every possibility, and was best equipped to undermine the stony but crumbling Buchanan.

'When your daughter came home and told you she was expecting a child, what did you do?'

'What any decent parent would have done. I'd no' hae disgrace brought on my house. I . . . I sent her away again, before she could flaunt her shame aboot the place.'

'No, Mr Buchanan. You flew into a rage and murdered her.'

'I'll not deny I raised my hand to her. Chastising her, as every father has the right to do.'

'Chastising? You call murder—'

'I'll answer to God, not to you.'

'You struck her. Hard enough to kill her.'

'That was never meant.' He stopped, gulped, and the bluster ebbed away into a bubble of spittle.

'You stripped her of her clothes – burned them, I suppose? – wrapped her in a sack, and buried her in the moss. Nobody would ever be likely to find her there. Then when there was a danger of the site being dug up, you desperately went for the building contract. And then' – Lesley let a vibrant silence hang in the air for a moment – 'you dug her up and moved her into another of your projects. Entombed her again, this time in the Academy flue. Clumsily smashing her hand in the rush.'

'That's too stupid to answer.'

'Come to think of it,' Lesley went on, 'this would have been about the time that Jamie Lowther left the district. Very abruptly. And seems to have been quite well provided for. Was he trying to blackmail you?'

Buchanan came to life. 'He was a reliable worker, Lowther. No reason to blackmail *me*. And I'm no' the kind to be blackmailed by anybody. That sort of filth would never work with me, that I can tell ye.'

Lesley was sure that this, at any rate, was true.

'Why did he go away so soon, then? So suspiciously close to the time you shoved your daughter into that flue casing?'

Instead of denying or trying to excuse the murder of his daughter, Buchanan shrugged, still anxious to show that he was and always had been the man in charge. 'One thing I *will* tell ye,' he condescended. 'A good reason for Jamie Lowther being keen to get away was that young Adam was beginning to look more and more like his real father. I'd seen it all along. I'm a good judge, young lady. Sooner or later there'd have been others who'd notice.'

'Notice that Daniel Erskine was Adam Lowther's father?'

'Spreading his foul seed everywhere.'

'So you leaned on Jamie. Persuaded him to help you shift your daughter into that metal casing. You couldn't have managed it on your own. In a way, *you* were the blackmailer. Got him to help you with your dirty work, drove him out of Kilstane because of the fear of being sneered at, and paid him well enough for his services. Making it clear, I suppose, that there'd no longer be a job for him if he stayed?'

'If he'd been a real man, he'd have taken matters into his own hands. Treated his wife the way she deserved to be treated. And that fornicator Erskine.'

'The way *you* treated your daughter? And Daniel Erskine?'

'I'll not be speaking of that.'

'Not even when you realize Erskine had nothing to do with your daughter's pregnancy? That you murdered him for nothing?'

'I'll say no more.'

But he sagged gradually as Lesley went on remorselessly spelling out the true tale of his daughter and Erskine.

'When she came back, ditched, did she actually tell you it was Erskine who had made her pregnant?'

'She wouldnae tell me, but I kent fine.'

'We've got Erskine's DNA as well, and there's no connection between him and your daughter's unborn child.'

'So you killed Erskine,' said Rutherford, 'for nothing.'

'I'll no' believe that. He was well out o' this world. And where he belongs. On the floors of liquid fire in hell.'

'And you felt you were appointed by God – personally appointed – to send his mistress after him?'

'I never laid a finger on that slut. Never.' Buchanan seemed genuinely indignant. Lesley sensed, along with Rutherford, that before long he was going to confess – proudly confess, now there was no way out – to the murders of his daughter and of Daniel Erskine. But his rage over this other accusation rang just as surely as the resonance of guilt in everything else he had been denying.

Rutherford turned off the recorder and indicated that Lesley should follow him into the corridor. 'I'll get a uniform to sit in with me. You take Elliot along with you to Lowther's shop, and see what he's got for sale. Or what bargain offers he can come up with today. Especially about his duet partner. I want to know more about them making beautiful music together. And why it all went out of tune. Have I got the jargon right, Les?'

Nick Torrance stared out over the view that he had learned to love. But now it was contaminated. His bird's eye view of the stage and the taped-off area was partially obscured by the roof and open doors of the police van. Another murder had happened on his property. He was the laird, he ought to be in charge. Or at least liaising with the police after they came on the scene. But it had been too much – going down after that first alarm was raised, seeing what lay in the shadows, and wanting to throw up over the grass. Coming back here, he could think of nothing to do but wait for them to come and report and interview him. Yet what could he tell them?

He thought of Adam Lowther going down the stairs with Mairi. It had been obvious they were still in a sensual daze, and he knew what Mairi could be like in that mood. And remembered what the music had done for himself and Lesley.

He couldn't just sit here or stand here, waiting. There was routine work to be done. The festival had ended – more brutally than anticipated – and there were loose ends to be tied up, bills to be looked at, farewells to be said.

216

Adam Lowther ought to be attending to that.

But did Adam Lowther know what had happened to Mairi? Had he been told yet? After he had left her, had someone been waiting, hating, ready to pounce? Or . . . No, he wasn't going to let that even cross his mind. Mairi, aroused, might be capable of violence. But not awkward, meek little Adam.

He had to see Adam. It was something to do.

He half expected to find the police there, but the shop door was closed and there was no sign of life. Nick had to ring the side doorbell in the pend. When Nora came downstairs and opened the door, her eyes were blank and unwelcoming.

'Is Adam about?'

'No, he's not.'

'Has he gone to see the police?'

'Why'd he do that?'

'Mrs Lowther – Nora – may I come in?'

She turned mutely and led the way upstairs. In the sitting-room she seemed incapable of offering him a chair, but stood there like a housewife who wished she hadn't let a salesman on to the premises and now only wanted him to leave.

'You haven't heard?' said Nick. 'Adam . . . he hasn't heard?'

'He's gone.' Her voice was flat, almost bored. 'Gone off with that woman. I knew he would, in the end.'

'He hasn't. I can assure you he hasn't.'

'What would you know about it? They've been planning it ever since she got here. Ever since she . . . they . . .' She made a vague gesture down at the floor, towards the shop underneath.

'He hasn't,' said Nick. 'She's dead.'

'No. That doesn't make sense.'

'What time did he get in last night?'

'I don't know.'

'After that recital, you must have been here when he got back. The two of you must have had things to talk about.'

'I've been sleeping in the spare room since . . . since I knew what was going on. I don't know if he came back at all. You ask me, I'd say they went straight off, just the way they'd been planning it.'

'Mairi McLeod,' Nick emphasized, 'is dead.'

Doubt stirred in his mind. She was so frozen, so sheathed in something impermeable, some armour of her own stubbornness, that it was impossible to tell whether she was in a state of shock . . . or denying, as murderers are often said to do, what she had just done.

Could she have been the one to murder Mairi?

He didn't believe it.

Nora, still remote, managed a curl of the lip. 'Dead or alive, I can tell you one thing – there'll be his fingerprints all over her.'

'But where is he? Nora, the police are liable to show up any time now. They'll want to know.'

'That's *their* job, isn't it? Up to them to find him.'

The doorbell rang. Nora Lowther went back down the stairs and opened the door.

'Mrs Lowther, is your husband at home?'

Nick recognized the cadences of Lesley Gunn's voice.

3

Nora Lowther had answered questions about her husband's possible whereabouts with a vague flutter of her left hand. A couple of times she raised it to her lips like a child just about to suck its thumb. Whatever had happened to Adam or to Mairi McLeod seemed to be a matter of complete indifference now. She had reached the end of a road which had promised little in the first place. She either didn't know where she was, or where Adam was, or she didn't care. The past was something to be smudged over because it didn't matter any more. And the future didn't matter because there was no such thing as a future.

She came out with only one helpful remark. 'They've been planning to go off and sort through Daniel Erskine's papers. He's very proud of that. I think it means more to him than she does ... than she did.' It might have been a last strand of comfort, but was hardly worth the effort of holding on to it. 'Well, they won't be doing that now, will they?'

Back in the caravan, Rutherford was waiting for Lesley. He was happy that Buchanan, now deciding after all that he needed a solicitor before saying another word, must have realized the game was up. He was safely locked away with time to think, probably pondering whether to be arrogant and try to bluff it out or to be arrogant and boast of his rectitude in slaying his sinful daughter and sinful Erskine.

'One thing, though,' said Rutherford. 'He's been twice as gabby on the subject of Mairi McLeod. Not sorry for the deaths of the first two. But quite adamant that he had nothing to do with the McLeod woman. So . . . what have *you* come up with?'

She told him. And told him that she had checked that Adam Lowther's car was missing, and that he had filled up at Marshall and Corsock's at just after seven this morning.

Rutherford barked an instruction to the girl at the switchboard to put through a call to the Northern Constabulary in Inverness. He was far from satisfied with the result. 'They'll *try* to spare a man to *keep an eye* on the house at Altnalarach.' He emphasized the words with heavy sarcasm. 'But their resources are stretched at the moment, puir wee dears. Two days of a big demo along the north coast, protesting about Dounreay poisoning the firth. Some real tough troublemakers out for a punch-up. But they will *try*.'

'And if they don't get there in time?'

'In time for what?'

'We don't know what Lowther may get up to once he's there. If that's where he's going.'

'Where else would he go?'

'Exactly. That has to be it. But if he's aiming to get into the house and start going through papers or scores . . . Is he out to steal valuable manuscripts – or destroy them, d'you suppose? Works by Erskine, or Strepka, or—'

'Here we go again. Les, the sooner that stuff is destroyed, my heart won't bleed for it. Probably better for the listening public, too.'

'But don't you see, it could be valuable evidence. Could be the whole story of who wrote what, and whether Erskine was a cheat, and what part Mairi McLeod really played in transcribing the work – or faking it somehow.'

'That's a matter for some music critic, not for us.'

'It's a little matter of murder,' she reminded him. 'And the motive for Erskine's murder and Mairi McLeod's could well lie in those manuscripts.'

Rutherford grunted. 'We've got three stiffs on our hands right here. And when Buchanan cracks, you'll find that the first two were simple cases of personal vengeance. Family stuff – the way it is in most cases. And as for the third, Forensic will come up with enough from the McLeod woman without us needing any musical theories to convict Lowther.'

'But don't you want to *know*. . . ?'

'Not specially. Just background music, as far as I'm concerned.'

'But if Adam Lowther destroys that evidence, and then disappears—'

'We're playing this by the book, Les. We put out a call to all traffic patrols between here and Sutherland. You've got his car registration number?'

'Yes.'

'Good. Then settle down to chasing it. That's police procedure, Les. Nothing to do with fugues and fantasies or whatever. The Northern Constabulary will round him up before long, mark my words. There aren't many places he can run in that ruddy wilderness. And if you ask me, he's the sort to give himself up. Once he faces up to what he's done, he'll just collapse and give himself up.'

'I still think one of us ought to be up there – someone who knows him, and what he's likely to be doing.'

'Oh no, Les. No way. I've let you go wandering off too many times already. You do not go chasing off into someone else's territory. When we send anyone up there, it'll be as escort for a prisoner who's already been taken by our oppos on the ground.'

The phone rang. The constable at the switchboard said: 'Sir, Mr Wilson's arrived at the nick. Enoch Buchanan's solicitor. He's asking for you.'

'I'm on my way.' Rutherford patted Lesley condescendingly on the arm. 'And right now, you can make yourself useful checking reports from the A9 patrols and plotting possible escape routes.'

Nick Torrance edged the Laguna up on to the pavement to allow the dustcart to grind its way out of a courtyard, and found himself a few yards from the incident caravan. Lesley Gunn was standing on the top step, her head back as if desperately breathing fresh air into her lungs – though the smell from the truck wouldn't have helped very much.

He said: 'Want a lift?'

Dragged back from whatever it was that she had been contemplating, she looked at him the way she might have sized up a stranger. 'Where to?'

'Altnalarach.'

Her laugh was mirthless. 'I'm supposed to be having a coffee break and then sitting by the phone waiting for news from that part of the world.'

'I'm prepared to take you to that part of the world personally.'

'Why do *you* want to go?'

'Somebody has to. You know that as well as I do. Better than your hidebound colleagues do, maybe?'

'I'd lose my job if I—'

'Good. But I'll tell you one thing. You'll lose your prey and a lot of important evidence if you don't come. Right now.'

She slid into the seat beside him. 'This is crazy. I don't know what I'm doing.'

'You do know damn well that if we don't get there in time we may lose something invaluable.'

She couldn't argue. He could tell she was not going to. But he could also tell that, now she had committed herself, she was terrified of the outcome.

There was no point in vague conversation. They both knew the main object of this drive, and nothing else was worth discussing.

Nick wondered if they might even catch Adam before he reached Altnalarch. Unlikely, but the Laguna was capable of speeds a lot higher than Adam Lowther's clapped-out old estate, worn down over recent years by the weight of musical instruments, loudspeakers, disco equipment and keyboards.

'If I get pulled in for speeding,' he said, 'I hope you can flash your warrant card at them and tell them what it's all about.'

'They'll be even tougher if they find out that I'm trespassing on their patch.' Lesley glanced along the fascia board. 'May I use your carphone?'

'Go right ahead.'

She murmured a brief message for DCI Rutherford, and then said: 'Can I switch it off so that we don't get him replying and threatening me with a firing squad?'

'Done.'

As they crossed The Mound, the sun came out from behind a thin veil of clouds and shot sparks of light like pebbles skimming across Loch Fleet. It was a day for relaxing under a display of changing, skittish skies. As the road hugged closer to the sea, the brightness intensified, and the broom burned more and more golden on the slopes. But they were not on holiday. Not this time, thought Nick.

He broke the long silence. 'Since you're expecting to lose your job, isn't it time we talked about—'

'For the time being I'm a serving police officer. I'll complete this investigation and prove to them why it's important, and then I'll take my leave.'

'Yes, officer. All right. But maybe on the way back we can talk.'

'On the way back,' she said, 'I hope we'll have company.'

The fitful sun was setting the western skies over Ben Loyal aglow as Nick manoeuvred the Laguna along the winding single-track road. Ahead, the hunched white shape of the house at Altnalarach darted from left to right as the road twisted from west to north, to the east and back again. When it was held steady for a few moments, there seemed to be a spiralling wisp of cloud above the house. As they came closer, it was clear that smoke was pouring from the chimney: not the blue tinge of lazy peat smoke, but dark fumes full of flecks of torn, burning paper which fluttered away like crippled birds across the lochans.

It was not until the Laguna had swung in beside the house that they saw the police car already there. 'Beaten us to it,' said Nick.

The door was ajar. Inside, a uniformed police constable lay

223

stunned across a coffee table which Nick remembered from that first visit, when Mairi had been alive . . . vibrant with life. A fire was roaring in the grate, fed with a wedge of music manuscript slowly blackening in the middle and shredding into flaring fragments round the edges.

Lesley let out a small sob and took a pace towards the fireplace.

'Stay where you are.' Adam Lowther was holding out a canister at arm's length, his thumb trembling. 'You know what this is?'

'CS gas,' said Lesley.

Nick said: 'Don't be stupid, Adam.'

'I don't want to have to use it.'

'Then don't,' said Lesley. 'It's police property, Mr Lowther You'll be in serious trouble if—'

'I thought I was in that already.' He spluttered a shrill laugh. 'Is this going to make it any worse?'

'Probably not,' said Nick. He kept it calm and compassionate. 'Adam, exactly how much do you know about the death of Mairi McLeod?'

They waited for him to deny it, to say they were crazy, he loved Mairi and was here only because she had asked him to come and sort some things out for her. To pretend, maybe, that he didn't even know she was dead and didn't know what they were talking about. Instead he looked back at them with what in the army might be condemned as dumb insolence. His eyes were not denying; just not registering. Nick marvelled that in this state this man could have driven safely this far. Trying to jolt him out his trance, he said: 'How many more manuscripts did you hope to destroy?'

'Perhaps it would be simpler,' said Adam dreamily, 'to burn the whole place down.'

Suddenly Lesley said: 'Mr Lowther, aren't you worried about your wife?'

'My wife? What's she got to do with it?'

'Mairi McLeod has been murdered. Your wife had as much

cause as anyone to want her out of the way.'

Shocked, Nick tried not to look at her. He had not realized she could be so ruthless. Without seeing her face, he knew it must be as he had seen it once before – the feral face of a predator, laying a trap and poised for the kill.

But it worked. Something flickered behind Adam Lowther's staring eyes. 'Nora? You must be mad. Nora would never summon up the energy to kill anybody. She's too . . . well . . .'

'Too nice? Too gentle? A perfect wife?'

'She'd never have the guts.'

'People can be driven over the edge, you know.'

'Yes, I do know. But leave Nora alone. I'm not going to have her blamed for any of this. Leave her out of it. She's innocent.'

'You've got reason to be sure of that?'

'Yes.'

'And any reason for who *did* kill Miss McLeod?'

The gas canister in Adam's hand trembled even more. The policeman stirred, groaned, and began to grope his way up to his knees.

Lesley said: 'Mr Lowther, there are three of us. Even if you try letting that gas off, three of us will still be able to cope with you. And I don't think you really want to set it off anyway. You've done enough damage already.'

Adam stared at the canister as if it was the first time he had noticed it. With a sigh he put it on the coffee table, close to the coal shovel with which he must have knocked the police constable out.

Lesley was implacable. 'If Mairi McLeod wasn't killed by your wife in a fit of jealousy, who else would want to kill her?'

'All right. I killed her.'

'You understand what you're saying, Mr Lowther?'

'Yes. I killed her. Isn't that what you want?'

'Why did you do it?'

'Because she killed my father.'

'Your father died years ago, Adam,' said Nick, bewildered. 'In Leeds.'

225

'I'm talking about my real father.'

'He means Daniel Erskine,' said Lesley quietly.

Nick stared at her. 'There's something you haven't told me?'

'Oh, why did he have to come back?' Adam was close to tears. *'Why?'*

'We've wondered that,' said Lesley. 'Why did he?'

'She told me she thought that . . . oh, that *he* thought that the corpse – in the Academy – might have been. . . my mother. Only somehow when he got here and met me, and asked about my mother, he knew it couldn't have been because we'd gone away and . . . oh, I don't know.'

'We'll never be able to ask him now. I think,' said Lesley, 'that you'd better tell us all the rest. About Mairi McLeod.'

'I've told you. She killed my father. Killed him as far as I was concerned. And laughed at me. She *laughed* at me.' He slumped down into one of the sagging leather armchairs, again staring at something or somebody not in this room. 'She thought it was *funny.'*

She had laughed. At first with lust as she let him strip her clothes from her and toss them aside. And then with satisfaction as his weight thrust her naked body down in the darkness on the damp grass. And then she was laughing when she said she was getting cold, and it was his turn to get a dose of the night ague in his backside while she clambered on top of him.

'This is how I usually had to do it for your father. Made it much easier for him.'

He revelled in the rhythm of her dancing on him, but still he could gasp out: 'What d'you mean, my father?'

'Oh, hadn't you realized by now? Why do you think Daniel was so prickly about everybody else but got so mellow towards you? He recognized you right away. Maybe you've got your mother's eyes.' She stopped, poised on her knees for a shuddering moment, then descended on him again. 'Not that I can see your eyes right now.'

When she had finished and rolled off him, dragging his arm

around her damp shoulders, he said: 'You can't mean Daniel Erskine. . . ?'

'Of course. Quite the local stud, from all we've heard, right?' And then she told him why Erskine had changed his mind, and come back to Kilstane thinking of that woman, and then found Adam's mother had gone away with her husband and died a natural death. 'I think he felt quite sentimental about that one. Your mother. Relieved everything had been . . . well, normal.'

Adam thought of Jamie Lowther, the man he had thought of as his father, and remembered Jamie's hatred of music. How he had tried to drag Adam away from anything connected with music, and snarled at all the things he most liked listening to. Barging into the room when he was listening to an Erskine Nocturne and switching the radio off. 'Showing off.' Sitting in a room alone, listening, to whom was he supposed to be showing off?

'Is that why . . .' In the dank darkness, close to her body yet feeling that she wasn't in the same, ordinary world, he was at a loss. But he had to be sure of one thing: when all this was sorted out, and they were together somewhere, together permanently . . .

'When we've gone through Erskine's manuscripts – my father's manuscripts,' he said, letting his right hand stray on to her chill breast, 'we'll have to decide how I wrap things up with Nora.'

'Wrap what things up?'

'Well, I'll have to get a divorce, and make reasonable arrangements for Nora. And then decide where we're going to live. Maybe look for concert engagements together.'

Then came the worst laughter.

Her face was only a vague mask in the faintest of lights seeping in below the ends of the stage. But her teeth were startlingly white as she smiled and began a gurgling hiccup of a laugh.

'Don't be ridiculous, Adam.'

'What d'you mean, ridiculous?'

'Once we've sorted out the manuscripts, I'm going to try my

hand in Moravia. Take the music back where a lot of it belongs. You don't think I'd want to be hanging around here, do you?'

Her hand wandered idly over his body, more in consolation than in returning desire.

'Moravia?' he echoed, baffled.

'You've heard of your father's old buddy, Jan Strepka? Or Ian McCabe, as he was in his incarnation here.'

'Oh, when I was a kid, there was some talk of the McCabes . . . but I don't see . . .'

'I've pleasured both fathers. And managed it with one son, agreed? May as well keep up the tradition.'

'But I thought the family went back long before you—'

'I met him in Hodonin when it was still behind the Iron Curtain.' She snuggled closer, as if expecting him to be happy sharing her nostalgia. 'He was my real love. They were great mates, Jan and your father. Rivals for the fun of it. Fighting over their women, and getting a hell of a kick out of it.' She licked his shoulder, but it was not Adam she was really tasting. 'And giving their women a hell of a kick, too. But I learned long ago that Daniel wasn't going to let his old pal stand in his way. Your father never let anyone stand in the way of his career. Or his appetite.'

'I don't get it. What are you on about?'

'Oh, I wormed it out of Daniel long ago. He was rather proud of it, vicious bastard that he was. ' She said it quite affectionately. 'He more or less confessed that he'd leaked a few facts to the STB about Jan's likely defection from Czechoslovakia. Jan was going to get out and claim his music for his own – and claim me as well.'

'His music?'

'Who do you think wrote the really great stuff attributed to poor Daniel? In the end I had to make do with Daniel. Though they did have a few shared talents.' She was gnawing at his shoulder – or a remembered shoulder. 'Interesting variations. But Jan's music was the real thing.'

'Until he died?' Adam fought for a glimmer of understanding.

'And then Erskine . . . my father . . . came into his own.'

Her laugh was growing crueller.

'You don't really think Daniel was up to that? He'd covered for Jan all this time. Then disposed of him. But there wasn't any more music coming out. You don't think he was capable of following Strepka's genius, do you?'

'Then what—'

'Who do you think went on composing in his name? He became the recluse, the great man shut away from the world with his amanuensis transcribing masterpieces. Not coming out too often in case he was rumbled.' She pushed herself up on one elbow. '*I* wrote all that music. Every note of it. Nobody would have been interested in it under my own name. So I fed his vanity. And he . . . well, he fed me in other ways. He wasn't bad. Not bad at all. Like you, Adam – not the greatest, but not at all bad.'

'You killed him,' he marvelled. 'You were the one who killed my father.'

'Rubbish. He was too useful to me.'

'Like this . . . this Strepka . . . the time had come when you wanted the truth to come out. But he wasn't going to wear it. So you killed him.'

'Adam, don't be ridiculous.' He was tired of being called ridiculous, and he was heaving himself up and turning so that his hands were on her neck, but she went on. 'I don't know who killed your father, but it wasn't me.'

But of course it had been Mairi. She had killed his father – killed the adoration Adam had felt, killed his love of music that had all been a fraud, nothing to do with the Daniel Erskine whose name and work had meant everything to him even before he realized that the man was his father.

Killed him in every way.

Killed the music and all it had meant. Mockingly destroyed all the foundations on which Adam Lowther had built his beliefs.

And she was laughing again. Laughing at him, mocking him, discarding him.

His fingers tightened around her neck. Her body began writhing, but not in the sensual delirium he had loved and now wanted only to destroy. She was trying to gasp out words that he refused to hear. His weight was on her body again, this time with the strength to bear her down and suffocate her.

Her last strangled sobs of protest were music in his ears.

'I had to do it.' He faced Nick and Lesley with his hands spread wide in apology. 'I had to shut her up. She had destroyed everything, and I didn't know what she was going to say next and I didn't want to hear another word of it. Don't you see, I *had* to shut her up.'

'Yes,' said Lesley gently, 'I do see.'

4

There were two funerals in Kilstane in quick succession. Enoch Buchanan, remanded in custody, was offered a few hours' liberty to attend his daughter's funeral, accompanied by a policeman. Adam Lowther requested a similar privilege for Daniel Erskine's cremation service, though without stating that in effect this would be the second father's funeral he had attended. Mairi McLeod's body was kept in the mortuary while attempts were made to trace any living relatives or anyone who would accept responsibility for her remains.

Enoch Buchanan turned down the permission to attend his daughter's final, hallowed burial. He would accept whatever sentence was imposed on him, and ask no favours of anyone other than the God whom he knew to be always on his side. His only message to his fellow worshippers enjoined them under no circumstances to allow their austere meeting house to be contaminated by a service implying forgiveness for such a wanton creature. He was overruled, though nobody came visiting to tell him this to his face. The presence of the laird, Sir Nicholas Torrance, was gratefully acknowledged with stiff formality by a middle-aged man with long, pale features which expressed pessimism about the human race but would never become as red and outraged as Buchanan's.

The service was short and bleak, in the presence of no more than a dozen men and women all dressed in musty black. As it was about to start, Nick noticed a stranger at the back, ruddy with drink and sporting a bright Donegal tweed. Towards the end, he was the only one showing any tears, wiping his eyes and murmuring something to himself which sounded like a more heartfelt prayer than the drab clichés droning across the bowed heads in front of him.

When the sparse congregation moved out into the open air, the man strode briskly away without a word to anyone. Two women whispered together. 'Would that not ha' been. . . och, it *was* that Gaffney, was it not. . . ? That Irishman who . . . only old Enoch would never have believed his daughter would . . .' A hiss of agreement: 'Och, aye, I did hear that was the way of it. He'd rather blame a man o' some repute than one o' his ain labourers.'

The late Daniel Erskine's memorial service in Kilstane's parish church of St Finian and St Andrew attracted a much more substantial gathering, the pews packed with local folk dressed in their best. No descendants of the deceased were officially present, but there could well have been a number of them, knowing or unknowing, in the congregation. One, Adam Lowther, was flanked by a uniformed constable on one side and by his wife on the other.

Captain Scott-Fraser was wearing his kilt and sporting two unidentifiable medals on his tartan jacket. His wife was resplendent in purple and hunting green, and before the service began stood up to inspect townsfolk already there and those who were arriving in twos and threes. Nick would not have been surprised if she had placed herself at the head of the aisle and marshalled them to left and right, like a self-important usher at a wedding.

The minister had done his homework and was determined that everyone should know it. He spoke warmly of the contribution the Erskines had made to the community, from the days when Dr Kenneth Erskine, father of the deceased, had been the much loved rector of Kilstane Academy to the times when his son had built up an international reputation as a composer of genius, sadly cut down in his prime.

The tributes went resonantly on and on, while some of the congregation nodded gravely, others silently consulted one

another with raised eyebrows, and a few leaned forward
devoutly in order to disguise the fact that they were dozing off.

Ten or fifteen years from now, thought Nick, some pedant in
need of a bursary or a grant from some literary fund would
concoct all kinds of interpretations of Erskine's music, perhaps
by then knowing enough to dig into the Strepka connection, or
even more profitably concocting a tale of sexual obsession with
his amanuensis, and maybe tales of illegitimate children all
along the valley from Kilstane, aimed at a sale of serial rights to
some Sunday tabloid.

Yet, really, what had Erskine been? A shell, inhabited by other
people.

His mind and his gaze wandered. Duncan and Deirdre
Maxwell were sitting together, a decorous young couple going
through the correct motions at one of the events of the year most
likely to be talked about long afterwards. And under the British
Legion flag in the north aisle, in a dark grey two-piece which
was definitely not regulation issue, Lesley Gunn sat with her
head bowed, either in reverence or in contemplation of her own
future.

Coming out at last, while the organ plodded through some
mournful, unrelated chords, Nick took her arm.

'Making sure the final loose ends are tied up?'

'I'm not on duty.'

'Your day off?'

'Several days off. Two weeks' suspension pending an official
investigation.'

'But shouldn't you have another feather in your cap? Or
another crown on your shoulder, or something? Cornering
Buchanan, and then handing over murderer number two intact.
What more do they want?'

'I broke official procedure. Mitigating circumstances' – she
tried a rueful laugh – 'but my future will have to be reviewed.'

The Scott-Frasers bore down upon them.

'Well, that's that, then, Sir Nicholas, hey? Hm?'

'A sad conclusion, yes.'

'Always said you should have stuck to what we real Kilstane folk know in our bones is best. Ought to have had a pipe band and a military band contest. Have to think about it seriously next time, hey?'

Cynthia Scott-Fraser's head was turning to watch Adam Lowther being led away towards the unmarked police car. At least, thought Nick, they had had the decency not to park a Black Maria conspicuously by the church gates. And the decency to let Nora walk beside her husband, just as she had sat beside him in the church, upright and imperturbable. Out in the daylight, she was still looking almost proud of Adam and what he had done. Maybe Adam himself was tacitly admitting that Nora had been right after all: he ought never to have come back to Kilstane. Obviously she would go on believing this but would wait loyally for him to serve his sentence, and would visit regularly, and adjust her life to the new circumstances without flinching. The unchanging rhythm of it would allow no doubts and no further questions. It would all be quite cosy. Nora Lowther was that sort of wife.

Nick tried to catch Lesley's arm again as she took a few steps towards Adam.

'Mr Lowther. I'm . . . so sorry.'

The police escort was taken aback. 'Inspector Gunn, I don't think you ought to be-'

'I'm sorry,' she repeated.

Adam stopped, polite and perfectly calm. 'It's all right. Really it is. I'll cope. I'll always be able to hear music in my head.' And before she could risk asking any more, he said: 'No, not Daniel Erskine. I think I'll learn to get over that.' As the policeman urged him towards the car, he added over his shoulder: 'There's always Bach.'

Lesley looked despairingly up into Nick's face. 'I feel so awful. So bloody lousy. The way I led him into confessing, the way. . . oh, the way everything had to be done. I hate the whole thing. Myself included.'

*

Rutherford said: 'I'm tempted to put in an unfavourable report on you.'

'Why haven't you done that already, if that's what they're asking?'

He had come out of Superintendent Maitland's office and joined Lesley on the uncomfortable bench in the corridor. Like being back at school, she thought, waiting to be summoned into the headmistress's study for some misdemeanour that would be blown up out of all proportion.

'Nobody's leaned on me or anything like that,' said Rutherford. 'It's my own idea. To make sure you get it right this time. For your own good.'

'My own good? So that I'll be more respectful, and stop doing things off my own bat, and stick to doing everything according to the book, and count myself lucky I'm not back in uniform?'

'No such thing, Les. I let you down once before. Persuaded you to stay on when you ought to have got out. I want you to make the right decision this time.'

'Is it going to be left to me?'

'I think so. But get it right this time.'

The door opened. The superintendent's secretary smiled frostily. 'Inspector Gunn, Mr Maitland will see you now.'

Rutherford patted Lesley's bottom gently as she went on her way into the office.

'Sit down, Gunn.' Maitland wasted no words in courtesies. 'This won't do. You do realize that, don't you? It's clear you don't take the job seriously.'

'I took it seriously enough to work with DCI Rutherford on pinning Buchanan down, and then—'

'And then going off on to another force's patch on one of your own wild goose chases, without authorization.'

'And bringing the goose back ready to be stuffed, sir.'

'We can do without the jokes. This isn't a television series.'

'Sir.'

'I've already considered those extenuating circumstances. But I still think you're quite out of your depth, Gunn.' The Super leaned back in his chair and rocked it from side to side with a discordant creak. 'I suppose I must accept some of the blame for putting you on to something a bit tougher than pretty pictures and knick-knacks.'

'You're asking for my resignation, sir.' It wasn't a question. She waited for the chop.

'Never said any such thing. There you go again, you see. Shooting off on your own without balancing things before you jump.'

'What things, sir?'

'I've had a vote of thanks from the Arts and Antiques fossils in London. Very pleased with that operation over at . . . where was it. . . ?'

'Dalspie, sir? That one?'

'Yes, that one. Thanks to your tip-off, they've rounded some villains up. Shouldn't imagine they faced much in the way of violence from seedy operators like that. But anyway, they suggest you might care to go for an interview there.'

'*They* suggested it, sir?'

'Absolutely. And I wouldn't want to stand in your way.'

Meaning, she thought, that he would be damned glad to step aside and let her hurry past, out of sight and off his manor.

From the high window of Black Knowe it was possible to see the line of road along the ridge, descending in a slow arc to the outskirts of Kilstane. Tall delivery lorries flickered between the trees and then were briefly exposed before swinging down that slope. In late afternoon the sun struck sudden flashes from car windscreens. Through a gap between the trees Nick caught the glint of a pale blue hatchback which he recognized as Lesley Gunn's. Heading back in to finalize things in the caravan incident room, he supposed, or to sign off at the police station, or to collect personal belongings from her digs.

He wondered whether to drive down himself into the town and intercept her. There were things that had to be said. There were going to be no mistakes this time.

Before he could leave the great hall, the Peugeot was stopping below his window, and Lesley was heading towards the entrance. He waited, motionless and apprehensive in the middle of his own room which had all at once lost all its reassuring qualities.

Mrs Robson announced 'that detective lassie'.

When the door had been closed, Lesley said: 'I've come to say goodbye.'

'They want you back at the nick, after all?'

'No. I've been offered an interview in London. Possibility of a transfer to what they call the Dusty Attic Department.'

'But you're not going to take it.'

'I've no alternative.'

'You know perfectly well you have. Right here.'

'I've come here to say goodbye.' She must have rehearsed it and steeled herself in the car on the way here. 'I turned down that post you were offering me twice. I've not come here begging this time.'

'The accommodation here's much more comfortable than you'll get in London.'

'Oh, that would look marvellous, wouldn't it? The laird's bidie-in, visiting his aristocratic friends in the pretence of keeping an eye on their treasures, and coming back to perform other duties.'

He thought her anger was gorgeous, her voice so warm and vigorous, her whole body so tense and ready to give battle. And in the flash of a wonderful second he knew that she didn't really mean a word of it: she was fighting desperately not to acknowledge the truth.

Happily he said: 'You didn't come here to say goodbye. You came here because you had to.'

'Sir Nicholas, just because of a momentary lapse—'

'Lapse be damned. That was the real thing. And "Sir Nicholas" be damned. That's not what you were calling me when—'

'I don't remember.'

'Liar.'

'Please, we'd better both forget the whole thing. I'm not holding you to anything. It was just a—'

'Just a glorious experience,' he said.

'And if I were on the premises, trying to work, I'd be available
whenever you fancied another experience. On a regular basis.'

'That's enough.' He put his hands on her flushed cheeks,
pulling her face impatiently towards him and kissing her a long,
demanding kiss. 'You're staying.'

She tried to step backwards but he held her firmly by the
shoulders now.

'This won't do. It would never do. Can't you imagine the
snide remarks? They still snigger about my probationary period
here, and then I messed up their pet legend about the Bareback
Lass, and now—'

'They'll not dare make snide remarks about Lady Torrance.'

He could feel her trying to stay rigid and unresponsive; but
she couldn't. Her protest was only a helpless mutter. 'This is
crazy. I couldn't . . . I mean, just because . . .'

'Yes,' he said. 'Just because. Lesley, please. My dearest Lesley.
Will you please stop pretending, and say you'll marry me?'

'Nick.' She was giving up the struggle. 'Oh, it's crazy, but . . .
only, you know you don't have to marry me if all you want is—'

'Shameless hussy!'

'I'm afraid so.' She put her face up to his, and her lips parted.
'I came here to say goodbye,' she whispered. 'Really I did.'

'And made a mess of it.'

Their hands began moving greedily, and their mouths tasted
greedily, and when he had drawn her closer to make it clear that
he was never going to let her go, he said: 'You *will* stop arguing
and marry me?'

'Isn't it the deflowered maiden who usually has to ask that?'

He stroked her hair and let his fingers stroll possessively
down her back. 'You don't have to ask. I'm the one who's doing
the asking.' His hands reached down to her hips, still gripping
her, absurdly afraid to let go. 'No. I'm not asking. As laird of this
domain, I am exercising my right to insist. You *will* marry me.'

Her head burrowed into his shoulder. 'Well, I've been so used to taking orders for so long, I suppose I have to say yes.'

Later, when he had opened a bottle of champagne and sent downstairs for smoked salmon, he said: 'We've been having too many funerals lately. I must see about arranging a wedding. And some suitable music for the service, of course.'

'Of course. As poor Adam Lowther said, there's always Bach.'

'What else? Thank heavens, there's always Bach.'